# Tortured Skins
## and Other Fictions

# Tortured Skins
## and Other Fictions

MAURICE KENNY

Michigan State University Press

*East Lansing*

The paper used in this publication meets the minimum requirements of
ANSI/NISO Z39.48–1992 (R 1997) (Permanence of Paper). ∞

Michigan State University Press
East Lansing, Michigan 48823-5202

Printed and bound in the United States of America.

05  04  03  02  01  00    1  2  3  4  5  6  7  8  9

LIBRARY OF CONGRESS CATALOGING-IN-PUBLICATION DATA
Kenny, Maurice, 1929–
Tortured skins and other fictions / Maurice Kenny.
p. cm. – (Native American series)
ISBN 0-87013-531-7 (alk. paper)
1. Indians of North America—Social life and customs—Fiction.
I. Title. II. Native American series (East Lansing, Mich.)
PS3561.E49 T67 1999
813'.54—dc21
99-006954

ACKNOWLEDGEMENTS
"Blue Jackets" first published in *Gatherings* (Fall 1992), and reprinted in *On Second Thought: A Compilation,* Norman: University of Oklahoma Press, 1995; "Fear and Recourse" in *Earth Songs, Sky Spirit,* edited by Clifford Trafzer, New York: Doubleday Anchor, 1996; "What's in a Song" in *Blue Dawn, Red Earth,* edited by Clifford Trafzer, New York: Doubleday Anchor, 1996; "Salmon" in *House Organ,* edited by Kenneth Warren, 1997; "Forked Tongues" in *Drama & Theatre,* Jung-Fredonia.

Cover design by Heidi Dailey
Book design by Sharp Des!gns, Inc.
Cover artwork by Jaune Quick-To-See-Smith
Photo on back cover by Karen King

Visit Michigan State University Press on the World Wide Web at:
*www.msu.edu/unit/msupress*

*for*

LORNE SIMON

*in memory of great times, great trips,
but greater raps at En'owkin*

*". . . the best I can do, Nancy"
"yes, Ron . . ."*

*and*

SARAH . . . *friend*

# Contents

# Black Kettle: Fear and Recourse

*A Documentary Fiction*

## I.

THE FREEZING MOON HUNG OVER THE VILLAGE.

Ash and willow were bare. Cottonwoods held but few leaves. The starched leaves, which in weeks past had ribboned the winding creek golden and orange, now were rattled by heavy winds.

A mile off from the village, ponies grazed under the watchful eyes of young herders, boys too young for the hunt or war. The near-skeletal frames of the thin ponies were coated with thick fur. Even the herders' half-wolf camp dogs wore heavy coats and nestled as close to the fires as they were allowed.

Snow would fall early. The narrow river where the camp had been pitched was freezing. The women would soon need to chop holes in the ice to draw water.

Monahsetah dreaded this cold weather. It meant she would need to go out on the plains and pull roots for the pot, as again food was in short supply. Not only was this her duty, but the belly would grow very angry. Would there be no end ever to this hunger? Would the buffalo return to their lands? Would the pony soldiers and the whites leave the country? Would it ever be easier to endure, to survive? Would the war end? If she lived to be a hundred, she would never forget the horrors at Ponoeohe, the slaughter of her sisters and brothers, the screaming women in the village, the fury and hate of the white soldiers as they thrust sabres into the pregnant bellies of the young women, her own terror as she escaped, eluding the guns and knives of those butchers. It was survival, as now pulling roots from the frozen earth was a matter of survival. Her people could never be out of danger as long as the whiteman remained. Their villages grew larger as her own village grew smaller. She couldn't count the dead at Ponoeohe, but their numbers were staggering. Some people left the village to go north and never returned to the leadership of her father, Little Rock, and Black Kettle. She truly mourned their deaths, and also that of White Antelope, who was a good man, kind and thoughtful, gentle, loving, and wise. She would even miss Jack Smith with all his brutish, sardonic sullenness. "White Eyes"—that's what they called him. Half-breeds were never to be trusted, although they had all grown up together. They lived in two worlds, half-breeds, never really a part of either, and they were considered as much a cur, a mongrel, as any half-wolf camp dog. Jack's mother's milk must have been bitter when he sucked. But the Bents also were half-breeds, the sons of William, the trader and the chiefs of the band trusted George. Charlie was wild, certainly, untamed, irresponsible—and he always would be. It was the white blood. His father, William Bent, was greatly respected. A man of courage, he had tender moments—a tenderness not passed down to Charlie, who was a ball of fire streaking across the horizon.

She looked up from her thoughts. Day was approaching. Light filled the morning sky. The sun was rising. She watched as men prepared to go to the creek, the Washita.

Though the air was bitter, there were daring men who clung to the old custom of bathing immediately upon waking. Black Kettle was one. He walked along the edge of the partially frozen stream, prompting those too timid to take the plunge, encouraging the bathers.

A child, naked but for moccasins, leaned against a gray chinaberry tree. The boy was crying. The old man stopped and inquired the reason. The boy pointed to the ice forming in the brittle grass that hugged the shore. The chief reared back, startled. The boy's whimpering and his naked flesh awoke painful memories. He placed his blanket about the child's shoulders and with a pat and half a shove sent him on to his mother.

The shouts of the shivering bathers reached his ears, and he stared at their frolic. Yet his glance shot back to the jagged ice like teeth along the banks, and he saw a trickle of the boy's blood soaking through to the hard winter ground. The child had attempted to follow his older brothers into the stream, but had slipped and fallen and cut his leg. Now the blood stained the river. The Washita ran red as had Sand Creek—Ponoeohe—four years before.

Apprehensive, weary, the old sachem returned to his lodge. Chilled by the short excursion into the morning cold, he took the horn of broth that his wife, Woman-here-after, offered. He sipped slowly, first blowing on the steaming liquid. He pulled an old robe about his head and tied it around his waist. He thought of the boy, his wound, his blood on the river—only a spot, a trickle. He remembered his young men laughing and sporting in the freezing stream, and his thoughts clouded. He saw these same young men floating on that river, their faces down, their backs riddled with black holes from which blood seeped in profusion. The Washita ran red.

Shuddering, he spilled the broth on to the floor. Woman-here-after came quickly and covered his eyes with a robe, and she too then turned to the wall of the lodge. For a brief moment they remained quiet and shielded. The dust disturbed by the fallen broth might well cause blindness. The old rituals were still observed. It was necessary to cover the eyes until the dangerous dust settled once again on the dirt floor. The old woman hobbled off to the rear of the tipi and left the man once more with his thoughts. He dragged the blanket off his head. He recalled that this same blanket, now more brown with age and dirt than purple with dye, had belonged to his older brother, White Antelope. He closed his eyes to honor his brother's spirit. When he opened them, his gaze was blurred. White Antelope had been shot before him while standing in front of his lodge. He visualized the thin ribbon of blood weaving out upon the sluggish current and how it had stained the forming ice. He had watched as his brother slumped into the freezing water, his arms still folded across his chest, his face showing less pain than utter shock, surprised not that he was dying but that his white brothers had betrayed his people. Now there was the child's blood on the Washita.

He called to Woman-here-after and sent her to fetch the holy men.

Though the village lodges were warm with burning twigs and buffalo chips, the pots were nearly depleted of roots. The provisions that the Tall Chief Wynkoop, their newly appointed agent, had dispensed in the summer were nearly consumed. The hunt was poor. Hunters returned with only a few rabbits. Buffalo and deer had wandered into distant mountain canyons to escape the fierce winter that had settled upon the land. The mountains were too far for the weakened ponies to travel, ponies that were eating little more than bark stripped from the cottonwoods at the river's edge. The hunters themselves were too weak from lack of proper nourishment to make the long trek to the mountain preserves.

He would again send runners to the Tall Chief emphatically imploring for provisions.

With her mother and other women and children, Monahsetah went daily to the hills to dig and pull roots, but the stacks of withered turnips grew thinner. They gathered dried sage leaves and made a drinkable tea. They beat the bush to frighten whatever fowl were still sitting, though most had gone south. The women looked to the dogs. One by one, the old dogs no longer strong enough to pull a travois, or young enough to bear spring pups, lost their lives to the empty pots. A woman would call her cur, perhaps first to give him a handful of cold bear grease, and then, as he nuzzled her skirt for warmth and affection, she would take his neck between her strong fingers and wrench out the little whine of life. Or she would bash his head with a hefty club.

There in the Washita valley between the northern Antelope Hills and the southern Wichita Mountains, the Cheyenne awaited winter's toll, even though their agent, Tall Chief Wynkoop, had advised them to move out and away from this valley. There was danger. Though Edward Wynkoop could not say for sure just what the danger was or where it would descend from, he sensed an ominous presence of wrong, of evil. The vibrations of this pronouncement stirred throughout the encampment, yet the headmen would not move the village. It was warmer here in the valley of the Washita. The earth's depression and the woods along the shore provided some succor from the cold—surely more protected than the vast open plains on the south, where, yes, they could hide from, perhaps escape, whatever evil Tall Chief spoke of, that pursued them. Whatever happened, winter with its cold and hunger would claim its due. Children and old men would die of exposure or from lack of nourishment. An old grandmother who had no young son to care for or feed her, would inconspicuously wander, stumbling, out onto the snowy plains and search for a place to drop her bundle near a small pile of rocks. She knew that in fact her people would share what hot broth or dog bone was in the pot with her, but she didn't wish to be an extra burden on the food supply—there were hungry children. She knew that in the spring, when the encampment broke up and moved on, they would pass the pile of rocks and perhaps find her special and curious beadwork and know it to be hers. They would call out her name as they passed either north or south, and hail her spirit, because probably that's all that the wolves would have left, her spirit. But should there be a bone, a friend might place it on a small scaffold on a nearby cottonwood and leave some vestige of food for her spirit's journey into the world of shadows. She would then be at peace.

Such fears weighed heavily upon the chiefs and hunters of the band, the Hairy Rope people. Yet they had known hardships and hunger before. The People would survive.

Now, however, the village felt the teeth of hunger sink into the very tissues of their bellies. Game was scarce. Not a covey of quail could be routed out of the bush, or turkey found, not even frozen in the snows. Young boys did manage to dig out the burrow homes of chipmunks, and they climbed trees for birds trapped north by the weather. Proudly they ran to their mothers to present the trophies skinned and cleaned for the pot. While the fires cooked the thin stew, an older brother, or perhaps an uncle, angry, grumbled in the rear of the lodge. Once the chipmunk had been boiled with a few herbs and some frozen roots, the mother called her friends to the feast and praised her young man's prowess, and spat ridicule upon the men of the lodge, calling out that if they were women they should dress as such; then perhaps she could find them husband-hunters to care for them.

Any and all excuses were taken to celebrate when there was a provider, and the feast, no matter how small on such insignificant game, produced an important support to morale. At such times, good feelings were necessary.

Yet, in the time of the freezing moon there was little to eat and less to celebrate at a foolish feast. Hunger was so great that some women had taken rawhide straps and boiled them down to a nourishing soup. Dogs had become very scarce in the village, and even a boy's pet raccoon was sacrificed to the stewpot. Snakes, when found, were prized, and even the twigs of certain trees were boiled.

Black Kettle expected Major Wynkoop would arrive in the camp with a little flour, a side of bacon, some sugar, a sack of coffee. Perhaps General Hazen at Fort Cobb would have a herd of cattle driven to his hungry people. He had sent a small party of young men to Hazen to inform him of the starvation. Once more, he would implore Wynkoop to send seeds and implements for spring planting, to bring men who could teach them how to plow and raise cattle. The buffalo herds had thinned, depleted by both the Indians and the newly arrived white settlers. The People would all die of hunger.

Twenty years before, Chief Yellow Wolf had begged the government to send the instruments of farming, knowing bad days would come for the Wuh-ta-piu. Still the government had not answered the old chief's request. But the whiteman had raised greens on the plains, berries in jars, and beef hanging from rafters. The whitemen had . . . he had pushed the buffaloes away and brought hunger to their bellies. The young men would grow angry again, dissatisfied, when they saw their children and their wives starving. When they bury the first child who dies of hunger, Black Kettle thought, they no longer will tolerate this ugly predicament. In the spring when the ponies are fat on sweet grass, they will paint the face and the belly that had been full of hunger, and burn those very barns, and probably murder the ranchers. It would be out of his power to stop them. He wasn't even sure if he truly wanted to hold up his hand. There was no way to counsel with ravaging hunger. It does not parley, only cries pain in the belly.

In the time of the freezing moon, the moon of the mean face framed in hoarfrost, when leaves were crisp on the rocklike ground and ice formed teeth along the banks of the leaden streams, there was more than just hunger in the village to trouble the minds and the hearts of the Cheyenne chiefs. Rumor spread that the pony soldiers would ride to destroy the village, the same as they had ridden four years earlier when the Cheyenne had come in peacefully under the protection of Fort Lyon at Ponoeohe, Sand Creek. Perhaps the headmen should give ears to the Tall Chief who warned of bad omens.

Runners had appeared in the village, reporting that a great party of bluecoats was assembling and readying for war. Hunters found pony soldiers' scouts on the plains. Traveling warriors, returning to camps farther down the Washita, had entered the village to seek out the chiefs, with information. There was thunder in the north, and the rumbles were heard in the south, in the safe campgrounds between the Antelope Hills and the Wichita Mountains.

Men had been called out to form a war party and go upon the plains to meet the bluecoats. Black Kettle knew now how ridiculous this was. Now in his village there were few warriors young enough to fight, and their ponies were weak. Most of the warrior-age men were out hunting. A few of Tall Bull's Dog Soldiers were at his fire, and it was these young men who called for a war party, to paint and call it "a good day to die." The old sachem knew this was foolish. You do not war in the cold and snow on weak ponies and empty stomachs.

All grew uneasy. All knew some of the young warriors who were still out on war parties in the north, who would return only when their ponies, exhausted in the freezing weather, were stumbling from hunger, as the grasses were stubbled beneath blankets of snow. Black Shield, Red Nose, and Crow Neck were still out. When they returned they would bring many scalps, perhaps a captive, and they would hold a great victory dance. The chiefs knew those young warriors would also bring the long dark shadows of the bluecoats and their guns in pursuit. The chiefs sent messages to these men with word to cease all warring and to return to their home village. They warned that they must travel peacefully through the lands held by the whites and make no depredations. The moon of freezing had risen, and there was still no sign of Crow Neck or Black Shield, no sign of Tall Wolf or Red Nose or Porcupine, only persisting rumors of the gatherings of angry bluecoats:

卍

As George Custer wrote: *We pitched out tents on the banks of the Arkansas on the 21st of October, 1868, there to remain usefully employed until the 12th of the following month, when we mounted our horses, bade adieu to the luxuries of civilization and turned our faces toward the Wichita Mountains in the endeavor to drive from their winter hiding places the savages . . .*

*To decide upon making a winter campaign against the Indian was certainly in accordance with that maxim in the art of war which directs one to do that which the enemy neither expects nor desires to be done . . .*

*His {General Phil Sheridan's} first greeting was to ask what I thought about the snow and the storm, to which I replied that nothing could be more to our purpose. We could move and the Indian villages could not. If the snow only remained on the ground one week, I promised to bring the General satisfactory evidence that my command had met the Indians . . .*

*I consoled myself with the reflection that to use this strategy was an unpleasant remedy for the removal of a still more unpleasant disease. If the storm seemed terrible to us, I believed it would prove to be even more terrible to our enemies, the Indians . . .*

*I would, in the absence of any reports from him {Major Joel Eliot, sent ahead as scout}, march up the bluffs forming Antelope Hills and strike nearly due south, aiming to encamp that night on some one of the small streams forming the headwaters of the Washita River . . .*

*One of them {an Osage scout} could speak broken English, and in answer to my question as to "What is the matter?" he replied: "Me don't know, but me smell fire." . . .*

*The battle of the Wishita commenced. The bugles sounded the charge and the entire command dashed rapidly into the village. The Indians were caught napping . . .*

Wrote a disillusioned Army officer George Custer: *There was no confidence to be placed in any of these Indians. They were a bad lot. They all needed killing, and the more they were fed and taken care of the worse they became . . .*

江

The plan of [Generals] Sherman and Sheridan was to launch an extensive and carefully prepared campaign to drive the tribes into the reservations set aside at Medicine Lodge, and to pursue and kill those who refused to go. The drive would come at the approach of winter so as to place the Indian at the greatest possible disadvantage.

And as a footnote, consider this, from military historian William N. Leckie:

*It is worthy to note that at the time this decision was made no preparations of any kind had been made for receiving the Indian at the reservations.*

## II.

A BITTER WIND SNAKED ACROSS THE VALLEY, DRIVING BEFORE IT A thin veil of snow. Here and there, in the darkening hours of twilight, snowy whirls cycloned to the steel-blue sky. Five silent men turned up furs against the blustering winds that nipped the ear or ruddy cheek, or rankled in the stiffening joints. Drifts covered the trail. But there was still light in the gray sky to show the way to the south.

The old chief, Black Kettle, rode at the rear of the party. Chilled and worried, he slouched over the pony's mane, his knees barely clinging to the only warm spot in the night, the animal's sweaty flesh. His cold fingers, naked to the winds, loosely held the stiff reins.

Before him rode Little Robe, huddled in fur, one hand touching the icy metal of a carbine. Beyond, Big Mouth, Little Rock, and Spotted Wolf of the Arapaho clucked their ponies on through the blizzard. A mile behind, a few young men followed.

As the party traveled on into the night, the snow ceased and the winds calmed somewhat, leaving only the icy sting of winter. The blue night was quiet and cold beyond endurance, yet the five men did not halt their march to build a warming fire.

It was so cold that leather reins snapped; it was so cold the earth cracked as if a blistering sun of summer had baked and seamed the soil. Frost appeared on the fur of their robes, and tiny icicles hung in the shaggy hair about their ponies' bits.

The old chief stayed at the rear of the party in the hope of saving the strength of his pony, which was wont to lead as if in a charge. Forty miles stretched before them, and the animal would easily exhaust itself too early in the ferocious weather. The old man talked to the beast as it lumbered across the hard ground. In the crust of snow its unshod hoofs beat out a soft, squashing crunch, and the bell tied to the bridle jingled solitarily, echoing over the quiet of the plains like the sad sounds of a sodden drum.

To the left and right, in the distance, on the ridges beyond, came the baying of coyotes. He heard their cries and knew their hunger. This night not a rabbit scurried across the trail, nor a prairie dog darted from its earthen burrow. Not even the flaming tail of a red fox thrust up like a sleek feather from behind a snow-covered bush. Tonight his brother the coyote would go hungry, like many of his people in the village. There had always been a brotherhood between the Cheyenne and the coyote. Coyote brought the People from dark into the light of this world. The Great Spirit had sent this cunning little fellow to traverse the whole of the known world and to talk to the Cheyenne, as the ancient stories told. A warrior society had taken the coyote's name and gave him much respect. Tonight he was hungry, and there was not a berry on the bramble nor a mouse beneath a sage leaf. Like Brother Cheyenne, Brother Coyote was hunted down and slaughtered by ranchers and bluecoats alike. He too was despised; he too was an unpleasant disease deserving of the removal that meant, of course, death and extinction. Coyote also was being driven from his winter hiding place. Like *pte*, the Wolf; Beaver, in the streams; Eagle, in the skies. Why was it the whiteman found these creatures so despicable? And the Indian, the Cheyenne? Yes, even the earth they plowed up, tore up, crisscrossed with irons roads? Was there nothing that pleased the whiteman except the sight of Indian blood on the snow? He destroyed all he touched.

Again the male coyote called out to his female on an opposite hilltop. No food in sight. Only a party of humans stumbling on their horses through the darkness. They were friends. No danger.

Stars appeared in the crystal sky and shimmered in the hard blue coldness. Slowly, moon rose and bathed the night with a pale ghostly sheen. Beneath this not quite full moon, the snow sparkled, icy twinkling in the flow of a fast river. Once more Coyote howled, and his cry was followed by the deep whine of a wolf, who also was out in the darkness on the hunt. The wolf smelled death.

The chiefs moved on at the same steady, slow, determined gait. None spoke, nor looked back, nor made a motion that he recognized his trusted friend and worn companion. They barely noticed the ponies' lowering heads and the snorting spurts of steam jetting from their nostrils.

Little Robe silently chewed a hunk of cold, greasy pemmican; Big Mouth, Little Rock , and Spotted Wolf stared straight ahead while warming their tingling fingers within their furs; the older chief, Black Kettle, bent lower over the neck of his pony. The young men following behind had stopped to build a fire.

He was weary. The great Moke-to-ve-to, head chief to all of the Arkansas Cheyenne, the Hairy Rope people, the Wuh-ta-piu, was indeed weary. It was a tremendous effort to stay saddled; it was an effort to hold the reins; it was painful to keep his fur robe from slipping off the shoulders, to urge his pony onward down the long trail, this same trail he had ridden hundreds of times since young manhood in war parties, horse raids, hunting parties, that he had ridden hurriedly in escape, ridden joyfully to new spring campgrounds where buffalo grazed and the pronghorn stared down the mountain and elk bellowed through canyons; ridden to offer, to make peace. Once more, perhaps the last time, he would ride this trail south for his people.

The five exhausted, worried men rode to Fort Cobb, where they would appeal to their friend General William B. Hazen, commander of the fort. They would beseech him for military protection. Knowing the bluecoats were marching on a winter campaign directed against the Cheyenne, Black Kettle could only presume out of past experience that his peaceful village was vulnerable and consequently would be attacked. His people were so weak they would not stand against the cavalry's barrage for long. Sand Creek was never far from his thoughts. After a long council, it had been decided that these five chiefs would journey across the night to Fort Cobb. Once more, if necessary, Black Kettle would place his mark upon a paper to save his people. He would prove to General Hazen that he was friendly and wanted peace.

The pony stumbled on the slippery crust of hardening snow. It jolted the aging man; he nearly lost his balance. He pulled his furs tightly about his shoulders and stared on ahead, down the cold trail. The wind whipped again into a fury, angry with the night and the five tired humans who possessed it. The wind drove against them.

For a time he attempted to put fears of attack out of his mind. He tried to recall the faces of old friends, friends he had known first when he came south from the Pa Sapa territory. There had been Yellow Wolf to greet him, to make a place at the campfire for his small band, to welcome the young brave eager to prove himself in raids against the Kiowa and the Comanche. Probably Yellow Wolf had had more to do with his intellectual growth than any other man. When young, he had often sat at the older man's feet in council and listened in rapt attention. Then, Yellow Wolf was aging but wise. Peace was always his first thought, peace and trade with the whiteman. There had been those, Indians and whites alike, who had laughed at the old chief when he had implored the Indian agents to bring them farming equipment and seeds and to hire a whiteman to build them a wooden village and instruct them how to raise cattle. Yes, many had laughed. And no implements had ever arrived in the wagons crossing the plains. As Yellow Wolf had fled north, now Black Kettle fled south for protection from the bluecoats and the Great White Father who could never understand the Indian way nor his way of life. Yellow Wolf was finished: a soldier's bullet had taken him down at Sand Creek, had taken him as it had his friends War Bonnet and Standing Water and White Antelope. Those were bad thoughts to keep alive, like burning coals in Black Kettle's mind. Think only of the People still living, hungry and waiting! And yet how fully and frighteningly he realized that the whiteman thought them a bad lot that needed killing. At present they were not pursued to be placed on a reservation, but hunted like game to be slaughtered and nailed to the wooden village walls like the stuffed heads of deer and buffalo trophies. Did not some bluecoat carry in his pocket White Antelope's scrotum used as a tobacco pouch? Black Kettle's anger commenced to warm his body. The sting of the wind did not cut as rawly into his cheek, which now burned.

Moke-to-ve-to had been hostile once. He had painted and rolled his pony's tail for the warpath. He had even placed his knife below the skin and torn away the scalps of his enemies. He had found the Ute after they had captured his first wife, Vo-ish-tah (White Buffalo Woman), and taken her to their village, never to return to her young warrior husband; they had taken her away from him as though they had ripped a rib from his chest, the loin of his thigh. He had raided Pawnee and Crow for ponies; he had attacked the ancient enemy; and it was true, he had at times led depredations against the white settlers and the pony soldiers. They had advanced too far into Cheyenne lands. They had ripped the Mother Earth with the deep blades of their plows. They had driven off the buffalo when their bullets did not stop him in his roaming tracks. They had carried their diseases under their blankets, and they shook those same blankets of disease out upon the People. They gave his young men rot-gut whiskey, which made them mean, lazy, and weak; some young men and women went to the whiteman's coffee pot and never returned to their village fires. Perhaps even worse than those atrocities, they had brought the bluecoats and their guns who found it a sport to kill innocent children, women pregnant with the nation's young; who smashed the heads of infants, raped young girls, sliced off the manhood of his warriors and dignified old chiefs. These were cruel men, men whose hearts were not sweet but bitter like the gall of their oxen. These were vicious men who wished only for the extermination of the Wuh-ta-piu. Oh, the Cheyenne had been so wrong, so thoughtless, to open their robes to those men! So he had danced in the firelight of the darkness, had thrust the point of his lance into the earth, and had ridden off to battle calling hookahey to his followers. Yes, it was good day to die for your principles, for your blood, for your nation and Creator and the Mother Earth. Hookahey. And so he would return to the village, his face painted black for victory, his hands already vermilion with blood, and would dance the great victory of celebration with the white scalps dangling from the tip of his lance, blood still fresh on his war club.

The hunger for revenge that had once driven him to war, now again, on this night of the freezing moon of the hard face, blew upon the old ashes protecting the coals smoldering in his heart. He took warmth from this fire and urged his pony on into the darkness.

One day amidst the thick of battle it had come to Black Kettle that he and his people were to be exterminated by the whiteman. He saw, as in a vision, that all the People had fallen down, and all the buffalo had fallen down, and all the horses had fallen down. The war club beat, the arrow flew, the carbine smoked, but all the People had fallen down. All that remained standing were the whiteman's fence posts, his singing trees along the roads, and the steam from his iron horse.

Black Kettle had turned immediately and had ridden among his war-riors calling for a cease-fire to end the kill. He, Moke-to-ve-to, head chief of the Hairy Rope people, would war no more. He would bundle his lance in the skins of coyotes; he would dismantle his carbine. He would break his arrows. He would raise a white flag above his lodge. Not because he loved and trusted the whiteman or his peace treaties, which benefited only the whiteman. He had watched for many summers the death struggles of all the creatures of the plains and the mountains. He had watched the sharp axe fell the cottonwoods. He had listened when women called out that the hackberry bushes were plowed under and the turnip had been crushed by the pony soldiers. He had seen the lands loaned to them by Mother Earth grow more and more constricted until they were insignificant islands in the middle of the whiteman's sea of grass. He heard the bluecoats' gunfire and had watched their guns kill his strongest men, his most powerful braves and his wise chiefs. He had watched pregnant girls die, bellies cut open, and the children of his people's blood smashed. He had watched as hun-dreds died with the blanket disease, and had observed those great holes, the gashes in the faces of those who had survived the blanket's weight. He learned you could not fight and win against the soldiers the Great White Father sent into his lands. They fell upon them like rain but with the strength of a blizzard and the power of lightning. They could not be stopped, nor be driven back to their lands on the eastern shores. They sprang up again like new grass after spring rains. Peace must be made. The lance must be put down for the plow, the war club for the hoe. The People must learn new ways, a new Cheyenne way. They must plant seed in a garden, raise cattle to graze. The voices of the shadows came to him. Yellow Wolf spoke, Tobacco spoke, even the traitor One Eye spoke. The People must survive. They must grow strong hearts, strong bodies, strong minds. His young must firm up every muscle of their beings, and throw off the bad gifts they had accepted from the whiteman.

That is why this great warrior, when proclaimed chief, became a man of peace, a statesman whom the young men laughed at, ridiculed, and cursed. The war lord Roman Nose scoffed at this peace chief and persuaded the old man's young braves to join him and Tall Bull with the Dog Soldiers and the hostile Lakota warriors. What did it get Roman Nose? Death. What did it get Tall Bull? Death. His bones bleached at Summit Spring.

The big soldier chief, General Sheridan, had called him a worn-out and worthless old cipher. Others of his own nation named him a fool. At the signing of the Medicine Lodge Creek treaty, his own men went against him and threatened not only to kill his stock and horses but to take his life. None of this mattered. Nothing was important but the endurance of the Wuh-ta-piu. Not even his death by assassination would be important.

Black Kettle gathered his family and relatives about him. He gathered trusted friends who like himself believed in the peace, and they villaged together. There were those in his camp who sneaked off to raid the whites. One day they too would stop thumbing their noses and slapping their buttocks in derision and settle down on the lands of the reservation at peace with the whiteman.

Moke-to-ve-to had been lied to, tricked, made a pawn in the game of survival, yet he was proud to think he had never lied to his heart, tricked his people, or played games with anyone's life. He had spoken out for war when he thought it was necessary, justifiable; and he had spoken out against war when killing involved innocent people. He finally came to realize that it was impossible to fight the swarms of whitemen. The "pale-eyes" meant to stay, in the belief it was their destiny, an act of progress in the advance of their most-materialistic civilization. Not only had they built wooden lodges, but they had planted trees in the clearings where there were water holes. Victory could never be achieved. The Indian would never push the whiteman back to the eastern shores. Black Kettle now fought bitterly, with all the strength of his body and mind, for peace.

For sixty-seven years he had watched the cottonwoods turn green, then orange along the riverbanks, and he lived now to ensure that, for sixty times sixty years more, his people would continue to ensure the greening of the timbers and to feel and hear the falling of the rain and the rising of the winds. He could not imagine a time when the ponies would not grow fat on new spring grass, or the buffaloes would not roam the plains, or the wild pea would not flower on the bluff, or men would not ride off to hunt while women waited on the knoll to skin the game killed, dry out the meat, pound it into pemmican with wild berries, and build lodges with the skins. He could not imagine a time when boys would not go to the sacred hill for their dreams, for visions of their future.

The Cheyenne way was good. Why did the whiteman wish to wipe it out? They had been brothers once, and they must hold hands again.

A gust of wind brought him back from the shadows of the past. Once more he found himself heading south to Fort Cobb.

卍

*"I will say nothing and do nothing to restrain our troops from doing what they deem proper on the spot, and will allow no more vague general charge of cruelty and inhumanity to tie their hands, but will use all the powers confided to me to the end that these Indians, the enemies of our race and our civilization, shall not again be able*

*to begin and carry out their barbarous warfare on any kind of pretext they may choose to allege."* (Sherman to Sheridan, October 9, 1868)

*"The more we can kill this year the less will have to be killed next year for the more I see of these Indians the more I am convinced that they will have to be killed or be maintained as species of paupers."* (Sheridan)

*"The only good Indian I ever saw was dead."* (Sheridan)

卍

The men rode on through the cold night with the young braves following behind. At last the dark sky was streaked with ribbons of light. In the distance the tent peaks of Fort Cobb were sighted.

On arriving at the fort, which was really a supply depot composed of army tents, the chiefs were taken to General Hazen's quarters and offered food and sugared coffee, which they enjoyed greatly, before sitting down to council. A pipe was brought out from under a robe, and a smoke exchanged before the chiefs spoke.

Little Robe and Spotted Wolf spoke first, claiming their rights to the Washita reservation. Black Kettle raised his glance from the cooling ashes of the pipe. He sat cross-legged, his blanket loosely pulled about his shoulders, his expressive hands lightly clenched, folded in his lap. His wise, sad face showed heavy signs of fatigue and was shadowed with a mask of fear:

"We only want to be left alone. All we want is that you yellow faces keep out of our country. We don't want to fight you. This is our country. The Great Spirit gave it to us. Keep out, and we will be friends."

His colleagues nodded heads in agreement. The chief spoke slowly as always, but as if in pain:

"My camp is now on the Washita, forty miles east of the Antelope Hills, and I have there about eighty lodges. I speak only for my own people."

Why should the bluecoats attack, as rumor had it? The Cheyenne were there on lands granted by the Medicine Lodge Creek treaty. Grey Blanket (John S. Smith) and the Little White Chief (William Bent) explained the boundaries. The Tall Chief (Edward Wynkoop) had advised against it, but George Bent had suggested they camp there on the banks of Okeahah, the Washita, under the winter protection of the cottonwoods and chinaberry trees.

Black Kettle explained that the whitemen were to blame for all the murders. They had fired upon the hunters. He admitted that he could not keep a strong hand upon his young men. They would not forget Sand Creek and lived in dread that the massacre would be repeated. When fired upon, they returned fire. Sadly, tragically, deaths occurred.

Big Mouth, the Arapaho, voiced fear that the rumors would prove correct that the bluecoats were on the march.

The general listened quietly, intently, to his interpreters. Clear-eyed, not totally unsympathetic, but in full knowledge of their destiny, he allowed his lips to part in a half smile as though to negate the rumor and pacify the chiefs. His thin fingers crawled along his weather-beaten cheek to his mustache, which he stroked nervously, Still a young man, not forty years old, he was a veteran of the Civil War between the states under Sherman's command, and a seasoned Indian fighter. He was still suffering from a wound received from an Indian. An intelligent commander, he was cognizant that the Indians had been dealt an injustice. He was well aware that the whitemen, emigrants and soldiers alike, fervently desired the Indians' demise by whatever means were available. The faster the better. He knew there were commanders in the field who hungered for glory and game, and should the extermination of "savages" be the road to this end, then the road would be traveled gallantly. Under the guise of a punishment expedition, extermination would commence. New stars would rise over the plains.

Doubtless Hazen was a good soldier, a firm commander, and an intelligent man not totally devoid of insight into human misery. Though old grievances rankled in his memory, he could do nothing but carry out orders. He was aware that General George Armstrong Custer was on the prowl for scalps and recognition. General Phil Sheridan, his immediate superior, was on the march, and his aversion to Indians swept like winter winds across the plains. Hazen possessed full knowledge of Sheridan's march into Cheyenne territory and his purpose. This was not a routine patrol.

He made an attempt at honesty and fumbled with his words in explaining that he could not stop the soldiers from attacking hostile villages. Nor could he promise protection at Fort Cobb. Black Kettle's band, with the Dog Soldiers of Tall Bull, were known hostiles:

"I am sent here as a peace chief. All here is to be peace, but north of the Arkansas is General Sheridan, the great war chief, and I do not control him, and he has all the soldiers who are fighting the Cheyennes and Arapahos."

The chiefs grumbled amongst themselves.

"Therefore you must go back to your country, and if the soldiers come to fight, you must remember they are not sent from me, but from the great war chief, and it is with him that you must make your peace."

The worried chiefs all seemed to stare at a wisp of smoke still smoldering in the discarded pipe.

"And you must not come unless I send for you, and you must keep well beyond the friendly Kiowas and Comanches."

This offered nothing—wind in the hand.

Hazen stood as if to dismiss the men and paced the small office tent. Turning abruptly, he looked directly into Black Kettle's worn eyes, which reflected the chief's fear and doubt, and were not untouched by anger and disappointment. He said,

"I hope you understand how and why it is that I cannot make peace with you."

He added that he had heard through Comanche chiefs that the celebrated peace chief Black Kettle had lost favor with his young men and that they no longer listened to his counsel nor were under his command.

Black Kettle did not dispute this accusation. He reasoned that under Cheyenne custom he could not speak for all the bands and all the People, that each person was an individual, and that as headman he could merely advise and not command.

To this Hazen offered a frugal smile as he concluded their talk.

Before the men left the fort, the general had sugar, coffee, tobacco, and a little flour given to them to take back. Then they were dismissed.

He was positive that he would never set eyes upon the "old cipher" again.

## III.

"HEAP INJUNS DOWN THERE . . . ME HEARD DOG BARK," INFORMED the scout.

卍

*"I was rewarded in a moment by hearing the barking of a dog in the heavy timber off to the right of the herd, and soon after I heard the tinkling of a bell. . . . I turned to retrace my steps when another sound was borne to my ears through the cold, clear atmosphere of the valley—it was the distant cry of an infant; and savages though they were and justly outlawed by the number and atrocity of their recent murders and depredation on the helpless settlers of the frontier, I could not but regret*

*that in a war such as we were forced to engage in, the mode and circumstances of battle would possibly prevent discrimination."* (Custer)

卍

On the night of November 26, 1868, the moon of the freezing face, the chiefs, upon arriving in the village, found a small raiding party there under Crow Neck and Black Shield, with fresh scalps. Already they had urged the women to build a fire for a victory dance to be held at moonrise.

Two Kiowa warriors, just back from a pony raid upon the western Ute, had entered the village and spoke with the headmen. They told how their ponies had crossed the heavy trail stamped into the snow by many horses that wore shoes. Ar-no-ho-woh (Woman-here-after) offered these warriors hot broth, and soon they left for the Kiowa village downstream.

Black Kettle prepared for the eventual attack. He tethered his best pony to the poles of his lodge. He placed a sentinel on guard and arranged in his mind how he would ride out to the soldiers before the attack and speak with them. He would tell them, his white flag above his head, of the peace in his heart, that he did not want to fight and they should go home.

From a safe distance Monahsetah observed, dismayed, the celebration. She knew it was foolish, crazy, what with the premonitions of danger about. She knew some of these youths, hot-tempered young warriors, knew that they would do as they wished and that her father and the other chiefs had no control over them. It was cold. It was time for her to go to sleep. She closed the lodge flap and disappeared into the darkness.

The joy of the dancers drummed the night. Shadows cast by the fire fell against lodge walls. Black Shield led a young woman by the hand to the dance, and joined the celebrants. An old woman broke between the lines and stacked dry buffalo chips in the fire.

Black Kettle stepped out into the lateness of the night, looked up at the waning moon, and shivered. He looked off south beyond the camp. There he saw the small fire of the pony herders flicker. He had warned the young men that bluecoats were on the march. They had laughed at him. They laughed now and ridiculed him for being a worried old woman. They shouted that it was winter, snow littered the ground. "Look, now it's falling," they said, pointing. It was the moon of the hard face. Pony soldiers did not fight in this bad weather.

There was no way he could counsel these men; they had already forgotten that Mashane (Chivington) had attacked the village at Sand Creek in the moon of the hard face. They refused to listen. Black Kettle's admonishments fell upon the snow and were scattered by the winds. Peace would come at a heavy cost, and the night's revelry would be paid for with flesh and blood. He hoped that at least Double Wolf would not join the celebrants, wear out his energies in the exhilaration of the dance, and slip into sleep on guard. This might be the very night the bluecoats were stalking the outlying hills, preparing to creep upon the village.

A dog barked. The tinkle of a pony bell struck the night. The herders were probably asleep. The vigil fires flickered in the distance. He heard the cry of a baby.

Now the burden.

Hearing the baby's cry, he remembered the young child's blood smearing the ice edging the creek. He shuddered and entered the lodge.

# Blue Jacket

*For David Petty (Dead February, 1992)*

## I.

"THEY CALL ME BLUE JACKET."

The old man stood straight as though he faced a judge or jury, or possibly like a potentially mischievous child. Eighty, maybe a hundred, he had an almost timeless air about him. Ageless. It was early spring and yet his exposed flesh, face and hands, was nearly bronzed. He wore a somewhat ragged black suit coat and baggy trousers which seemed not to have been pressed for many years. A single dark hair rose from a mole on his chin, determined and adamant.

"What you doin' in those blackberry brambles?"

Before he allowed me to answer, and without pause:

"I watch you closely."

Straight as Aaron's rod. Not necessarily extremely tall, but he stood thinly straight, a warrior, a matchstick, proud of his being and carriage.

"Yes, siree. I watch . . . very closely.

I could not but notice that his arms—sleeves rolled high to the elbows—were heavily covered with thick black hair. At the moment I paid little attention to, really, what appeared to be fur running the length of his flesh from wrists to elbows, but thinking back now, the body hair should have been gray, if not white, for a man of his age. I seemed more struck by the glint, sharp and penetrating, in his eyes rather than his hairy arms. My glance moved from his glint down across a wrinkled face to his shoes planted on the muddy ground. They were curious, the shoes, or sneaks rather: red, raspberry red; and they looked oddly store-bought new, possibly worn that morning for the first time, as though he had just emerged from his winter house and wished to meet spring in a handsome manner.

It was early May, the ground was muddy, and I feared his new red sneaks would become readily soiled in the oozing mud. Water squished away from his bulk, thin though he appeared. Behind his imposing figure I could not help but notice his tracks, prints, where he had walked in from the woods' cover. I looked again, expecting to find moccasins, but no, the red sneaks were there on his somewhat small feet, each foot pointed outwards.

He stared me down, puzzled.

"You Indian, too?"

"Yes." I paused. "But not too much."

"Either you are Indian or you are not," he snapped. "Not a little, not a whole lot."

He demanded a more exacting reply.

"I'm Mohawk . . . a little" was my feeble response.

"Aaaaah. I guessed you'd be Indian even if you are pale as the inside of a cucumber or plucked chicken."

He seemed pleased even though my quantum wasn't much in his assessment. "I'm a big Seneca guy. What clan?"

His chest flared. His eyes softened but brightened like the flame of a night candle. Pride shone on his lips.

"What clan?" I thought. It had been years since I thought of clan. Seemed years since I thought of Indian and all that implied. Years since I had spoken with an Indian. Before I could answer, he said,

"My mother was Bear Clan."

I replied my father was Turtle Clan, from Canada. My declaration was met with something akin to a scoff. He waved his hairy arms as if to dismiss me. "I should have thought so."

Before he could ask, I admitted that I had recently, only the day before, come into the area from Ohio, old Shawnee/Delaware territory.

"Delaware." A laugh circled the word. "Delaware. They are all women. We put skirts on them folks two hundred years ago. Still wear 'em. 'Cause we never said those Delaware could take them off."

I had been associated with St. Margaret College near Columbus, Ohio, and was now newly appointed president of the local community college on the New York State Southern Tier at Jamestown. That day, that moment, I was looking the countryside over for a house that my wife, Helen, and I would be comfortable in for a few years, perhaps through retirement.

His mouth puckered at this information that I volunteered. He wasn't much impressed, I could tell. "Teacher, huh," he whispered through the puckered lips.

"So what you doin' in this here blackberry patch? It's the best in the whole state of New York and Pennsylvania. I come here every summer, every July, to pick these berries . . . big as your thumb, round as a full moon, blue as a star. Oh! And sweet, sweet. Sweet enough to tempt all the animals to squabble. Yup, I pick every season."

There was some question in my mind as to what the house owner might have thought of this statement about picking his berries. I knew that it would not please me much should I purchase this place and move in. "The owner doesn't care?" I asked.

"Not much . . . I guess."

He raised his right hand with two fingers curved as if to pluck a ripe berry from the bramble, the thorns gripping the cloth of his black jacket. I noticed long yellowed nails, thick hairs on the hand's knuckles.

"You gotta share . . . if you move into this house. He always did, even if he didn't want to share. Birds know when to get here, ya know."

"Well, I'm only house-shopping. I've several houses to look at and my wife, well, she has the final decision on what we buy."

He paid no attention to what I said.

"You gotta share. Don't be greedy. I'll share with you. I don't even know you. Here I am talking to a stranger that don't even live on this property. You will," he pronounced quite emphatically. "An' I'll share. Don't be greedy . . . even if you ain't much Mohawk."

I had to smile.

"Been comin' down here for long time now. Probably won't stop comin' down even if you do buy this here house."

He patronized me.

Shifting his stance, water still squeezing out of the mud around his red sneaks, he assumed a superior attitude: "I talk a lot. But I got the right— at my age. And I can. I'm a big Seneca guy. Seneca folks like to talk. They say we're pretty good at it. We learned that in council. You can pick those berries—the blue, the black, the red—if you get up before the birds an' others. They'll outsmart—every time you think them berries are ripe and ready, and you got a can swinging at your beltside. Well, they'll outsmart. What kind, Not-so-much-Indian, you say you was?"

I couldn't help but smile. He teased in good Iroquois fashion. He was testing.

"You a damn Catholic, too? You believe in Jesus Christ? You go to Sunday church? You know the prayer, the Book? You know what a Quaker are . . ."

He did not expect an answer. He wasn't really asking questions but making statements.

"My wife, Flower-who-sleeps-in-winter—hell, darn, that wasn't her name at all. Her white name, her white name was Maud Parker. An' my name ain't Blue Jacket. I just made that up to scare you a little, stranger. You might think I was the famous Red Jacket . . . my ever-so-great uncle. Remember him? He liked to talk a lot. They called him Windbag, or He-that-fills-the-air. Great man, my uncle. Remember him?"

I couldn't agree more. Red Jacket was famed across the world as one of the greatest orators. Every schoolchild knew this fact.

"What's your name, Not-so-much-Indian?" He didn't stop to hear my reply. "My Maud was the one who said I talked too much. If I worked the way I talked, I'd get the work done. Why hell, damn. I don't want to know your name. You got a name now: Not-so-much-Indian. I only wanna know if you'll share these blackberries when you buy this house. Share with the birds, an' the others."

He stared me down. Stood his ground, eyes piercing my very soul, or morality, or sense of fair play. But if I bought this house, this land, these couple of acres that came with the berry canes, then why should I have to share with anything, birds or whatever? It was mine. I could let the bloody berry rot if I were so inclined, no? He wanted an answer. He was deadly serious. The comic had disappeared. The glint in his eye held no laughter now. I opened my mouth, but as the words slid off the tongue he turned and left, left me holding the words on my dry tongue, stymied. He disappeared. Sort of vanished in the dark tangle of woods beyond.

Straining, I caught a glimpse of him striding through one small clearing after another in the forest, hunched over as if at any moment he would drop to all fours and amble away content in his purpose of the morning,

Chuckling, with a small grin almost of disbelief, I strode away from the thick, wide berry patch that rose out of the rich earth just off the running creek not far from the house I was considering. Surely this creek, or brook, held trout—rainbow—that would be tasty when sautéed in a frying pan. Trout was my second passion after blackberries.

## II.

IT WAS TRUE, A FACT, I MUST ADMIT HONESTLY, CANDIDLY: I HAVE A strong passion for blackberries. The most delicious of summer fruits, seed or no seed. Succulent, sweet as honey, healthy. I longed, now that I had seen this remarkable stand of canes, to stuff my stomach with the delectables. Old man Blue Jacket obviously had the same passion. I was consumed by it. I had never lived any place in the Americas where I was in complete possession of such a patch. Store-bought berries never satisfied my passion, my abnormal craving for the wild berries. There are those who crave cigarettes, or avocados, or orange juice, or even heavy gravies. Not I. My only flaw was the passion for these natural blackberries. A rustle in the brush beyond invaded my revelry. There sat a squirrel staring glassy-eyed at me. It grit its teeth together, but its lips parted. It sat on its hind legs, tail furred behind, its little claws empty of nut or acorn, or berry. The furry creature dropped his forepaws and stepped towards me, turned on a dime, and scampered off into the thick brush. What was he trying to tell me? No, no, my brother does not talk to horses. Nonsense. Animals do not talk to humans, only cats that rub against your leg when hungry, or dogs that wag their tails when they want to go out to hit the hydrant. But they don't speak except body movements, body language. That squirrel had nothing to say to me.

Coming through the woods, the stands of conifers and cedars, I could hear Blue Jacket's echo. "Don't be greedy." That would take some thinking. A major decision—whether Helen and I should buy this house—and I was going to pressure her into the purchase!

I was born and raised in the city, in Crown Hill, a crack in the Brooklyn cement. But I remember well my grandmother and old Granddad. Mr. Blue Jacket reminds me of Granddad. I can still vividly remember visiting the Rez with summer moons on the waters, canoeing, and fishing for lake bass and brook trout. How could you forget the wild strawberries and the

June festival, or going to the woods with Granddad in late July to pick luscious blackberries for Grandma's pies and jams? All those summer berries—the blue from the Adirondacks, and particularly the elderberry—and the wine Granddad brewed. He'd sneak me a sip from the tin cup out behind his stacked woodpile where Grandma couldn't see him. He'd mumble some special words and pour the wine with a wink as he handed the tin cup into my boy's hand and said, "Repeat after me, adowe, adowe. You must always remember to say adowe, thank you. Thank you for life taken and that you are about to drink or eat. An adowe to the Creator and that which has given up its life that you may live . . . gift or elderberry, corn, or opossum meat."

And I would repeat the adowe after him—thank you, Bush; thank you, Creator. Then I would take one small sip of the wine, give him the empty cup, and stagger toward the house under burning summer sun. Grandma taught that the sun was Brother; the moon, Grandmother; and all the fruits were sisters. Though I was born urban, Grandma and Granddad saw to it I learned a little, at least, of the natural world, especially to respect all living things because they were relatives and they too had their rights under the sun the same as we humans.

My father had been an ironworker as a young man. A Mohawk youth desperate for employment, without much of an education, perhaps two years of high school, he had needed to go to the states, to the city, New York City, to find a job in high steel. He liked the work and worked hard at it. In time, when he married, he proved to be a good provider, a good saver. Grandma and Granddad had taught him well, too. Nights, instead of going to the bars for beers, he stayed home with my mom and tried to learn a little more from books. He'd say, "You never know when you'll need to use more learning." Saturday nights he'd take us to the movies. And after our Sunday bath and castor oil he'd take us out for ice cream or some such treat. Never paid much attention to church, even though he had been

baptized Catholic. Never put, as he would say, much stock in church going. Best to pray alone or in the woods or at the river's edge. He always told
me that he prayed on the high steel and that was a good place to pray. Not
out of fear—my father feared nothing; he was a true warrior and hunter—
but how much closer could you get to the spirit world than there on the
iron foundation of a skyscraper? I guess he was a good man. I remember
him as generous and warm, though he could tease and test (yes, exactly like
Mr. Blue Jacket), he never taunted with ridicule or slander. He was a good
man. I wish he had lived.

Mom, my mother, was a different story; not that she wasn't a good
woman and mother. She was, but she wasn't Indian. A full-blooded white
woman, born and raised in the Brooklyn neighborhood she had lived in
when she met my dad, where she eventually died. Crown Hill. She was
Irish. My dad, Henry, always said she was more tribal that any Indian woman
he knew except his mother. She got fat, slowly, after one day he reached too
high to grab a beam. She claimed there wasn't a reason anymore to stay
thin and pretty. Her man had fallen from the heights, and she didn't need
another. Her big Mohawk wasn't there to appreciate her anymore. She ate
chocolate and lots of buttered popcorn before the TV on the couch. She
took a job as clerk in a dry cleaner store. And she never went back to the
Rez again. Nor did I after I was thirteen years old.

One night after I had graduated from high school we heard a knock at
the apartment door. A man stood there with a Manila envelope in his hand.
Mom asked him in and gave him coffee at the kitchen table. I went off to
watch TV. They talked a long time, and when they had finished, and the
man had left, and had left the Manila envelope on the table, Mom called
me in. I went to college that fall because the envelope contained a special
insurance policy my dad had taken out for me, for my education. It paid
my tuition, and I worked nights in a drugstore and sold aspirin, toothpaste, and condoms to shy, scared men and boys who stumbled up to the

counter when they requested rubbers. I wasn't embarrassed. It was my job. My night ended with mopping the floor. I got through my undergraduate years that way. Then grad school—a math major. I'd teach. My Dad would have approved of that, I think. I wasn't overly brilliant, an intellectual. I wasn't going to Wall Street, didn't have either the money or the smarts for either law or medical school. I'd teach. A good career, and I liked kids, students. I have taught math in one small college after another for all these years.

I met, fell deeply in love with, a very pretty girl, Helen Thorne, and have been happy since then. Like my mom, Helen is a full-blooded white woman. She gave me one son and one very beautiful daughter, who, thankfully, has the sparkle of my Dad's eyes, his coloring, his sensitivity, and his smarts. Now both my children are in college and working nights. My good Helen shared all the difficulties, labors, heartaches. She has been a librarian all the years of our marriage. And is a great berry pie maker . . . just like my Grandma was.

Born and bred in Brooklyn, my mother didn't go berry picking. She didn't make elderberry wine. She didn't say adowe before she bought a ham to bake or vegetables to cook. She did buy pint baskets of cultured strawberries, and we had terrific shortcakes. And she saw, when I was very young, that I spent summers on the Rez with my grandparents. It was my real college—living with Grandma and Granddad—and where my passion for blackberries developed. Nearly everything I own is the color of crushed blackberries: socks, pants, ties, pajamas, shirts, car seat covers, my sleeping bag for camping; even the pictures on my office walls are of canes and ripe berries with people picking, I demanded that we name my daughter at birth Sweet Blackberry. Helen discouraged this. Later, Tammy thanked me graciously and profusely.

I had to stand there beside this house under consideration and laugh at poor Tammy being named Sweet Berry. Old Blue Jacket surely would appreciate that jest, that honor naming. But would Sweet Berry have been any worse than Dawn or Aurora, or just plain Agnes? Sweet Berry would have been a great name. Perhaps I can tease Tammy into naming her first girl child this. I doubt it.

When the last echo of Blue Jacket's voice and crunching in the mud had faded, I found myself facing the stand of woods, a wide spread of sugar maples laced with white birch, witch-hopple, a single spruce, a mixture of sycamore, beech, and tamarack. A young oak leaned toward a white pine and near the house several cedars stood gallantly against whatever winds might rush off the hills. A mere foot away, a white trillium smiled up at me. A patch of wood sorrel colored the darkness. For a brief moment my eyes deceived me for I thought I saw Blue Jacket standing pine-straight within the shadows of the woods, spying on me, the house, the patch.

I shrugged, turned with key in hand, and approached the back door. Helen would want a fine report on what the house actually had to offer. After all, that was my mission that afternoon.

I inspected the interior. I was more than satisfied; I liked it sufficiently to bring my wife for approval. Three bedrooms, a study, bath and a half, and all the other usual rooms, plus a small attic, a large cellar, a medium garden plot, a three-mile drive from the college and town, and the closest neighbor on either side no less than a thousand feet from the line. Nothing really unusual, it was built soon after World War II. Neither a murder or a mysterious ghost in the night shadows, or so I was led to believe; no bad spirit rambled through the rooms. Adequate for our needs, I knew Helen would enjoy the rhubarb patch (if the creatures allowed), the garden, the day lilies, the lilac, and her hours slaving over the newly planted tomatoes. What totally satisfied me was the study and, of course, the wide and deep swath of blackberry brambles—forgetting the black flies, mosquitoes, and no-see-ums. There were also canes of raspberries on the property, a few blackcaps, and a single currant bush. Obviously there were wild strawberries in the general vicinity, and in the small woods beyond I guessed there would be blueberries and elderberries. I'd make the wine just like Granddad did those years back.

Being something of a prosaic man, as I've been told, I cannot, dare not, wax too lyric. But my heart leaps up when I behold—to copy Wordsworth—blackberry brambles. I could at that moment taste Helen's pies and the ice cream I'd churn in our old ice bucket. Come July we'd be rich in berries and growing fat around the middle.

I returned to my hotel and phoned Helen. She was so excited that she promised she'd drive on from Ohio the next day. I took in an early supper in the local Denny's, went back to the room to read, and fell comfortably off to sleep early.

On rising, I was somewhat bothered by my dream the night before: the berries were all picked, washed; Helen had them between crusts; and I was storing them in the deep freezer. I had the count up to two hundred and twenty-one when I woke in a hot sweat, remembering Helen's words "Did you pick them all?" and my response:

"Yes, every last one of them."

"You didn't leave any for Mr. Blue Jacket?"

"No. Only the berries dried by the sun."

In all honesty, this did prick my conscience. Had I made him a promise? I couldn't recall. I simply could not remember. My dream was of greed.

My report to Helen satisfied her needs. When we visited the house and land site, she agreed we would buy the place and have an enjoyable life there. When the kids emerged from study at Christmas, we'd hang real stockings from our fireplace.

On a sylvan May afternoon, late, the sun was slowly wending through the shafts of incoming summer light. In the stillness of twilight, the light yet remained brilliant, silver. There was not a breeze in any pine, nor a rustle of any tiny animal. Perhaps a deer or a raccoon stood off in the darkness below the birch or tamarack in the shadows. One bird sang, perhaps a thrush. I couldn't tell, as I'm not a true bird watcher. It seemed too early in the evening for a thrush. Not a cloud ruffled the sky. Nothing rippled, bent, shook, rattled, or warbled. I had the feeling of home in this silence.

The Buick waited on my cinder drive. I boarded, turned on the ignition, and glanced out the rear window to back out. As I turned to face the windshield, there he was, standing straight as an arrow, handsome in age, peering directly into my heart. I backed out of the drive and raced off to pick up Helen at the town library.

## III.

SHE HAD APPROVED; HAD FOUND DELIGHTS A MAN WOULD NEVER DIScover without a woman pointing out those special delights to his naked eye. She found more closet space, a hutch in the dining room, a dressing room off the master bedroom, and other attractions. She sang blissfully over the kitchen cabinets, whistled about the unusual bathroom tile; she nearly fell to her knees to kiss the waxed and polished parquet floors. She loved the place and couldn't wait for the furniture to arrive from our last home. The garden plot, she aahh-ed about. The front and rear lawns were a decent shape and size. She imagined lovely summer lemonade parties on the back deck. She ignored my blackberry brambles. When I called attention to them, she growled.

"They're thorny."

She had no interest. I found it a lone joy.

"Must be a graveyard beyond those trees," she ventured.

"How would you know?"

"Those brambles are too heavy."

I allowed that suggestion to drop. Corpses feeding my berries.

"There is one there." She was adamant.

While she ohhh-ed over the new, bright kitchen, I took a stroll through my woods. The stand was thick but not as deep as I had originally believed. And Helen proved right again. There it was. An old Seneca graveyard reared behind the woods, topping a sloping knoll beyond a rise of green hills. How did she know?

"I just did. I could smell it. I sensed it was there. Call it women's intuition, if you must. Remember when your granddad died, and Jeff March, our neighbor? Didn't I tell you their deaths a week before the telegrams arrived?"

"You're sixth-sensed."

Parker, Jemison, Jamieson, etc. I read and named the stones aloud. Weathered, chipped, some dropping, a few knocked over, names chiseled so light by time that names were fading. On one short stone I read a B and then blanks for the rest of the entire first word. Then there were more blanks and the last letter, a T. The date read 18— and something that could have been a 2 and a 9.

Obviously an ancient site. No new headstones with fresh flowers. Satisfied with Helen's prediction, I ambled back to the kitchen and confessed to my wife her intuition had hit it on the nail again. Over a beer, my imagination played with the blackberries, ripening, picking, eating. For safety's sake, perhaps I should construct a fence around my brambles.

We moved into the house. It all took a good deal of time and energy to settle things into proper places. Helen was most difficult, things had to sit at just the right angle for effect, colors had to complement. The dining room rug had to match the wax grapes in the bowl on the table. Helen said it was good taste, breeding. Time disappeared. Temporarily I forgot my brambles, but way in the back of my mind I hadn't forgotten them. I continued tasting their jam. From our bedroom window I had an excellent and clear view of the berry canes. While stretching for bathrobe and slippers, I could easily sneak a peek.

One morning, to my interest and great surprise, I watched, while stepping into my slippers, old Blue Jacket sauntering through my brambles. He'd lift a cane and drop it, lift a cane and drop it, lift another cane, check it quickly, and drop it. He must have lifted every cane there. I watched him closely for half an hour, then observed him in the woods. I knocked loudly on the glass pane, but he ignored my tapping, stone deaf. The next morning I'd beat him. I was there waiting when his first foot stepped out of the shadows and put down on the mown lawn.

"Good morning, Mr. Blue Jacket." I think I shocked him.

"Oh yes. Good morning, Mr. ah, ah, Mr. Not-so-much-Indian. Out for a morning hike. Keep in good shape that way."

"Yes, me too," I replied grudgingly. Under my eyes, he was lifting the sprays and scanning the ripening process.

"Heard a bear crawling around last night."

"Oh! Where? Near here?" I questioned.

"Yes, up by my house there."

"Where is your house, Mr. Blue Jacket?"

"Around up there some." He gestured to the hills beyond the woods. His mysterious response did not fool me, nor did it, or the gesture, answer my question. "You live near here then?"

"Not far up there some place near. Nice morning walk. Not far up there."

But not far up where? He wasn't going to reveal his house. Perhaps he was afraid I'd stop by and disturb, or maybe scare, his wife, Flower-who-sleeps-in-winter. I wouldn't dream of calling on them without first an invitation or at least a phone call to announce my visit. I was city born. Thinking about it now, I'm not sure if it isn't Indian, phoning before dropping by.

"Well, what do you think? Ready to pick soon?" Then I happened to remember that I had tramped all over those hills where he had pointed to his house, and I couldn't for the life of me recall a house on the hill.

"Yes, sir ready to pick pretty soon. Gonna make some bellies happy. Ready soon. Now don't forget to share."

He turned his back on me as if I would not be one of the happy bellies, and he waved his hand good-bye as he disappeared into the dark woods. He did not give me a moment, a chance, to explain my passion, that my life-long dream was to have a huge spray of my own of these luscious fruits, and that nothing would make me happier. His warning to share had unnerved me, made me downright frightened. What could I do? Well, yes, relax and accept the inevitable. Or, or, I could construct a fence! That afternoon I called the fence people, and the next morning the enclosure was there in place.

That afternoon I strolled out into the backyard for a breath of air after working on college papers at my study desk. And there was Mr. Blue Jacket smack in the middle of the brambles, lifting and checking and lifting. How could that old man have climbed over that fence? It was four feet high, and he wasn't so tall that he could simply step over, tall though he was. I blinked, and he was gone. I blinked again, and he was there again, lifting and checking.

"Mr. Blue Jacket. What are you doing? How did you get in there?"

"Morning. Morning. Nice day today again. Berries ripening nicely, no?"

I briskly marched to the shiny new fence. "How did you get inside my fence?"

"Oh, I just did somehow. These berries are real nice now. Real nice. Won't be long."

I was so unnerved that I continued to stare at him, probably open mouthed. Words would not rise to meet this outrageous occasion. The sun was hot that morning. Some humidity in the air. With my feet planted by the fence, I closed my eyes, shut them as tightly as possibly, with the hope that when I opened them up, truly he would be gone, not there, that my imagination played tricks. I kept my eyes shut for several seconds, and when I opened them up, truly he was gone out from the enclosure and tramping through the woods.

"How? How did he do it, Helen?"

"I have no idea."

"Today's Tuesday. Yes? No? Yes. Alright."

This time he was standing on the outside leaning against my new fence.

"Mr. Not-so-much-Indian, I'll wager that these berries will be ready by Thursday at sunrise. Mark it, sir. Sunrise. Thursday this. Some belly gonna be made very happy. Thursday, this. Sunrise." His brown hand dropped a bramble pushing through the fence, and he marched off slowly into the woods, his back bent, stooped. Suddenly he stood in his usual straight stance, turned abruptly, raising his arm to point at the silver fence. "That won't help much, Mr. Not-so-much-Indian. Won't help." He smiled showing old and yellow teeth.

Needless to say, I was stunned. I actually believed he was going to pick the berries on the bramble that he had held in his hand. But the shocker was when he turned about with his threat. And I knew that somehow he could climb the fence. How, I didn't know, but he already had. A stool maybe. A stone. I was positive he planned to pick the berries. Hadn't he said in our first chat that I must share with the animals? I was, am, willing to have a bird take a few, and to give some to the chipmunks and squirrels. But he meant himself, of course. And I didn't mind, wouldn't mind, giving the old man some. However, he had said some bellies, plural. Did he mean his and mine, or, or, whose? I must work out a strategy. The fence was not going to work to keep the "animals" out, and he could scale the fence. If the berries were to be ready this Thursday at sunrise, then I'd make sure I was there first. Before sunrise. I'd save him a few. I wouldn't be totally selfish. Share . . . some, a few. Not many. They were mine. I owned that land. For all the world to hear, I shouted, "I'll be there in the brambles amidst the sprays long before sunup when he places his ol' codger's foot down near the first cane!"

I went inside the living room, where Helen was still arranging the furniture and hanging freshly laundered curtains.

"You are being silly. Plain silly. That old man isn't going to rob your darn berries. There are brambles all over the Southern Tier. He's not planning to outsmart you. Though the way you are acting, he probably could. You're worse than a hen on a nest."

Helen was right, of course. Why would he steal all my blackberries? There are brambles all over the area, rich and thick canes heavy with fruit. He probably has his own patch near his house "up there somewhere near." I was blind silly.

Tuesday passed uneventfully. Then Wednesday dawned. The day was deathly quiet. I managed some work in my study with my eye slanted towards the backyard. No sign of Mr. Blue Jacket, nor even a robin, let alone skunk or chipmunk. I spent the day answering letters to old friends and family. Soon Helen announced supper was ready—a fine steak, rare. She teased me about it being fresh game, and the meal turned into a guessing game.

"It's good old-fashioned cow."

"Maybe. A deer peeked into the garden and I took good aim, and now you have it on your plate." She giggled, her fork in the air, the tines stuck into bloody flesh. "Actually, I think it tastes a little like porcupine, maybe bear. Yes, bear, I think."

The evening passed slowly, as they say like molasses in January. I thought bedtime would never come. I could barely read for excitement.

"Go to sleep. Turn off the light and stop mumbling. I can't keep my eyes closed for your growls."

Before going off to bed, I had left my garden shoes, my pants, and work shirt on the chair near the bed. Suddenly I heard the alarm go off and it was still dark. I had slept after all. Yet dawn had not yet risen over those hills. I knew the old stones in the graveyard had not been warmed by the sunrise. Why was I thinking of the graveyard? Imagining pies and jams and shortcakes, etc. I stepped into my pants. Pulled up the white socks. Pushed into my work shoes, stood, draped my arms with the sleeves of the Levi shirt. It was getting a little tight and would be considerably tighter after Helen baked the pies and cobblers. I was willing to suffer the consequences. I dressed quietly so as not to wake my wife. She'd have no sympathy. In fact, when I told her before bed my plan for the morning, she laughed outright in my startled face and cried out that I wasn't silly, I was certifiably crazy.

Downstairs I made instant coffee. No time for perked. I disliked imitation coffee, imitation anything. I wanted the real. Now I needed the brew and there was short time for the real. Half a cup down the gullet. A faint streak of light struck the low cloud cover. A cold, black cloud. Rain. No sunshine. Good. That would keep Mr. Blue Jacket out of my patch. I didn't mind rain. I fetched the raincoat from the kitchen closet, reached for my flashlight on a shelf nearby and a large water bucket. I'd win. I should have accepted his wager last Tuesday when he stood leaning against the fence. I found a thin pair of garden gloves. I was ready for victory, triumph. I was ready for my blackberries. All of them.

Dew glistened. The morning spit, the foam that we used to call rattle-snake spit, covered the leaves of the brambles, and the spit hung as if a human had passed through expectorating everywhere. I reached the first cane. A few bright pink berries clung to the stalk. No black. I moved left. The same. I moved right. Nothing at all. There was not a single berry of any color or degree of ripeness. I moved deeper into the canes. Nothing . . . nothing. Not a single dark globular fruit. Nothing. Not pink nor red nor black. Light was approaching, moving up into the sky. I could see now without the flashlight. Not watching my feet, I nearly stepped in a pile of scat. Still warm, almost steaming, fresh. Must be a rabbit. What else could manage the fence. Or a raccoon. Rabbits do not make that sort of scat, cylindrical like a dog. Must be a raccoon or fox. We'd sighted plenty in the area, one or two in our backyard. Fox eat wild grapes. Raccoons eat anything. Near the fresh scat I discovered prints. Five toes and the ball of the foot on the left, five toes and the ball of the foot and the heel on the right. No shoes. Didn't Mr. Blue Jacket wear shoes when he came to make his periodic visits? Of course, he did. So why did he come here this morning barefooted? As the light from the rising sun increased, I could more clearly see the footprints where they scurried throughout the brambles in the soft dew-moistened earth. The toes were somewhat off. The big toe was in the wrong position for a human foot. "Oh, my God!" In the wrong place for a human foot. It wasn't Mr. Blue Jacket, and it wasn't————Mr. Blue Jacket who would defecate here, in a berry patch.

I slid back to the house for my rifle. It well might be needed. The creature might still be there in the shadows of those woods whose shadows were lengthening across the patch. I had a most unwelcome friend, an uninvited guest. The brambles were high; there was a good growth this year after a strong rain and good runoff. The leaves large, the canes high— high enough to hide him if he were bending over, picking. And he could climb my fence.

Rifle loaded, I returned to the yard. The sun now had risen. Clear, clean light filled the air, streamed through the brambles. At the edge of the canes I noticed black fur caught on thorns. There were many tufts. I walked through the canes. In the interior the brambles were completely naked of fruit, clean as a dog's breakfast dish, and flattened to the ground. There was not a berry of any color. But tufts of fur were caught on spiky thorns. My canes were ten feet deep, at least, and it took me some minutes to wade through them. They were cleaned, trampled, but all were clutching bits of black hair.

I returned to the kitchen. Defeated. Helen was up, coffee perked, and now she had bacon and pancakes working on the stove.

"Well, how many buckets of berries did you pick?"

I grumbled inaudible words. Some of which were curses.

The kitchen window had a decent view of the patch, if you looked kitty-cornered, as they say. I looked for fox, raccoon, or whatever the creature or creatures were who stole my blackberries, my precious berries. I couldn't take my sight away from the window. I ignored the coffee, and it was real coffee this time, and I ignored the food Helen encouraged me to eat. Then, just then, I swore I spotted Mr. Blue Jacket in the canes behind the fence. I rushed from the table knocking over the creamer, spilling the coffee in its saucer. I banged through the screen door and spilled out into the yard. He was not there. An illusion. I'd had an illusion. Trick of the mind. Houdini of my imagination. Optical trick. My depression, my deep, deep disappointment, my painful and costly loss, had conspired to delude my vision. He was not there. Rubbing my eyes, I heard Helen calling from the kitchen door, imploring me to return to the table. My coffee was cooling, and the bacon and pancakes were frozen. Who cared? However, I did return to the house.

"What you think you saw? A blackberry moving out there? Dear, it was just a black bear. Or bears."

"It was Mr. Blue Jacket. I tell you. The old Seneca."

"No dear. That old man couldn't climb your fence."

No response. I slurped the coffee. Her irony deserved nothing, certainly not an intelligent response.

In the late afternoon, having finished off reading class projects for the new semester that was to start the first week of September, I completed a letter to a former colleague, a berry aficionado. It was then time for my daily stroll, a way of keeping the inner tube off the belly, airless and flattened. It didn't really do that much good, but I played the game each day. I got out an old walking stick that had belonged to Granddad, a canvas fishing hat I hadn't much used that summer, put a package of sugarless gum in the shirt pocket, and left the house, avoiding a talk with Helen, who had continued to smirk and laugh at me throughout the day. I didn't need her brand of humor, or sarcasm. It wasn't funny, the loss of my berries.

Out back I skirted the fenced but broken canes, stumbled through the woods, and headed for the hills, where the now western sun had shifted its declining rays onto breastlike mounds. I could easily see the tops of the headstones. That was my destination. Only a few weeks before, I'd been there on my walk. They stood straight. Now several were knocked over. Strangely, the grass and earth appeared disturbed near the one particular headstone that had been so difficult to read. B and T and 18-something, and then something that looked like a 2 and a 9. This time it could be read clearly. Not to say I was not utterly amazed. The stone had been smeared with a black-purple juice. The carving stood out broadly in the orange light of sundown. I stared, couldn't take my eyes away. I poked the broken pieces of the stone with my walking stick, lifting some tufts of loosened grass, then pushed the tip of the stick against a wad of black fur. A Canada goose flew overhead, honked a signal to its followers, and disappeared in the sky. From afar somewhere I could hear a dog bark. Weird, solemn, prophetic. The dog howled. It took a few minutes to find the tracks, the prints, but yes, there they were in the softened earth, the same prints that were on the loam of my blackberry patch. It was then I took a last look at the headstone. It read, "Blue Jacket Seneca 1829."

I ran down the hill as fast as legs could carry me. I dropped the walking stick. A tree limb caught the canvas hat. I reached the kitchen door. Slammed it shut. Bolted the lock. And stood leaning against the frame, heaving, pulling for breath.

Helen wandered into the room for a glass of water.

"What's wrong with you? You look like you've seen a bear."

There was no answer. What could I say to her? She'd laugh me into eternity.

I didn't sleep well that night.

The next morning on rising I called the fence company to come and tear the fence down. They could keep the metal for scrap. When the men had finished the work and had pulled out of the driveway with their truck, I went to the garage for a shovel and spade. In no time at all the ground was cleared and the plants stacked for a bonfire. I wiped the sweat from my brow and neck, and uttered a silent prayer. I was so pleased that I had not named my daughter Sweet Berry after all.

For the remainder on the summer I stayed in my study when not in my college office and kept my nose to the books.

One evening before dinner, Helen asked if I'd like to have a shortcake for dessert with dinner. "Raspberry," she said.

My abrupt answer was simple.

"No."

回

# The Girl on the Beach

THE SUN WAS SLOWLY DYING.

Bloody waves curled to the shore.

A young girl stood in the waves, the red water lapping her knees. She stood watching the scarlet sun go down far out behind the ocean. Long strawberry colored hair streamed down her back. She was thin, light against the faint breeze blowing onto shore. Her flowered skirt blossomed about her thighs. Both hands struggled with her hair flying helter skelter about her.

A man strolled the dunes also observing the falling sun. He appeared fascinated by the girl. He stopped in his hike, stared at her for a long moment. Isn't she pretty, he must have thought. Lovely, truly a painting, the sun coloring her figure nearly in silhouette, highlighting her youth and vitality. Yet, he may have considered her somber as she merely stood in the waves with neither a smile nor any indication of emotion expressed on her face. He approached closer, but stayed a distance off so as not to frighten her.

The sun at last dropped, the colors flailing as the sky darkened. The girl continued standing like a crane in the lapping waves, her skirt billowing, wet at the hem.

The man moved on down the beach, having climbed back up to the dunes where the sand was, indeed, blood red.

卍

He took breakfast such as it was on the deck facing the ocean. Coffee, black, please, and toast with orange marmalade. College-age waiters sprightly sprang around him, dipping to serve, bending to cart away used plates or to pour guests more coffee. A handful of people took breakfast. A sprinkle, a mostly elderly group who customarily rise early as time is speeding by and all time is important. He busied himself with his coffee, patiently spread his marmalade on little squares of toast. He made a ceremony of cutting the lightly burnt bread into little squares. It was a more elegant way of eating. He hated the proletarians who gobbled the whole slice of jammed bread, shoved into open mouths. Uncouth, he must have thought. He seemed very concerned that morning with one particular waiter. A young blonde woman who smiled and laughed lightly as she served her customers. Yet he thought how plastic the smile which showed teeth as white as snow. He knew she must brush with that new chemical toothpaste which brightens the enamel into an inhuman, unnatural tint. The teeth became almost blue, pearly. The old commercial jingle popped through his memory:

*"You'll wonder where the yellow went,*
*When you brush your teeth with Pepsodent."*

Carefully he lifted a square of toast from the plate and slipped the treasure into his mouth, and as he did, he glanced out to the beach. A pelican screamed flying low across the water. Two seagulls floated contentedly. The sky had never been bluer; a white puff or two hung over the horizon. No trace of blood now, no trace of the setting sun.

There stood the girl, the child. She was dressed in the same flowered skirt and white blouse and she stood in the water with the curls of waves lapping at her knees. Now her hair flowed gentle though loose down her back. It wasn't strawberry colored. Of course not, it had been the sun's sheen last evening.

Had she stayed on the beach all night? Impossible. He chewed his square of toast. The marmalade did not please him. Too sweet, it's all sugar and no orange flavor. His next square he would do without the preserve. He reminded himself to complain to the plastic college waitress when she came back to offer more coffee. But his intent was not so much with the sugared marmalade as it was on the young girl who then stepped back from the waves and headed toward the Inn. In fact, he took particular notice that she seemed to be moving this way. Wasn't she a charm, he must have thought. A charm . . . a charm dangling from a silver bracelet. The morning was silver and she was silver. She was definitely a charm.

Now he could observe her better and discovered her skin was a beautiful cinnamon color, tanned to perfection. He also discovered to his surprise that she wasn't nearly so young as he originally had thought last evening as he watched her standing before the setting sun. From his distance, first on the dunes, he considered her to be ten or eleven years old and wondered where her parents were and why weren't they attending her. But now, now to his new delight he realized she was nubile; what was the exact word he sought? She was more likely fourteen, fifteen at most. And she was a precious gem, an opal.

He must surely have been disappointed for the girl veered off from her original approach to the deck and leisurely strolled around to the right side of the Inn towards the front door leading into the lobby. She vanished. He spread a pat of butter on another square of toast and motioned for the blonde waitress to pour more hot coffee. He actually asked her to change his cup to a fresh one. She complied reluctantly and as she turned away from his table, a table set for two, she squinted up her face, puckered her lips and soundlessly moved her pretty lips to form a silent curse.

卍

He signed the check, left a newly minted quarter beneath the coffee cup for the plastic waitress, and rose from the table. The blue sky seemed to be graying. Rain had been forecast and surely it would fall ultimately.

He wandered through the French doors leading into the main dining room and continued to wander out to the lobby. There he was sure he would find reading materials, and decided to lull away the remainder of the morning with a magazine. On a coffee table sitting far to the right of the waiting area, just before a huge fireplace not kindled and flaming, he discovered the morning edition of the *Wall Street Journal.* Ah, he must have exclaimed, perfect. He lifted the paper and pressed it to his chest and ambled off to locate a comfortable chair under a lamp. He spotted the teenager, the girl on the beach. She sat knees together, the flowered skirt shielding her bare brown legs, a straight back against the overstuffed Morris chair, staring out into the depths of the lobby. Her chair was directly beside the reading lamp that he wished to sit under. He must have thought that a grand idea, to take the chair beside the young girl. May I, he might have asked her, before sitting himself. Immediately he opened the paper, spread it in the air before him, an eye cocked at the girl. She wasn't fourteen but to his eye she appeared far older, perhaps seventeen, eighteen. He gave a cute little smile, or more like a smirk, pressed his lips together, paying no attention to his spread *Journal,* and sank most comfortably back into the embrace of the chair.

"I'm India."

Startled, he let his paper fall onto his lap.

"I'm India."

"Miss . . ." was all he replied.

"You wanted to know who I am. I'm telling you. I'm India."

"I beg your pardon, miss."

He was ecstatic. He was relieved of the duty of opening the conversation with this, thin adorable creature . . . adorable because he could determine now that she was nearly of age.

"I'm India."

Obviously to him, she repeated this phrase over and over, her name.

"Your name is India?"

"No. I am India."

"Really," he replied, smugly like an Englishman might reply to a servant at his club upon saying, I am your servant, sir.

"Yes, I am India."

But how could he be smug in conversing with this charm, this silver charm, this opal of a gem . . . or as he now might have considered, this emerald of a jewel. Her eyes were green, and he noticed that immediately.

"You are from India?"

"No," was her only response.

"Then why are you India?"

"Because I am India. Do you know my father beat me when I was a small child, a very little girl."

Oh dear, he must have thought, the confession. What has been opened?

"My father was brutal. He beat me. I bled. I still have scars from his leather whip, his belt." She made as if to raise her skirt in proof.

He wanted to change chairs instantly. He wanted to rush out of the lobby. He wanted to return to his room on the fourth floor and lock the door. She was a prostitute. Wasn't that his luck. She'd cost money. Or she was setting him up for the police to descend and arrest him. Oh my God, he might have whispered to himself. Oh my God. What have I gotten myself into? I only wanted to while away quietly the morning which is graying and soon will be showered with rain.

"My mother left him because he beat me."

He didn't stir, did not budge, did not change his seat nor return to his room on the fourth floor. He stared directly into her gorgeous green eyes and waited for her to explain and recite the charge and details.

"My mother left him and took up with another man when I was still a tiny child."

Why can't she get to the point he must have asked himself. Why all this folderol of a confession. That doesn't really make this illegal act any more romantic. No. She's leading up to a higher price by reciting this list of violence and lewdness against her body.

"But I am India."

"What do you mean . . . India, if it is not your name nor where you come from?"

"You Americans. You Americans are not too smart."

"You're not American?"

"No, of course not. I am India. I am Olmec."

"Olmec?" He was not only puzzled, but totally confused.

"Yes, yes. Olmec. India. I am an Olmec Indian. From Mexico. The state of . . ."

"Oh I see. I understand."

"When I was six my new father . . . my stepfather . . . the new man mother then lived with . . . raped me."

Revelation. Revelation. He was both intrigued and horrified.

"She stuck a knife into his chest, and he went away. He did not take the clean shirts my mother had scrubbed on the rocks at the river. He did not take his machete to cut bananas with. He did not even take his bottle of tequila. He went away . . . he dropped out of sight . . . like the sun that dropped out of the red sky last night. Yes, yes. I saw you stealing glances at me last night at the beach. I watched from the corner of my eye you watching me. And I saw you too, true, on the deck this morning having coffee but staring at me."

He might have been dumbfounded, gagged at this truth.

"But, but . . . your mother didn't have him arrested . . . for the rape, I mean?"

"No, why should she? She stabbed him. And besides, men rape little girls and little boys, too, all the time in our communities. Men are cruel."

She emphasized our communities.

"He vanished. My mother said he surely would get his one day, in the gut. Some mother would plunge a stiletto into his guts and his belly would bleed his organs. And perhaps, with luck, some mother would cut off that ugly thing between his legs."

The gentleman squirmed in his chair. Folded and re-folded his *Wall Street Journal.* His tubby body tightened, near froze at the mention of cutting off the male organ. His own guilts began to pry at and warm his body, his mind. Beads of perspiration jumped out on his forehead even though the temperature of the lobby was cool, cooled by an air conditioner.

She was brutal. But the vicious acts upon her had been brutal too.

"I am India. I am Olmec. My mother is India and she, too, is Olmec. We know . . . we know how to treat such scum."

Before the man could make any attempt at reply or stop her from going further, deeper into the autobiographical details of her unsavory life, a voice came over the paging system. The voice announced that a Miss Margaretta Trini had an important message at the front desk.

India rose straight from her chair as though propelled by a jumping jack box or some other mechanical spring.

"My mother calls me. I must go . . . for now. I'll be seeing you."

He thanked Providence he had been spared further details . . . pretty as she was. He diligently perused his *Journal* but moved his chair to a darker corner of the lobby where he might not be spotted should she return.

But, but he must have watched her as she strolled off and noticed that she was not sixteen but a young woman obtaining a certain elegance in stride, and she was beautiful.

卍

The dining room was dressed in pink and each table had been lit with pink candles. The center buffet was flowered also in pink carnations and white. The main entrée of the evening would be poached salmon with a blueberry sauce and wild carrots. Tonight the dining staff was all male, dressed in black pants, pink shirts and black bow ties. He must have been happy that the young plastic waitress would not serve him . . . guilty for having left a shining new quarter for the breakfast tip.

The maître d' seated him at a table for one. An ensemble played romantic music on a violin, a cello and a bass. Divine, he probably whispered to himself as he shook the napkin and placed the pink linen over his lap, but he did not consider the pink motif of the room divine. That was gauche, sentimental . . . a luncheon setting for elderly spinsters. And he was neither elderly nor a spinster. He decided to relax and try to enjoy his meal. After all he had only two days remaining of his vacation at the seaside, and then back to the drudgery of the office and stupid young clerks just out of high school or college and inept receptionists who cared more for painting their nails than reading the mail. He quipped in rhyme.

Noticing a smart young waiter approaching his table, he placed the menu on top of his plate, and with a sigh of hunger, and a pleasant smile for the boy . . . after all, you do get more flies with syrup than with vinegar . . . he awaited the youth to ask his order.

"I believe I shall have the salmon and . . ."

He stopped, stone, cement. No words would budge. His mouth open as if to catch the fly which the vinegar would fail to do. He gaped across the dining room to one other table for one. There sat Miss India, Miss Olmec, Miss Margaretta Trini . . . alone.

"Ah, ah waiter . . . I'm feeling slightly . . . ah weak, dizzy. Could you fill my water glass, please, immediately."

There sat, no more than twenty feet away from his table, there sat, with the candle light shifting shadows across the face, there sat one of the most beautiful young women he had ever had the good fortune to see in his life. She was the nth of sophistication. Elegance beyond elegance. She sat like a Deana Durbin. She reared on her dining chair like a queen, no, a princess, Princess Grace herself. Perhaps more contemporary . . . perhaps Diana herself. She was more than lovely. She was . . . glamorous.

He kissed her a smile.

How could he ever have thought last night on the beach that she was a child. This princess of a young woman.

The waiter returned with the water, poured or splashed the iced liquid into his glass which spattered onto his chin.

"Be careful, young man." They don't train these days, college nincompoops, he more than likely breathed under his breath. He looked up from the water glass, its contents now spilling onto the pink tablecloth, at the young embarrassed waiter holding pad and pencil awaiting his dinner order.

A middle-aged couple passed by Miss India. They actually bumped into her shoulder just as she was to raise a glass of wine. It spilled. She rose from her table. He noticed that she wore a flowered skirt and white blouse, Not terribly fashionable, not a dinner dress. She rushed from the room.

卍

After dinner he went to the bar. It was nearly empty; a couple or two sat at separate tables. One young man was holding the lovely hand of a very striking young woman in slacks and red blouse. He pulled out a stool at the bar. The young college boy, the bartender, dropped a cocktail napkin and inquired as to what he "could get 'im." "Oh a brandy," you could hear him say. Remy Martin . . . probably was his taste. He pulled out a cigar from the inside pocket of his dress coat, tore off the wrapper and awaited his brandy glass. The youth sat it down in front of him on the napkin.

"All set?" the youth asked.

He despised that phrase . . . all set. Of course he was all set. He'd been seated for the last five minutes waiting for this idiot to serve him.

The bartender took off; a waiter had called him down to the service bar.

He dipped the cigar end into the brandy, retrieved it, brought the cigar to his lips and lit a match. That was the bartender's job he thought as the flame rushed against the tobacco.

"I couldn't finish my story."

A woman's voice was behind him.

"May I sit, please?"

He turned. It was India. It was Miss Trini. He felt his maleness turn; his groin grew warm; his palms were already sweaty.

She took a stool, nodded her head no to the bartender when he approached. She didn't care for a drink. She didn't drink.

He chose not to look. Nervously he swirled the brandy in his glass. Sipped. Puffed slightly on his cigar, blew the smoke off to his left so that it would not offend the lady seated beside him at his right.

"I was called away twice. Once by page, and once because that loathsome couple spilled my wine."

He turned his head. She was still dressed in the flowered skirt and white blouse. One knee crossed right. She leaned elbows on the bar. He gazed long and lovingly. She was indeed most lovely. Her black hair . . . but did he notice a bright fleck, a silver strand . . . her hair cascaded down her slender back, now arched, and fell across the right shoulder in tiny ringlets. He noticed how dark was her complexion. Honey, no not honey. Cinnamon. No. Nutmeg. Yes, nutmeg. His stare moved from her sharp but delicate chin to her mouth. Her lips were luscious, no lipstick, then the cheeks, full and round almost edged at the top. The nose beautifully long, beautifully long and thin, with almost a slight hump near the bridge. He remembered Barbara Streisand's gorgeous Jewish nose, and he for years had longed to kiss her nose, to press his lips upon it. And in the far back of his memory he recalled once he had met a poet, he believed a Polish-American poet, who had also a most beautiful nose. And how she covered her nose in self-disgust. And made noises as to how ugly the nose was. And it wasn't.

"I wanted to tell you. My third farther shot me in the left leg. Here, want to see the scar?"

He feigned, no. He waved the invitation off.

"My fourth father decided he was going to kill me. But my mother was always there. She called the police on my third father. He was sent to jail for four weeks. My fourth father . . . of course they were not biological, but stepfathers, or I like to think my mother had sort of rented them for sex. Don't you see! And my fourth father . . . well, she took the gun, aimed at my temple, and turned it on him. He fell to the floor his blood spattering my skirt. She then took the gun and shot herself."

He chugga-lugged the brandy and waved frantically at the bartender. He ordered a double scotch, soda on the side.

"Isn't that a fantastic story? Isn't it? But don't go. Don't go, sir. There is more to my life."

卍

This beautiful woman had become not only a horror but a downright annoyance, a bore. He would avoid her for the next two days.

Now in bed, beneath the light covers, he clicked off the bed lamp, allowed his book, *Profiles of Courage,* to slip to the carpet, and rolled to his left side. He slept naked . . . as a rule. He enjoyed the sensuality of feeling his naked skin embraced by the sheets. At home, he slept between satin sheets. Now his hands moved between his thighs. Feeling the fleshy muscles he most assuredly made some decisions to diet or exercise. The feel of the increasing blubber was hard to accept. But his thighs invited his hands. They slipped further and he touched his warm genitals. His flesh was then flaccid, but his palms felt it stir, move, grow. And he thought of this beautiful woman. This phenomenon of womanhood, this female aberration. Lust moved through his groin. Yes, she was an aberration. Ridiculous!

He pulled his hands away from the hot flesh. He threw them out from under the bed quilts. He allowed them to rest on the spread. He turned over on his stomach, and changed the pictures, the images in his mind. The plastic waitress with the chemical white teeth flashed and he remembered how cute she was. What a darling little butt she actually had. He'd give her a better tip tomorrow morning.

He awoke once in the night. Thought he heard someone on the balcony outside his French windows. Thought he saw a figure move in the moonlight. Was positive he heard a voice calling him. No. He returned to sleep.

In the morning, room service brought his toast and marmalade with a large pot of coffee. He then complained to the waiter that the preserve was all sugar and no orange flavor. The room service waiter promised faithfully he would tell the chef and have the brand changed.

卍

At one o'clock, he had room service bring a cheeseburger, rare, and an order of crisp french fries to his room. And, yes, he ordered a *Los Angeles Times* and the *Wall Street Journal.*

The room service waitress proved to be pimpled, stout and surly. Her dress hanky in a breast pocket was dirty, and her white shoes were in great need of polish.

He was most observant.

卍

Despite the mosquitoes, he took dinner that night on the deck. Tenderloin tips on a bed of yellow rice flavored with chopped walnuts. The vegetable was asparagus. Dessert, simple, a ball of raspberry sherbet. And of course his coffee. Because of the flittering bugs he was the only diner on the deck.

The sea was quiet. Barely a breeze. The moon was low. Barely a sheen struck the lazy waves, indulgent waves. Many clouds formed on the vast horizon.

He sipped the last of the coffee, gently placed the cup into the saucer and was about to pick up the waiter's pen to sign the check when he noticed a figure at the edge of the waves. It was obviously a woman because her skirt flared about her thighs. She turned and began a stroll up the beach away from the shore and towards the deck.

Surely he would have recognized the woman.

The waiter bowed and scraped as he lifted the check from the table. Quickly he stole a look at the check. A one-dollar tip on a thirty-dollar bill. What kind of cheapskate is this old fuck?

In moments, brief seconds almost, the woman was at the deck and heading to his table. He thought it was okay. He was over whatever slight passion he had felt earlier yesterday when he discovered she was not a child, or a teenager, but a full blown and sensuous woman. And not only was he a man, an adult, a successful man in his career, trade, whatever, but he had no fear of the weird nor the occult, nor a dangerous woman who told outrageous lies concerning her life. He was brave, solid, stolid and had a broad shoulder for this poor thing's troubles. Let her come, let her cry on his shoulder. At least then he could breathe in the scent of her femininity.

She came directly to his table. Pulled out a chair and seating herself she opened the conversation . . . directly;

"After my mother died. Remember, I told you she shot herself to avoid prison after she shot my fourth father who had aimed the gun at my temple. I was eight. Eight years old. Orphaned. Penniless. My mother and I never had anything but a shack, a pot, and rags. The men she rented her body to never gave us anything but misery, squalor, their spit, and the back of their hand or the slice of a machete or the muzzle of a gun. They were despicable . . . half-breeds. My mother was a full-blooded Olmec. Proud. My real father, the man whose snake entered my mother and bred me with semen. He, too, was a full-blooded Olmec. Proud."

He listened intently. He remembered books he had read in college. He had taken a lit course, a survey of world literature. He was forced to swallow a book titled *Crime and Punishment* by some maniacal Russian. He now remembered the story of this book. The crime of a young student axing two women to death, an old crone and her younger sister.

The man was not repulsed by her story, not sick to his stomach, nor horrified now. He was interested, seriously. And he would let her ramble on until she had spilled all the blood and guts, the bile she had stored up these years.

"I am India. I am Olmec. I am proud, too, like my dead mother and my dead father, my biological father, not those monsters who rented my mother's body after my good father died."

She paused. He probably expected to see a tear staining her cheek. But there was no tear. No redness to her eyes. She was stoic. Not an impression of emotion on her face, nor lips.

For some odd reason the lights on the deck came up brilliantly sharp, blinding . . . just for a moment. A moment, a splash of time, long enough for him to take a keen, deep look into her face.

Her hands in air, fingers open wide, she was disclaiming, or what to him seemed disclaiming, a part, a role in a play. He stared into her eyes, the pools of green, but no longer were they green but jet-black. He looked and found little tiny lines growing around the eyes. He looked at her nose . . . the beautiful nose he had admired so much before, and the sharp chin which now appeared weak, with an ever-so-slight tremble. He looked into the depths of her black hair which had shone brightly with the highlights of the moon yesterday. Now, now there were near splotches of gray, white hairs ruffling through the black.

"I went to the streets of my village. I begged. No one offered a single tortilla. Nor a rotted tomato. Not even the cooked balls of their roasted pig, nor the eye of a dead fish. They brushed me away with a kitchen broom. They pushed me off. I was eight. I tried to rent my body to old men and very young men. Not even the little adolescent, masturbating boys would buy me, not even with a Chicle nor half of a brown banana covered with fly shit. There was nothing to do. But leave my village . . . my village contaminated with half-breeds. Olmec blood was slowly dripping out of the veins into the sands which the northern winds blew down the emptied streets and into the doors of the huts."

Suddenly she stood. For the first time he may have noticed that she was tall, taller than he had originally conceived, and certainly taller that he falsely believed an Indian would be. She stood straight, back straight, legs straight, feet firm on the carpet. She did not lean over to whisper in his ear but in a natural voice, level, exclaimed:

"I went to the city streets and became a whore. I opened my legs for any bastard who wanted a sniff . . . as you wanted to sniff the other night when you walked off the dunes down to the shore to observe me. Don't lie . . . you wanted to sniff, and you smelled more."

Startled, he attempted to plead innocent. Then he remembered he was a man, male and like all males he was curious, no, not just curious . . . he too . . . like her second father, wanted to embrace her, drop her to the sandy shore, the beach, and enter, wallow in her womanhood. But a knife stabbed into his brain. She wasn't a woman. She had been a young child that night on the beach, her feet in the red water, her figure covered with the blood of the setting sun. What . . .

"To make a long story short, I did not live on the street too many years allowing those males to sniff me, their hands to move up my calves, to move up to my thighs, to move up to . . . I wasn't on the street too many years."

And she paused. Fell silent. Turned her head and stared out to sea, the sea, the sea. The air was rife with her emotions. He could have at that moment touched the air which contained her emotion, her dreams, her fears, but the sea, the sea seemed to hold her dreams as she wistfully glanced backwards to the sea, where only a half hour before she had stood in the curled waves and meditated upon the mystery of the sea, the same as she knew he pondered her mystery.

"I was found, a street urchin, a whore sniffed by the worst of humanity, rented by the rags of men, spat upon after their ooze rammed into my cunt."

She pulled up straight having hammered the last word of her sentence into his head, his brain.

"I was found, discovered crawling the streets the way lice crawl over the body. I was adopted by a kind stranger. A kind stranger. A kind, kind stranger."

At that moment the lights on the deck blacked out.

This was theatre he must have thought. Tricks, magic, show business. She had been hired an actress, to play for me, to play with me. To entertain me but not to bed me.

He looked up into the blackness. The figure of a woman stood before him, but not the slender, straight handsome woman who had sat at the table and confessed her sins.

Suddenly the lights blinked on. The deck was brilliant with white light. The woman, Miss India had left.

He stared out at the sea, the beach. He thought he could see the silhouette of a figure trudging down the shore. The moon had dropped. There was barely light.

卍

He was to leave the Inn early the next morning. He had a long drive to Tucson. Even though his car was air-conditioned it would be unbearably hot. Consequently, he wanted to leave early to avoid some of the heat. He would rise at five, breakfast quickly and take off. He packed his bag. Walking to the dresser he pulled out the heavy imitation mahogany drawers. In the top drawer he found his bathing trunks. He hadn't used them. He hadn't meant to use them. He did not like water, wild water, heavy waves.

Actually, he finally, for the first time, admitted he was afraid of the sea. It was too huge, too grand and noble and expansive. It held too many mysteries for a man like him, who had lived ninety percent of his life in the desert, in an office or before a court room bench. He actually hated the sea. He picked up the swim trunks . . . the ones his secretary told him he must buy for the vacation . . . and noticed not their stiffness or dryness or the smell of the newness of the cloth, but he noticed the crotch and he remembered Miss India and how she had "rented" her body to sniffers. He sniffed his swim trunks for the smell of maleness. But it wasn't there. It smelled of burnt cloth. He tossed it across the room to his suitcase, distressed, embarrassed, angry with himself.

It didn't take long for him to pack up all but what he'd need for the trip home. He'd leave out the toothpaste and such things he'd use in the morning.

Shortly he was ready for bed, tucked in under the quilts and about to click the bed lamp when he heard a knock on the door. He didn't know anyone at the Inn. Surely if the desk, the management, had business with him they would have phoned first . . . before coming to his room.

He pulled on his briefs and approached the door. The chain had been set and as he opened he asked who was knocking.

"Open. It is me, Miss India, as you like to call me."

"I'm in bed. What do you want?"

"We need to talk."

He closed the door, took off the chain and admitted her into his room.

"Ah, how nice, how very pleasant. It is almost sweet, your room. What comforts you have."

She walked directly to his bed, pulled back the loose covers and sat, her left leg crossed over the right.

He noticed she still wore the flowered skirt and white blouse. She was barefooted. For a second or two she played with the spread, smoothing it out with her palm. Then she rose, played with a button at the skirt waist. Her skirt dropped. She was naked. No clothing, no slip or panties under the skirt.

He stood with his mouth open. She did not look at him, but unbuttoned her blouse, button by button, slowly, and then angrily pulled the blouse from her shoulders and threw it on the carpet. She slipped effortlessly between the sheets of the bed. Her head on the pillow, her hair billowing about her face. She motioned for him to come to her.

Astonished was not the word to describe what appeared on his face. Perplexed he was, amazed he was, near fright moved him into a rigid stance. His heart did a few murmuring flip-flops. He watched her finger curl, and she motioned him to come to her again. He staggered across the room from the closed door where he had been leaning, bracing his paunchy body. When he reached the bedside he dropped his briefs and climbed into the open sheets she held for him. He submerged. Not daring to think, hardly capable of feeling. He was not aroused.

"My second mother adopted me. She brought me from my country to this place, this land. She took me from my people, my beautiful people, my people who centuries, centuries ago carved great figures, great heads out of huge rocks, round and smooth. They are there to this very moment, to prove to the world that my people, the Olmec, the Indias, once were a great nation, and a strong civilization. Then the sniffers came. My people dispersed, they ran into the jungle. They were afraid. They knew their lives were in danger. They hid the women and children from those who came to sniff the body."

She rolled her body against his flesh.

He struggled away.

"My second mother taught me language, your language. I speak your language as if I had been born to it, as if it had flowed from my first mother's breast with her milk."

It was true. Her English was clear and distinct. No accent whatsoever. Why had he not noticed it the first time she spoke, in the lobby of the Inn, when he was reading his *Journal.*

"So now we are here. And as you have wanted, you may now sniff. You may rent my body."

He said nothing, but surely he was heavy with thought. What to say? What to do now that this beautiful woman lay in his bed, her flesh warm against his flesh. He looked over at her. Her black eyes burned into his skin.

"You may buy me now . . . if you dare."

Her hair, her gorgeous long black tresses . . . they were white. Her face, her beautiful gem-like face was withered. Her breasts which had been firm, nipples the color of rose buds now sagged. And her nutmeg skin, that taut flesh highlighted by the moon and the setting sun, was thinly pulled across a bony skeleton.

She laughed and laughed. Hard, seriously, wildly, maniacally laughed, a banshee, a mad woman, a raving blood curdling laugh of insanity.

He jumped from the bed. Grabbed at his bathrobe laying across a chair but missed as he stumbled over the suitcase on the floor, spilling out its contents. He noticed his bathing trunks. He grabbed them up into his sweaty hands and ran out of the room.

卍

"We went for an early dip," the blonde plastic waitress with the chemical teeth was saying to a police officer.

"He was weird," the young man who served as bartender said, shaking his head. "He came to the bar one night, and sat there talking to himself and getting the answer."

"And he was cheap, believe me. He pinched me one morning at breakfast, my butt, and he had the goddamn gall to tip me a quarter."

"We found him just like he is now. On the sand. In his trunks. His arms stretched out like he had been nailed to a cross. His mouth open just like it is now. With seaweed hanging out."

"Did you ever see him talking with a young woman. Rather dark complexioned. An Indian."

"No."

"Not me. I only heard him talking to himself."

"The desk clerk said he was always asking for a young woman named Miss Trini. Said she was a Mexican Indian, you know, a Chicana."

"Nope. Not me," the college lad said. "Spoke only to himself."

卍

The sun was slowly dying.

Bloody waves curled to the shore.

A young girl stood in the waves. Maybe she was ten or eleven or possibly fourteen . . . surely no older. She stood watching the scarlet sun go down. The red water lapped her brown legs. She stood in the waves staring into the mystery of the sea.

卍

# Visitation

## I.

AGNES AND MONROE SAT AT THE SUPPER TABLE. A LARGE TUREEN OF potato soup steamed between them near a loaf of bread and a pot of butter sweating in brine, butter Agnes herself had churned that very morning. Their meal was meager, but sufficient and nutritious, and included a salad of thinly sliced red onions and green cucumbers, drowning in cider vinegar. The dark room was lit by a small blue bulb hanging directly over the table. It was a sparse kitchen, showing more of what it lacked than what it contained. No microwave oven or electric dishwasher; no vinyl cabinets, nor portable color TV, not even an electric can opener. An old iron stove sat against the right wall, beside a somewhat gloomy-looking refrigerator. On the opposite wall was hung a braid of sweetgrass; on a shelf sat an antique radio—now silent, austere. In the far corner was a large rocking chair, its back upholstered by a dull, though once brightly-colored, throw rug. The rug's design resembled lightning flashes striking barren ground. The seat was covered with a fluffy red pillow with fringe, some of which was knotted or missing, like the teeth of an old tomcat caught in too many fence battles at midnight. The tiny room was centered with the kitchen table and four chairs, and beyond, in the right corner, stood a tall and wide metal cabinet. There was a porcelain sink, its belly draped by a ruffled fabric of color so old that it could be of just about any hue.

The house was hardly more than a cabin. Besides the kitchen, a living room of sorts extended the structure and contained a narrow stairwell to the top floor, where the bedroom was. The parlor contained an old army cot neatly made and a twin rocking chair. The floor was littered with split cane, baskets unfinished, completed, and a stripped black ash log. The walls were covered with pictures of ancestors, and a faded pattern of roses and iris. Only two windows looked to a pasture and a barn to the right, and a chicken coop with a dense wood beyond. There was no inside bathroom.

Monroe spooned his soup. And when the spoon missed his mouth, the liquid spilled down his chin. Agnes reached over and sponged the spilled soup away.

"I'm going to make you a bib."

"Yes, ma'am."

"Look at your shirt. Nice and clean it was this morning. You drank your soup through your shirt." And she laughed, dabbing the sponge to his lips and chin.

"Maybe I should get you a little trough, instead of a bib." And she laughed again, a huge grin parting her lips and showing a missing tooth on the upper row.

"Here, take a bite of bread. It's buttered."

Monroe opened his mouth wide. No teeth at all. He closed his lips down upon the soft meat of the bread. Agnes tugged and his lips pulled, and finally he yanked off a hunk of the freshly baked bread. To the best of his ability he chewed and chewed the bread, his gums making hard work of the task. It was soon masticated and Agnes once more shoved the slice of bread between his lips; again she tugged and Monroe pulled. Success. He gummed the food until it had been chewed small enough to be swallowed.

She followed this with a glass of water. Then she again spooned soup to his lips, and once more sponged away the drippings which did not enter his open mouth.

The evening light lowered outside. The kitchen darkened. Shadows from the outside light flittered and played against the room's walls. Their own heads flat in silhouette on the wall. Agnes made no motion of pulling the light chain dangling above the table to illuminate the room. She ignored it.

They were both dressed in work clothes, she wore a typical print house-dress, a sash tied in the back. Monroe wore green work pants and a grungy white shirt buttoned at the collar. Suspenders held up his pants. They were both grayed, going to white; Agnes's hair was in a bun at the back of her head; Monroe's hair, fine and silky, brushed his ears and lay in a gentle fold against the temples.

Agnes sipped her soup slowly, lifting the large spoon from the soup plate, extending it out away from her ample bosom attempting not to spill, and then drew the spoon directly to her mouth.

"Ohhhhhh!" she exclaimed.

"What's the matter?"

"A bit of arthritis."

"You haven't taken your medicine?"

"Doesn't work," is all she replied.

"Won't unless you take it. Go get it, now . . . I'd suggest," he cautioned.

"I'll take it later. After supper is over."

They never called each other by their first names. She would say "you," or "he," or "him;" he would say "you," or "she," or "her." Never did they utter Mr. Bond or Mrs. Bond. Just simply "you."

"What's that cow bellowing about out there in the pasture?"

"Don't know."

"Go see!"

She rose from the table and went to the door, closed even though it was late June and the fair weather that spring had brought warm afternoons and pleasant evenings. Agnes was always a little afraid animals would come into the house, especially if she was outside doing her chores, and they would annoy Monroe. Chickens knew no boundaries, nor did squirrels, nor raccoons. She'd even heard of a black bear walking into a neighbor's place once and cleaning out the refrigerator. Monroe would have big trouble if a bear or raccoon got into the house. The door now opened, she scanned the front yard: the yellow rose bush, the huge maple at the beginning of the dirt drive, a wheelbarrow leaning on its side; and she moved her gaze toward the pasture where their one and only cow should be grazing. She had many times tried to get Monroe to agree to acquiring a small mutt which would give warning should a bear be in the yard, or a stranger. Even here on the reservation odd folks would show up from time to time, and she had heard of a recent house robbing, chicken stealing, things like that. Crime, minimal that it was, minor that it was, had finally left the city and arrived at the doorstep of the reservation. But Monroe insisted that a dog would only be under foot, its food costly. He also pshawed the whole idea of crime on the reserve. If anyone cared to rob them, all they'd get was a dumb radio that didn't work and maybe a sack of spuds. No dogs, he insisted. Animals belong outside, he believed. Agnes had agreed with that, it wasn't necessary for the dog to be in the house, even in the winter. It could house itself in the little barn, in the hay. And food, well, let it hunt for rabbits and so forth. It wouldn't be that much trouble, she reasoned. It could be helpful, warning with its barks.

She scanned the yard again. Her sight cleaned the pasture. The cow was standing still . . . not even a tail wagging, chewing grass. Nothing there. No one there. Not even the three hens that usually clucked about. Nothing but the scent of lilacs and the pungent smell of wild strawberries ripening beyond in the long meadow. She firmly closed the door, shut out the pleasant winds and returned to the table.

"You want onions and cucumber now?"

He nodded yes and she cut the vegetables in tiny pieces, speared some on the tine of Monroe's fork, and slipped them into his open mouth.

"You chew well. Remember before you didn't. You choked."

There was a certain care, concern, between these two elderly people, this married couple, two folks who'd married so many years before that they had almost forgotten exactly when they had married, when Agnes had accepted the gold ring; when Monroe had moved into her father's house. They were not blessed with children, but they were satisfied with their lives together. Monroe worked the small farm, and Agnes did house chores and wove baskets of black ash. She picked sweetgrass and wove it into baskets as well. She sold these to the market in town until the Museum opened ten years ago. She then began carrying the beautiful baskets to the young lady directing the Museum, selling them to her. Much easier for Agnes, and she made more money. Selling to the market, she thought, she was always under-paid and that man, Mr. Basely, actually cheated her. The Museum gave her a fair price.

Agnes and Monroe grew old together. As they aged, they watched the farm and its labors slowly outpace them. Monroe was not the best farmer in the community, not that he was lazy, but that he was meditative; wasn't much concerned with new scientific methods, chemical fertilizers, or raising more than what their own personal needs required. Two cows were enough. One for the milk sales, one for their own use. He kept a horse to plow the garden and to pull the logging sled into the woods for lumber, some of which he sold, but most he kept for their own woodstove, to cook and to heat. Chickens were okay, and in their early marriage they had some turkeys and a goose or two. No pigs. Monroe didn't eat pork. It wasn't traditional. He did like to hunt and bag a goodly variety of game: venison, rabbit, quail, etc. . . . and he trapped for otter and muskrat. Beaver was no more in the vicinity, had been trapped out years ago, or poisoned out. They kept themselves in fresh meat, fresh garden produce, fresh fruit and berries from the woods and meadows, and fresh dairy products from their cow. Their butter was the best churned on the reserve, and people were constantly driving up their dirt road to buy whatever extra Agnes might have to sell . . . no matter how much it perspired, being so salty in preservation. Agnes maintained the old way of preserving meat and butter . . . brined.

Now in their early seventies they knew a distinct comfort. They had small needs and enjoyed each other's company. Evenings, Agnes would read to Monroe as he sat in the rocker, puffing on his pipe. It was all the pleasure they needed . . . apart from walks up and down the country road for exercise and to help keep their weight down. To be overly fat was simply not good. Once a day they trekked a half mile down the road to Turtle Pond and back. Agnes would take him by the arm and lead the way. She was his eyes. When the berries were pickable, she led him to the meadow for the fruit or to the low brush for blueberries or whatever had come into season. His ears watched for deer.

Though their relatives figured in the high numbers, they were rarely bothered . . . even after Monroe lost his sight. Occasionally a nephew or niece would drive by to see if they were still alive. Occasionally Agnes's much younger sister would drive out to take the couple in to see a doctor, or to the grocery store for sugar and flour and sometimes coffee, which neither of them drank too much of. Agnes gathered wild leaves and made tea with them. Besides cold water, that is all they expected to drink.

If they did not have a happy, joyous life together, they were content.

Neither the man nor the woman held great expectations of life and were not disappointed or disgruntled when life occasionally dealt a blow or two, such as when Monroe lost his sight, or when arthritis began to cripple Agnes's left arm, making basket weaving difficult. Had they had children, life would certainly have been different . . . certainly had more problems, but a sense of joy and pleasure would have been within their spirits and the walls of their house. Children didn't happen. They took this in their stride, never complained, and never thrust guilty accusations at one another. Agnes decided she was barren, and that's all there was to it. Monroe decided he was sterile. And that's all there was to it. They managed to live their lives: peaceful though not placid; comfortable though not rich with material things; uneventful, but not boring, not monotonous, as there were many chores on the small farm, and enjoyable chores at that. They found pleasure in gardening and berry picking, raising flowers, and tapping the maple trees. Yes, to Monroe the sawing, chopping, and splitting of his own wood was a good feeling. Independence was supreme in their view, even after Monroe lost his sight . . . which again they took in stride. If it was to be it was to be. They believed there must be some purpose in not having children, not having sight. The couple felt they had much to be thankful for: dawn, noon, sunset; the stars and the moon, the sun; the small creek that babbled near the house and from which they took fresh water; the songs of the birds and particularly that of the hermit thrush at twilight. They enjoyed all four seasons as they came and disappeared . . . the leaves, the snow, the rain, and the sunshine. Even the occasional shrew which would get into the kitchen, was a thing of goodness, a reminder that life was there and to be lived, not a threat nor hindrance, not something to be ignored in boredom or covered over in fantasy, or drenched in jealousy or envy or corrupted with alcohol or crime. They plotted and plodded a good life, a simple life of common everyday things and experiences. The garden and the yellow rose bush were sufficient entertainment, and there was so very much beauty around them . . . wherever they looked, whatever they touched or tasted.

Another noise at the door called her back from the table. Agnes opened the door. She stared back at Monroe. He sat at the table undisturbed. His arms folded across his chest, his mouth slightly opened like a fledgling waiting for Agnes to spoon more soup into the gaping hole. He was calm.

No one stood on the top step of the small porch. No one. The knock must have come from the wind. As she began to push the wooden door closed a figure suddenly appeared in the opening. She was startled.

"Uuuuu," she exclaimed.

"'Scuse me, ma'am. Didn't mean to frighten you."

"Well you did. For a minute there. Did scare."

"I'm sorry."

"What do you want? Who are you?"

He was young, perhaps twenty-five, tall, wiry, a little stooped from his height. Dark. He wore jeans dusty from the road and a sweatshirt with letters stenciled on the cloth—University of Wisconsin, and in a crescent underneath, Green Bay. He wore a blue baseball cap with capital letters which, spelled out, would have said New York Mets, the brim of which pointed down and off to the left. His hair was long and black, loosely tied in a pony tail; his face dark from sun but dark also from a heavy beard. He carried a tote bag slung over his left shoulder.

"I was just walking down this road on my way to town. It's dusty. I suddenly got very parched and couldn't find a creek. Thought you might give me a drink of water, please."

"Who is it?" Monroe asked in a careless voice.

"Young man says he wants a drink of water."

"Invite him in."

"Yes. I think we could spare a drink. Then I'll give you the pail. You can draw more from the stream."

The youth grinned, pleased, and began to step into the kitchen; Agnes held her hand on the door, her arm stretched across his path.

"Wait here."

"Ask him in," Monroe called.

"He wants me to ask you in. Come in then."

This time the young man's grin broke into a wide and pleasant smile nearly from ear to ear. He showed beautiful white teeth in a somewhat large mouth.

"Thank you."

"What's he look like?"

The young man then recognized the man seated at the table was blind.

"Not much," she rejoined. "Pretty tall. Dirty. No, I guess maybe just dusty. Got shoes on. Not too much to look at. As I see it."

The young man laughed and shyly strolled into the now dark room.

"Have supper, boy?"

"No, sir."

"Set him out a plate. He's a guest now he's in."

Agnes's mouth formed a slur, but no words came. She angled back into the center of the room, shuffled about, found a bowl and set it on the table with a spoon and knife.

"All we got is soup and bread. Soup's cold now. Fire's out and can't be heated up."

"Thank you ma'am. I don't need it heated up. It's just fine cold."

"Sit down, son," Monroe invited.

He eagerly took a seat, but before picking up the spoon to commence the cold supper, Agnes noticed his mouth move, his lips, he mumbled, but she couldn't catch what words tripped out.

Now that there sat this young stranger at the table, Agnes felt there was a need for light. Before reseating herself, she pulled the chain and light showered down onto the table and its contents. She would now have a better look at him, and he at them.

"What you doin' on this back country road, boy?" Monroe asked.

"Going to town."

"Which town?" Monroe persisted in questioning.

"Any town that will have me." The uninvited visitor slurped the cold soup, and accepted the bread Agnes sliced from the large heavy loaf.

"I mean, sir, that I'm just traveling around."

"A bum?" Monroe asked, inquisitive.

"Not exactly."

He still held his tote bag in his hands and Agnes was slightly amazed to find this as she stared him down; her gaze moved from head to waist, as the rest of his body was hidden under the flat table. What, at first, in the doorway she thought was a heavy beard in need of shaving, the five o'clock shadow as it is often referred to, was really a thin beard. She looked at his arms. His sweatshirt sleeves were rolled high to the elbows. His flesh was covered with black hair. His fingers were short, too short for a man of his size. There was hair on his knuckles, and long fingernails turned under and pointed.

"What are you then if you're travelin' around with no place in sight? Just bumming. You aren't a bum? Are you a hobo as they used to say?" Monroe continued to quiz him.

"Some folks call me a hippie, but I'm neither a bum nor a hippie," he answered, "And I'm sure no hobo. I just got out of school, college, and want to see some country. So I'm walking the roads. I've got some money . . ." he reached for a billfold in his back right pocket then thought better of it and placed his right hand back to the spoon in the soup bowl. "They tell me that's what you do when school's over. You hike around and see things."

"They used to call that getting an education . . . the hard way," the old man suggested, and giggled, his laugh showing his toothless gums.

"Guess you're right," the young man agreed. "Soup's great. Just great. Ah, could I have that glass of water, please?"

Agnes stared at him. Startled, she rose from her chair. What had happened to his face! What had appeared in the doorway was now disintegrating before her eyes. He had been young, full of the blush of youth, eyes twinkling, lips parted in huge smiles; there had been something of a laugh in the way he spoke. But now, now his eyes were circled with lines, dark shadows rounded below. There were wrinkles at the sides of his mouth. Her glance moved down to his arms and hands. His hands appeared knotted with veins sticking high in the flesh, rough and reddened as though worked hard for years.

She stood straight and glared down at her husband Monroe, who had insisted upon inviting this stranger into the kitchen. What! Monroe's bent back was now straight. He'd been stooped for years, ever since he lost sight. His thick hair was white, but now this moment it looked . . . brown. It appeared as though someone had washed away the wrinkles about Monroe's eyes and mouth, they had disappeared. His large flabby ears were firm and silky.

Agnes backed away from the table. Her sight was gone. Her eyes had failed her. Her mind began to wander. This could not be happening. She turned and went to the water bucket. She filled a glass of water and brought it back to the table and placed it before the stranger.

She looked again at Monroe. A vivid imagination was a good thing to have, but when it played tricks on you it wasn't so good. Her imagination must definitely be playing tricks. Old crow, old coyote was tricking her senses. Yet, there it was. Monroe's hair had turned dark brown. His cheek had a shine, a blush. The rise of the cheekbone was firm and the flesh full as it had been when he was twenty. She sat down and looked again at the young man. He was bent over the soup bowl slurping in the liquid, dunking hunks of bread and slobbering the wet bread to his mouth. His back was bent now. What had been straight before, was rounded, aged with years and burden. Wires of black hair curled out of his ears and nose.

Knocking over his half-empty glass of water, Agnes jumped to her feet and staggered away from the men. Slowly, she stepped back, back to the wall where she knew a braid of sweetgrass hung. Her hands fumbled up the wall until she grasped the braid, pulled it down from the hook, and turned.

"Slice the boy more bread," Monroe said.

"I've had enough, sir," the boy growled as though he was angry, mad with the food he'd been given.

In a moment, Agnes had a kitchen match lit and the sweetgrass set aflame. She strode toward the table, then blew out the tongue of fire. Lunging, she circled the table, first stopping to allow the smoke to engulf her husband's frame. Then she held it directly over the table.

The stranger looked up at her. His nose was now a muzzle, long, pointed, sharp, wet. His face was covered with black fur.

"You don't need to be afraid," he growled . . . all youthfulness of voice having vanished.

"Can't you see! He is not a stranger," Monroe said.

She made no reply, but continued to dust the room and Monroe with the smoke of the burning sweetgrass. She noticed suddenly her husband's eyes had a glint of light where before they had been covered with a film of mucous. It seemed as though he had regained his sight, as if he could see.

What had happened when she went over to the door? she asked herself. There had been no one there at first, but the spring wind and the cow out in the pasture, and the smell of heartberry blossoms. There had been no one on the porch. No one! Now this . . . this creature, this animal, sat at her kitchen table and her husband, Monroe, Mr. Bond, was transforming before her eyes. Was she dreaming? Was she awake? Was she dead? Had lightning struck her when she opened the door? Was it so ferocious she had not felt the snap and burn as it shot through her body, her mind, her brain? Was this the death world?

She leaned into the table, and fell against Monroe.

Or had she fallen asleep at the supper table over her soup? She had done this before. Monroe was always falling asleep at the table. Now had she done it, too? Had she had a heart attack at the table? True, she was tired, exhausted. She had worked in the garden that morning, worked on her baskets that afternoon, churned the butter, and cooked the potato soup. She did these kinds of things every day. Nothing new. Daily chores, tasks. They had taken their usual stroll, the hike to Turtle Pond and sat there for a while on a log watching the life of the water swarm about, the water spiders and a muskrat swimming to the far shore. They listened to a kingfisher rattle and a crow caw. That was it. That nasty old crow had followed her home. Bewitched her with its black magic. Its powers. Somehow she had offended the crow, the trickster, and he had taken revenge by blanking her mind, destroying it with this outrageous fantasy. What now could she do to ward off this evil, to strike this evil thing away, to call off the magic of the crow? How, how did she offend it? How! She always left crumbs of something or other by the bottom step. Bits of bread, or corn bread, a handful of corn, suet. Why that very morning she had left the churner for him to peck and lick if he wanted.

She steadied herself against the table. She brushed the smoldering sweetgrass braid in the air, the smoke caressing around Monroe and then rising and disappearing into the spirit world. Waving the sweetgrass braid and its rising smoke over the table, she looked down. There was Monroe slicing bread for this creature. Was he the crow, this evil thing at her table, a creature she had somehow offended? Maybe this was why her hens did not lay. And when they did, the eggs were often spoiled.

"Have butter. Fresh this morning churned. The woman churns it herself. Want honey? I'll get some from the cabinet," Monroe offered to the stranger.

The stranger made motions, signs with his hands that yes, he would enjoy a taste of honey on his buttered bread. She watched her husband rise from the table and walk stealthily, steadily to the large metal cabinet. He opened the door and pulled down an earthen jar of honey, honey she

collected last year herself from a beehive found at the edge of the woods.
Monroe was blind and stupid and old. Useless to himself and the world.
Useless to her. He couldn't plow, saw wood, garden, read the newspaper.
He couldn't even lift his soup spoon to his lips without missing the opening of his mouth. Yet here he was, there he was, traipsing to the cabinet on
strong, sturdy legs which had weakened years ago, and pulling down the
honey jar, a jar moments ago he could have only recognized by the shape
and the smell. And he didn't turn his hands around its oval shape, didn't
pick it up to lift to his probing nose. He immediately, without any prior
thought or act, pulled it down, returned to the table, and placed it right in
front of this stranger.

"Don't be afraid, good people. I'll explain," he said in a soft growl.

Now that he had honey on his bread, on his tongue, his voice lost the
husky growl, it became the sweet voice of the young man she had found
standing in the doorway, who Monroe had invited in for a glass of cool
water and a bowl of her potato soup, potatoes grown by her own hands, in
her own garden last season.

There was nothing she could say. Her tongue was stone. She couldn't
speak. It was as though all the words had been cut from her mind, her
tongue, as though she were totally deaf and dumb to language and the
meaning of words. She stood silent, waiting, waiting for the worst to happen, or had it already happened? Yes, it had happened. She had died, was
dead, struck by the lightning, her old heart. She was in the dream world,
the death world and had brought these scenes of life with her. It was no
fantasy. Her imagination was not that rich. She had died and had brought
both Monroe and this stranger into death with her. She went to the sink.
She placed the burning sweetgrass down on the porcelain. And then she
realized she should not have listened to Monroe. She should have gotten a
big mad dog.

"Wife, you cooked a good supper tonight. I want to tell you that. And I want to tell you how good you look," Monroe said.

"Yes, there is a special beauty about women who are kind and generous and thoughtful," the stranger added to Monroe's words. Above the sink was a small cracked mirror. Dare she glance into it? They say if you are dead there is no reflection in the glass. Dare she look? She wasn't sure she wanted to turn her back to the scene at the table. Her husband and that creature consorting against her. How had she offended this man whose body she had lain against all these many, many years, so many years it was hard to remember the count. The temptation would not go away. She did very much want to look in the mirror. Very much. She had to look, to see what they were seeing.

"How did you know who I was," the creature was asking Monroe.

"Oh, the blind have a way. The blind see better than the seeing. We smell better, we taste better, we have more strength in our hands, we feel, and we hear much better than the seeing do. I heard you first walking through the woods. Then I smelled you. You have a peculiar scent, you know . . . like no other creature. And your knock was furry soft. Like wind brushing against old wood."

The stranger chuckled in a knowing way. "You know I bring you no harm."

"Yes, I know. I know. But the woman there, she is not ready to believe. She won't turn and look in the mirror there above the sink. She's not ready."

Agnes decided not to look at the face in the mirror. She didn't want to know what it was, the reflection. There was enough craziness already happening around her. She refused to look, told herself if she looked the glass would shatter and fly out to cut her face to ribbons.

"Did you know I would come?"

"One day."

"How did you know? Or were you guessing. Were you just hoping?"

"No. I knew. In my darkness, I knew. That night when I was milking the old cow, she kicked me in the head . . ."

"The eyes."

". . . yes, the eyes. When she kicked me and sight was lost and all that there was were fuzzy colors swirling around before the total darkness came, I knew. I could smell you in the woods. I knew you would come one day. It took a few years. But here you are sitting at the table eating soup and licking honey from her buttered bread."

"Why do you suppose I came?"

"To give my sight back."

"But you are blind. You will always be blind. And you are old. If you could see I would say go to the mirror your wife refuses to look into and you will find nothing, no refection but darkness. I have given you these few moments to see. When I leave, so shall your sight leave and your hair will turn white again and the lines will crinkle your flesh and your back will stoop, and all the aches and pains, the worries and fears of the aged will return. And to your wife, too. Now she is young, beautiful again, and she will not look into the glass to see how lovely her face is, and how bright her hair, and how age has melted away from not only her face, but her figure. Look at her slender waist, the delicate ankles, the firm calf of her leg. See the music in her feet, her hands, her arms, the music of her mouth. The melody of life on her lips, the rhythms."

Leaning against the sink, she stood adamant, and refused to look into the mirror, refused to touch her hair, her cheek, refused to feel the slender waist this stranger spoke of, to allow the music, the rhythms, to move her feet, her hands. She said nothing. She stood mesmerized, comatose, against the sink as if all breath had left her lungs, all life risen from out of her aged body, a body now young again.

"Will you stay long?"

"I came only for a glass of water. I was dusty and thirsty. You good people gave me water and cold soup. You quenched my thirst and added the surprise of the soup and the bread with the honey and butter. No one else on this road welcomed me in for drink or for food. I'm pleased. And I shall go soon."

This is all ridiculous, this entire scene, Agnes thought. She believed in spirits. In ghosts, in the other world. She believed you could visit with the dead, commune. She spoke with her mother often. In her dreams she spoke with ancestors. She knew out there in the woods and in the rivers were good spirits who protected you and bad spirits that would suck your soul if you offended them. She believed in the power of the crow, the trickster who played jokes constantly. But it wasn't a crow seated at the table. It was a huge blue-black bear slurping her soup and licking honey from her buttered bread, butter she had churned and bread she had baked. She believed a person's spirit could rise and leave the body and then return. She believed all these things and knew, from teachings, there was a time when humans and animals talked and lived together in the same world, the same woods. Only after the great separation did they stop talking and become cruel and mean to each other. Had she been cruel? Had she hurt an animal, a bear? What! What brought this spirit in the shape of a bear who first entered her kitchen as a young man looking for a glass of water, carrying a tote bag on his left shoulder, hungry and tired, but nearly hairless and with a nice smile and handsome glint in his eye. Now there it sat covered in black hair, a snout for a nose, claws for fingernails.

They'd get a dog now.

"You are an old man. Your wife is an old woman. Surely you have very little to share, give away. Even the water you use and drink, your woman must carry from the creek in the woods. And you offered me that water. You raised your own potatoes to make this soup. Your woman bent down and grew and picked these good things, and bent again and harvested these fruits for your table. You were too old and blind to help in the garden, but your support was there. She churned this butter this morning. She gathered this honey last season. She walked to town for the flour to make this bread. How could I not come and accept the glass of water, the bowl of soup, this bread? It was my duty, as it was your duty to have these things and to offer a taste of your labors and harvest to me. I will go now. I will become the young man again and go on my way. You must not be frightened, neither you nor your good woman. You have nothing to fear. Not the dark, not the night, not any creature or spirit that walks the dark night or the light of dawn, and then noon."

As the stranger spoke, Monroe kept his eyes closed. Agnes had remained leaning into the sink.

He rose and left the chair. He did not rise as a human would rise from a seat. He fell to the floor, making a loud, soft crashing noise. Monroe opened his eyes to see the blue-black bear on all fours waddle to the door. One paw shot up to the handle and opened the door, threw it wide, threw it open to the porch, the top step. And then he stood. The young man dressed in jeans and a sweatshirt, wearing dusty shoes and his cap, a baseball cap aslant to the left of his head, his long black ponytail lifted by the evening breeze. He did not turn, but stepped down the stairs. And disappeared into the now darkness of night. Not a star shone. With him he took his smell.

Monroe remained seated at the table. His mouth agape. His eyes wide with lids open. Agnes hesitantly leaned away from the sink as if to move toward her husband, yet, somewhat fearful of leaving the safety of her station.

"You. Woman. You! I can see."

Agnes had never cursed a single word in her entire life, but now she let out a howl like a dying beast and cursed:

"You damned fool. You can't see. You're blind as a bat, and ignorant, and crazy. And so am I a damned fool, and crazy. Age. Or death. We are dead, I say. You do not live. Your blood has curdled. And mine is frozen."

The sweetgrass braid continued to smolder. The smoke filled the room, ever so slowly rising and falling with the light wind entering the still-open door.

"You, woman. I can see. I tell you I can see."

"Then look at me and tell me what I look like. You damned old fool. Am I young and beautiful as he said a while ago? Am I as slender as a reed or an iris? Do I dance the way he said I dance? These fallen arches; these old legs arthritic and humbled by too many years."

She moved nimbly to the table. She stood beside him, her hand touching his shirted shoulder. She placed her hand on his head and turned his face toward hers.

"As an act of respect I have never called you by your name before. Monroe Bond. You are blind. You have no sight. I am old and crippled with arthritis. We have reached our last years. Soon they will come to cover us with earth. That is good. That is as it should be. We have had a long, good life even though we have brought no little feet or sweet laughter into this world, onto this earth. It has been good. I have been contented. You also seem to be contented with the burden that we have had. But you are now blind. Tonight never happened. We dreamed. That's all that happened. Two old folks had the same dream. You hear me? You are blind."

And she was quiet. Agnes had never spoken so many words at one time before.

"If I am blind how is it, wife, that I see a blue bag sitting on the floor next to the chair where the stranger sat?"

Agnes looked down. There was something humped on the floor. She walked around the table from Monroe. She pushed the thing on the floor, figuring it would disappear at the touch of her shoe.

It didn't disappear.

## II.

NEAR DAWN, AGNES WAS AWAKENED BY MONROE'S RAUCOUS SNORES. His snorts traveled from his cot in the living room up the narrow stairwell, to the large bedroom and Agnes's sensitive ears. Being blind, she long ago decided, her husband should not trust his feet on the stairs—especially as he was prone to sleep-walk, or rise in the night for a glass of water or the bedpot. Downstairs, he might well fall and suffer some minor injury but should he stumble at the top of the stairs there could be more serious consequences. Monroe concurred with his wife.

The sun rose in its usual eastern sky, rising beyond the pasture and woods. A reddish light veiled the treetops. The usual birds sang, a robin pecked worms in the dew-glistening grass, and a single crow cawed in the front yard's lilac bushes.

She stretched, rubbed her elbows where the arthritis burned in the bone joints, and brushed back her hair. Some strands tickled her withered cheek. She made the decision to rise and make a pot of coffee. The first scent perking out of the pot always woke Monroe.

One foot, then the other, she gradually left the feather-tick mattress of the bed. Her feet shuffled into slippers, her arms stretched out for an old robe hanging from the brass post, and slowly she ambled to the head of the stairs. Step by step she forged down as she steadied her descent by clinging to the rail. At the bottom, Agnes inspected her sleeping husband. A blanket was pulled to under his chin; both arms were to his sides. His figure was straight, even the toes pointing up. He looked as though he was laid out on a slab, ready for the pine box coffin. There was a catch in the rhythm of her heartbeat and her right hand flew to her breast. But his loud snores reassured her that he was very much alive.

She crossed the room silently, though almost in a hobble. The old legs did not want to start the day and its chores. But light and coffee awaited.

Entering the kitchen, she could smell the burnt sweetgrass of the night before. Again Agnes felt a clutch around her heart and both hands raised to her breasts, and then to her throat and mouth. The events of the night flooded her mind. The potato soup, spooning it into Monroe's mouth, the knock on the door, the young man with the Mets baseball cap, and, oh, the horrible, terrifying creature he turned into.

"It was a dream," she whispered as she ladled water from the bucket on the sink board into the enameled percolator. "A nightmare."

There were still red coals in the woodstove. Agnes gathered up some kindling, dropped it onto the coals, and blew. Orange flames shot up and attacked the splints. Then she pushed into the stove's belly heavier logs. Shortly, the coffee would be perking and steaming away.

"No rest for the wicked, they say," she mumbled to herself. And then aloud to the empty kitchen—"for the wicked! Is that what I have been? That why I had the nightmare? The soup must have poisoned me some-how. Ridiculous—him regaining his sight. Wishful thinking. And me, me, ancient me, being young again, and, and, well, he said it, pretty."

She rumbled around the room, glancing out the window into the pas-ture. Their cow still stood in the meadow chewing, and yes, two of the Rhode Island Reds were there, pecking away. Reaching up into the cup-board, she brought down two cups and saucers, and the sugar bowl. Deftly carrying them against her waist, she moved to the round table centered in the kitchen. There on the oilcloth cover she spotted the honey jar. She stood frozen to the spot for a mere moment, then tossed back her head in defiance and placed the bowls and cups down onto the cloth. As Agnes reached across the table to put Monroe's cup and saucer in his usual place, she caught sight of a large object on the floor. Gripping the table edge, she slowly padded around. She bent down—though not without some agony (a streak of pain shot down her back) and picked up the object. A blue tote bag. As if it were a wriggling rat, she dropped it instantly and screamed.

"Oh no! It wasn't a dream! It wasn't a nightmare!"

She rushed to the mirror. She hadn't changed, her old face was still wrinkled, and her hair was white.

Agnes limped into the living room where she commenced shaking her husband, who woke immediately.

"Let me see your eyes. Open them. I say open them up!"

Monroe babbled morning nonsense, but opened his eyes. They were covered with a white film.

"Can you see me?" she shouted.

"I'm blind."

"Can you see me?" she repeated.

"Can't see my own hand," he said, raising his head from the pillow.

Agnes abruptly turned about, retraced her steps into the kitchen where she grabbed the tote bag in both hands and marched to the stove. The fire was blazing under the coffeepot. With great force she pushed the blue bag into the tongues of fire and shut the door. Turning around, she faced the empty spot on the wall where the braid of sweetgrass had hung.

"It was a dream. The fire has eaten the dream."

She realized then that she should never again open the door at night.

She moved, and slumped down at the table. She rested both elbows in the red oilcloth and cradled her head in her palms. Monroe was getting into his clothes. She could hear him grunt as he fingered the floor for his pants and shoes. Over the rich scent of coffee perking she smelled the "wild," a smell of burnt grease, or oil, the very same oil used in the lamps of the longhouse. Bear. And she remained sitting, staring across the room at the locked door as Monroe shuffled into the kitchen.

Quietly, gently, she uttered terrifying words:

"It wasn't a dream."

回

# What's in a Song

*(for Harold Katchenago, at Menominee)*

MARTIN FELL FAST ASLEEP WITH HIS HEAD RESTING NOT SO VERY COM-
fortably against a sleek log, his feet nearly to the river edge, his arms akimbo,
one hand stoutly holding a flute. He hadn't actually come to the river to
sleep. That was not his purpose, yet there he was snoring as loudly as any
crow could caw in the cedar over his head. When he'd arrived that morning, considerably earlier, he carried a small bag of cold corn bread and a
glass jar of water. The river's freshness could not be trusted anymore. After
eating and sipping the water, he simply leaned back against the log and
fell sound asleep. Now the warmth of noon cuddled around him, heavied
his arms, weighted his eyelids. The yawns arrived softly at first and then
protruded rudely into his reverie.

Summer flies began to dance about his ears, then attacked his rather
pug nose. Hands flew out to subdue the insects' buzzing attacks, but to no
avail. They continued to snip at his nose; one had the audacity to light on
his lip where a tear of water from the jar stealthily clung to the fleshy
corner. He swatted and swatted. The flies continued annoying the young
man. At last he gave up the battle, settled back with his round derriere
firmly planted on the earth covered with last autumn's leaves. He slowly

allowed his head to find some comforting spot on the log. The first snore, light and musical, gobbled from his open mouth where a last fly entered. The breeze of the snore was strong enough to evict the fly. His mouth shut, tight. The fly, having lost the battle, flew off and gave Martin the moment to rest, which, it would seem, he needed.

Martin had not gone to the woods and the river that late spring morning merely to eat cold cornbread and sleep. He could more comfortably do that at home on the sofa, or on the grass beneath his leafy apple tree. He had an important reason for his trek to the river, a far more imaginative reason. The night before he had felt music in his bones, as he would have said, had someone asked. His spirit was twitching, he also may have suggested. Notes and rhythms were floating in his inner ear but not making a true composition. He lay awake most if the night hearing notes and the rush of water, a river in his ears. The house he owned with Matilda was a goodly distance from the river. There was no water leaking in the tub or sink, nor rain running off the roof. At four A.M. he knew what he must do. He should rise early with the dawn, pack a light lunch, and trek to the river to see exactly what would happen.

It was the loveliest of mornings: the sun bright and as warm as bread Matilda might take from her oven; robins were singing, a red cardinal flew across his view to a telephone wire and sat there, watching him move across the meadow to the woods; clouds, thin and lazy, hung in the bluest of skies; the meadow was covered with wild blossoms . . . black-eyed susans, daisies, fleabane . . . and one ruby-throated hummingbird hovered before a single common tickweed. He felt good; he felt music in his feet, in his itchy fingers, and his head swirled with notes so immediate he thought he could see them in the air. He carried his two flutes in a deerhide bundle strapped to his back. He carried his lunch of cornbread and water, also tobacco. He lunged across the meadow as though wading through deep water; he plied waves, though the waves were really just a field of forgotten wheat. Plunge though he did in his hike, he thought he walked as sprightly as a dancer, lightly on the earth, touching the center, the earth, as though a drum of beaten hide, soft as skin, undulant as clouds floating above his head. He was light and airy, almost dizzy with expectation. He knew that morning he would have a new song, a song of the river, because the water had called him in the night to come and freely take its music. Shortly, he entered the woods. The river was only a quarter of a mile further through the trees. Birds and squirrels hopped from one branch to another. An elderberry bush, black fruit hanging, dangling in a shaft of sunlight, took his glance. Witch hobble, now barren of flowers, tripped him as he ambled through in a daydream He staggered, but confident in his mission, he paid no attention and stumbled on to the river which he could now easily hear. He was so excited that he ignored the morning dews dampening his moccasins. Matilda had sewn them for him only this past February. They were wet and loose. He thought of the new song, a fresh original composition, the creativity, the making of notes, order from chaos, beautiful rhythms which would flow from his flute so thrillingly that he failed to see a chickadee flitting about his path. It would perch and flit, flit and perch, fly off into the leaves and then return to perch on a pine branch directly over Martin's head. It sang "fee-bee, fee-bee," the second note much lower in tone than the first. Martin, of course, did not hear the bird's fee-bee. It flew down to the path where the young man hiked. He nearly stepped on the feathery bird. When he realized his foot nearly killed the chickadee, he awoke at the very edge of the river. Thin ripples washed to the grasses and stones sitting out from the shore. A heron, which stood in the shallows, heard Martin's approach and flew off into the air, leaving circles of waves fanning to shore. He wandered down river looking for a rock, a large stone where he could sit, meditate, hear all the notes of the new song. Half a mile down the river he found such a rock, a foot high, a foot wide, and fairly flat. He placed his lunch bag safely away from the water, shook off the hide bundle which contained his two flutes, pulled off his moccasins, and dropped his feet into the water, where the river tickled his hot toes. And he listened. And listened and listened. His toes curled the water, made a slight noise, but not the noise he had come to the river to hear. He pulled his two feet out of the coolness of the slow-moving waters and held them out to dry in the sun on the grasses surrounding the flat stone. And he listened and listened. He could not hear the river; he did not hear his new song. The chickadee clucked and sang: chick-a-dee-dee-dee, dee-dee-dee, chick-a-dee-dee-dee, dee-dee-dee.

"Go away, chicky. Go away. I came to hear the river's song . . . not your silliness. I can't make a song from dee-dee-dee. Go away."

The chickadee, indifferent to his command, continued to peck the earth for insects and to sing as it pranced about Martin on his rock.

"Chick-a-dee-dee-dee," the bird sang, and the song seemed to grow louder and louder, to the point where nothing of the water's rhythms, the river's music, could be heard at all, even though a few yards upriver huge stones jutted out of the riverbed and caused rapids not only to spray the flow's surface, but make bellowing music, shrill and deafening. Martin was not able to concentrate on the rapids' music. All he heard was the song of the chickadee.

There was a powerful song in the river. Powerful. Magical. He had to hear it. Didn't it keep him from sleeping most of last night? He had to capture the power of the river. It was speaking, singing to him . . . or would, if that damned chickadee would go away.

"Shush, shu, shuuuuu. Get out of here. Go away."

It wouldn't leave, but continued circling his stone. It hopped up on his flute bundle. "Get off my bundle. Get off my flutes, you nasty bird. Go away."

And he listened, and listened, and listened. The river made no gurgle, offered no song, seemed to have lost its power, its magic. His flutes remained tied in the bundle. It was then that he decided to eat his breakfast, the cold cornbread, and have a swallow of water. On opening his plastic bag which contained the bread, a sweet scent of baked corn careened into the air. The chickadee caught the smell and made a fast rush to Martin's feet. He began to feel guilty, having food in his stomach yet knowing that possibly the little bird was hungry. It was a female, her white cheeks and pale gray belly feathers looked bedraggled and thin; her wing feathers, tucked to her side, appeared ragged. Martin tossed the chickadee a small hunk of bread. With a cluck she thanked him and pecked away at the corn. "Now go away," he requested gently. As if she understood his words she left, left Martin alone on his rock, munching his lunch, satisfied with his altruism, content in what he considered the fact that he was not only a good Indian, but a thinking, feeling human, a man of respect and sensitivity. Now he would listen to the river, the powerful music of the waters, and compose his song.

And he listened and listened and he continued to listen some more.

The sun was moving higher in the sky. Shadows shortened. The birds of the woods sang less and less. A breeze that had wafted across the morning stilled. It was quiet. So quiet that he could easily hear the powerful song rise from the river. But it refused to rise. Refused.

From the rock, he strolled along the river's edge. A water snake slithered off the shore and sank into the river. He watched as a gray-white kingfisher perched on a thin tree stump rising a foot out of the shallows. No fish or minnow swam into the birds' ken. The kingfisher shrilled and rattled loudly, rattled more, and took off from the stump to hover a few moments over the flowing water, before quickly disappearing into the vast sky.

Martin knew he could compose the kingfisher's song or the hummingbird's song, the bird he heard earlier in the morning on his trek to the river. He knew he could accomplish that. Not difficult at all. But no, no, no. He came for the river's powerful song. He wanted a big song. A huge song for his flute. No kingfisher's rattle, no hummingbird's mouse-like twitter. He'd as soon record the raucous caw of the bluejay or crow. No, he came for the river. Wasn't it the sign of water? Wasn't his sleep disturbed by the rush of the river? Yes. He'd wait.

He ambled back to his stone, but the sun was now straight overhead and the stone was too hot, as his hand dropped to test the rock. He spotted the sleek log, bereft of bark, a young beech caught in a lightning storm and brought down to the earth. He strolled to the log, dropped his plastic bag and his hide bundle, took a seat on the earth crossed-legged, and waited the song from the river. And he listened, and listened, and . . .

"Chick-a-dee-dee-dee. Dee-dee-dee. Dee-dee-dee."

Startled he awoke. The chick perched on his moccasined toe. He could hear the river. It grumbled. He took up his bundle, untied the thong, and pulled out one flute, the flute he had carved with his own nimble hands, fingers. It was carved in the shape of a loon's head, the waterbird. It was handsome, and the music from its mouth was always beautiful. Today his flute yearned for the music of the river. He held the instrument straight out before him. Placed the lip against his mouth, and blew. It grumbled the same as the river now was grumbling. His flute seemed angry as the river seemed angry and disturbed. He took the flute from his lips, held the loon-shaped instrument to the sun now passing into the southern sky. He lowered the instrument, and as he did, the chickadee flew up and perched on the slender flute, and stared Martin directly in the eye. He made no motion of tossing her off, though he verbally encouraged her to hop down, "Go away. Get off my flute." She continued to stare him down. "Dee-dee-dee," she said softly, mellifluously. "Dee-dee-dee." She hopped down, and flitted into the woods, away from Martin now sitting straight before the log, the flute in hand, raised to his lips. And he blew his new song.

The chickadee tried so hard to tell him, to give him a lift. He continued to ignore her, to push her off, to chase her away. He was blind. He was not only sightless, but deaf, stone deaf. He heard nothing, even though he listened, and listened, and listened. He listened to the wrong voice. He listened to the river, which did not want to sing that day. He failed to hear the black-capped bird with the silly song, "dee-dee-dee." A song was a song, all given by the Creator. As each creature was unique, each of their songs was different. But that did not mean they had no beauty . . . even the hummingbird singing his mouth-like twitter, or the sheer rattle of the kingfisher, or the ugly caw of the crow, and certainly the chickadee held a certain beauty and pleasure. Her charm was magic; her magic was his song.

He heard. He blew, and blew sweet air into his instrument, the carved loon flute. He blew and blew and magic filled the air. No, it wasn't as powerful as the river song he had come to obtain, but the "dee-dee-dee" had its own power which was pleasing and light and delightful.

He played his song over and over until it was memorized forever.

He finished eating the cornbread and drank a deep swallow of water from his glass jar. The sun was beginning to move down the sky. A light wind was rising. He felt a late afternoon chill on his shoulders.

Martin pulled out a small soft hide bag from his pants pocket. Pulled open the strings, and pushed fingers into the bag. He extracted some fine tobacco, and dropped it where he had sat when the chickadee hopped onto his flute. He spread the tobacco as though he were spreading corn to the birds. Shortly he had his flute tied into the bundle, and he left for home.

That night, Matilda had a surprise supper ready for Martin: macaroni goulash, his favorite dish. After the excellent food, he took out his flutes and entertained Matilda by blowing a wolf song, bear song, and the new song of the chickadee. She was pleased, delighted, and thanked Martin, for he had played the new piece to his wife for her fine cooking. He put down the loon flute and patted the round of his belly contented . . . for the time being. Martin really loved good food. Maybe tomorrow he would go to the woods near Duck Creek to gather mushrooms. Maybe he'd hear a song, a song of bears eating blackberries. You could never tell, it might be very powerful. Or maybe just some squeaky song of red fox.

# She-Who-Speaks-With-Bear

## I.

"IT'S ONLY A BAG."

A silent room can be overpowering.

"It's just a bag."

A completely darkened room is a tomb.

"What do they want my bag for?"

A large dark silent room is frightening, terrifying to a single occupant. Alone.

"There's not any drugs in it."

A room or a place without a June breeze, a meadowlark's trill, the scent of clover or wild milkweed; a room without a candle, lantern, or at least a flashlight to search corners, or a crack of moon falling under the door or across the transit is eternity.

"My Grandmom told me to never give my bag to anyone."

A room which in reality is an enormous theatre or school auditorium where mice can't be heard scampering across a waxed floor, ghosts' flights, rats clawing or a chilled wind whistling in rafters, a lost cat's meow, a wolf howl or bear growl.

Mary Margaret Buford hated being alone. She had never experienced aloneness, being completely by herself in her entire young life. There was always someone from her large family nearby. Always. Aloneness was the most dreaded state ever. Cut away from all human beings would be unbearable for her.

"No," she exclaimed adamantly. "I won't give you my bag."

She shivered at the thought of being locked up without light.

"Sister Henrietta, you yanked my bag off my neck. Why did you do that?"

Mary Margaret had always enjoyed the open spaces of the vast plains of her home Montana country, with mountains framing the distance, clipping the horizon in jagged edges. She despised zoos, libraries, movie houses, spaced walls. Freedom, light, and noise of any kind from a machine of whatever description was a companion she could not exist without: a radio, TV, stereo, a car backfiring in the dark of night, the thud of a horse's hooves pounding earth, a drum, she thought, the whine of a coyote perched on a hill in the night. These were all sounds she welcomed. A bear speaking from a stand of autumn cottonwoods.

"I haven't done anything wrong."

The fourteen-year-old child faced the nun. Tears spilled. Right then she didn't much care if it wasn't Indian to cry. Besides, it was really the men who shouldn't cry, shouldn't show feelings. Her taut features tried to remain stiff at first; then stark fear began to show on her countenance. She weakened before the nun.

"It said my mother was sick. She was dying. I had to get home."

"This is your home now," the nun smiled, but it . . . it . . . "what is this?"

"Bear," she answered and hesitated. "The bear in my bag." She could not say, mouth the words . . . "my medicine bundle."

"Mary Margaret, be sensible. No bear could fit in this bag. It couldn't even hold a handkerchief, hardly two coins."

The stern nun attempted to untie the string folding the mouth of the bag together. She yanked but did not undo the knot.

"What bear?"

"Bear speaks." Mary Margaret was biting her lip. A speck of blood spurted out onto the flesh. "It tells me . . . things." She bit deeper into her lip. "Things . . . I'm supposed to know about."

Sister Henrietta Bourquin had forced the child into the school auditorium. She meant the girl to spend the night alone in the dark. Sister was unmoving, seemingly void of compassion, and ignored Mary Margaret's pleas to punish her in another manner, though she had done nothing wrong to deserve any punishment whatsoever. But if she was to be punished for the crime Sister thought she had committed, then do anything but lock her up in that hateful auditorium, huge and baffling, frightening in the dark across the long night.

Sister did not see the girl's anguish nor hear the child's silent fear, her fright.

All the child could then think of was home. Montana, the open plains coddled by the sun and cleaned, brushed by free breezes. She hated this place; she truly hated this school . . . House of the Faithful, this prison, really. She didn't want to be faithful to this house, these nuns and their religion and duties, or their commands. This was no house nor home, no house like her Mom's where she could amble to the fridge for a cold soda anytime the whim struck. Or fry up some tortillas and beans. She wasn't even allowed to walk through the gates for a stroll in the open air unless she walked single file with the other girls, supervised by a nun. She needed space, and the multi-sounds space offered. Not this walk with a horde of giggling kids, this walk which was referred to as "taking the air."

She'd give just about anything in the world to go home. She'd jump the walls. Break the windows and slip down and out of the "house." Mom was sick, dying maybe. Bear said so. It never lied to her. And Bear knew. Bear knew everything. To go home and be with Mom and Grandmom and the other kids, her sisters and brothers. Away from this hellhole, the "house" as the other students called the school, this school for wayward girls, students at risk. She wondered why the nuns didn't call it a school for wayward Natives. Indians. "That's all that is here," she realized. Only Indian girls are at risk? She pondered this often during her stay at the school.

The nun's cold hand reached for Mary Margaret's shoulder, and tightened onto her flesh, brought her back to the reality that Sister Henrietta was pushing her into the bleak empty shell of the auditorium.

"This . . . this bear thing. This bear thing told you to run away from school . . . your home now. Told you your mother was dying."

"Yes."

"You speak with this thing, this . . . bear . . . all the time?"

She didn't wait for the girl's reply.

"You've a rich imagination, my child. Very rich indeed. You should apply it to your studies. Let's see if spending the night in the dark will enrich it even more, or shed some light of truth on it."

This was the typical form of punishment that the Mother Superior recommended.

Sister continued to struggle with the string to get the mouth to yawn open, but she had no success.

"Bear talks lots to me, and tells me lots of things."

"Such as . . ."

"Not to eat certain foods because they will poison me. It tells me . . ."

"Mary Margaret, you are lying. Lies. You lied about your mother's condition, sick and possibly dying. And you ran off. Now you lie about this, this bear thing. And this bag. You have drugs in here, don't you." She yanked again at the string. "I believe, in all sincerity, you will have the opportunity of replenishing your spirit . . . and banish these bad thoughts . . . by spending the night alone in the dark. You can pray your sins away."

Mary Margaret retrieved the bag from the nun and shortly had it opened, the mouth loose.

"Empty it," the nun commanded.

The girl clutched the bag to her cheek. Her mouth puckered.

"Empty it out, I said. Now. Mary Margaret, empty it."

She had been stripped of weekend furloughs; movies for a month; sent to bed without supper for three nights running; beaten with a horse whip; shorn of her braids; made to sleep in a bed soaked in the urine of a class-mate bed-wetter . . . she actually had been punished once in that way; they made her scrub the floors of the "house" with a single brillo pad on her hands and knees. Mary Margaret pleaded silently. Only her eyes betrayed her fear.

"I can't show you."

"You are disobeying my command."

"Grandmom told me never show. It is secret, sacred."

"Grandmom is not in charge here. Empty."

Sister Henrietta grabbed the bag out of the girl's hand.

"Then I'll empty it."

Sister knew. How wise were the nuns. Shrewd. They knew all the cor-rect methods. Had centuries of experience and study. And now the nuns knew that punishment was good for a child. We will also teach them skills of the world, and a work ethic here at the House of the Faithful. We will not only save their souls but their minds as well from sloth, ignorance and paganism. They will live in the home, the breast of God, in the warmth and splendor of Holy Church.

Mary Margaret well knew what this warmth and splendor was.

Sister Henrietta was determined to save this child's soul and her mind. It mattered not in what fashion correction or education took place. She was committed as much to this purpose as she was to love and to her love of Christ. As well as keeping, of course, the House of the Faithful running in good order.

Mary Margaret had been punished before. She was caught speaking her language to another student. She had witnessed the dour nuns punish many of her fellow classmates. She watched children dig graves for their roommates who had mysteriously died in the night from some strange disease or another. She had watched the bed-wetters wash out the soiled linens in cold water on a frosty morning outdoors in huge tubs. She'd seen boys plow up the nuns' garden with a mere hoe and shovel, their hands so raw and red afterwards they could barely hold a pencil in the classroom. And oh, the many times she had weeded those gardens, the onions, carrots, squash, which would eventually be cooked into their supper stews. Yes, she knew punishment. And she would rather dig a garden with her fingernails than be forced into the auditorium for the night. She remembered having worn her moccasins once and how she had been punished by scrubbing the latrines for a week.

"Hurry up. Empty the bag."

The girl shook the hide packet. One object fell out.

"What is that?" the nun exclaimed in horror. "It's ghastly."

There was a soft tinkling sound as it fell onto the desk, then flopped over and fell off to the floor.

"Pick it up," she demanded.

Mary Margaret stooped and retrieved the object and held it tightly in her fist. She attempted to compose herself.

"What is this devil's . . . thing?"

"Grandmom gave it to me long time ago . . . when I was little."

"The work of the devil. Satan is with you. It is meant for working black magic. It is evil. Give it here to me."

Mary Margaret reluctantly handed it over. "It isn't evil. It is good. It is my bear. Grandmom said it would do good things." She paused and looked down at the desktop where Sister Henrietta had placed the odd object. "It speaks to me. Bear speaks."

It was only then that the nun registered the object, recognized what the thing really was.

"Come with me. Now!"

She collared the girl, clutched her blouse and dragged her from the office. Down a long corridor, the nun pulled Mary Margaret and pushed her through the open kitchen door. The corridor was cold and dim. Most of the "house's" rooms were cold and damp and dim. The nuns insisted upon saving the electricity. The kitchen was bright and warm. The woodstove burned logs the boys had chopped early that fall. Sister shoved the girl up to the stove. Making a clattering racket the nun lifted the lid. Flames shot out of the belly of the stove. She handed her the object.

"Throw it to the fire."

Mary Margaret hesitated though her fist had loosened around the object.

"Throw it to the fire. Instantly. Now."

She grabbed the girl's closed fist and held it over the leaping orange flames. She shook the child's hand over the flames as though it would automatically open and drop the contents.

"Let go. I said let go, Mary Margaret."

She shoved the girl's hand into the flame itself. The bear claw fell upon the red coals. Mary Margaret watched and heard it sizzle. Flames had caught it. A pungent odor rose from the fire, penetrated the kitchen as Sister Agnes Marie entered the room.

"What's wrong, Sister?"

The girl observed the crescent claw, saw the nail move into the shape of a circle. Quickly it turned to ash, and the ash fell between the burning coals . . . She held her right hand to her breast; her left hand shot up to her brow. She squeaked unrecognizable sounds. She mumbled. And then words of a prayer in her language escaped her lips. Sister didn't hear the prayer for she was confronted by Sister Agnes Marie.

"This monster's been carrying a bear claw around her neck. I was sure it was drugs in that bag. Might as well have been. This is worse. Devil worship. Satanism."

"Are you sure, Sister?"

Sister Agnes Marie questioned the other nun, her superior, and then turned her astonished glance upon the frightened girl. "Are you sure it is devil worship?" she said staring into the child's eyes. "Mary Margaret, are you a devil worshiper?" No response from the girl. "I hardly think so. Sister, this child is . . ."

"We will worship and cleanse the dark where the devil resides," were Sister Henrietta's only words.

Sister Agnes Marie's hard glance slowly moved into a gentle warm smile. She drew the girl aside and hugged her.

"It isn't as bad as that. She's a good girl."

"Yes, yes. All good girls lie and attempt to run away. She ran away, I tell you . . . And lied. Said the bear, this thing in the fire . . ."

"The what . . ."

"She claimed this bear had told her her mother was dying. And when I refused a furlough, she ran away. They found her at the bus station in town attempting to board the bus without a ticket. She lied."

There was no convincing Sister Henrietta that the girl was innocent of devil worship or black magic. That she was only attending to what her old Grandmother had told her when she was a child. "The bear is very important to Indians. It is a large part of their culture. It is part of their rituals. Very big in Indian thinking. It is a form of medicine. I've heard it said that the bear has powers . . . very special powers." She was trying to ward off the punishment that the child was about to receive from the Superior.

"Bear worship is equally as bad, sinful, as devil worship," Sister Henrietta proclaimed sullenly.

"Not worship, Sister. Not worship but perhaps respect."

Sister Henrietta clutched the girl's wrist and once more dragged her out of the kitchen and down the darkening corridor. Without turning her head she addressed Sister Agnes Marie:

"I think I know what is best."

## II.

MARY MARGARET HUDDLED IN THE CHAIR. THE VINYL WAS COLD. SHE had neither a coat nor blanket to wrap in. She had been humiliated by the nun. She was forced to kneel on the naked floor which had never been carpeted due to lack of funds. She was told to recite four rosaries, and then she was left alone in the dark. She was shamed.

All night she cried bitter tears; she sang songs; she prayed; she told herself stories; she spoke to Bear and to the bear claw she herself had tossed into the burning flames of the stove. She listened intensely and intently for Bear to speak. But Bear did not. She spoke to her grandmother, her mother; she drummed on the vinyl seat of the chair; she spoke to her brothers and her sisters. She prayed to the Great Spirit. She wept. Her grandmother did not hear her. The Great Spirit did not hear her prayers. Her mother did not answer. Bear remained silent. Her tears and drumming, her songs and prayers did not alleviate any of the shame she felt nor the cold which penetrated her flesh to the very bone, nor her fear of being alone in that great dark hole. Once during the night she thought she could hear her mother's voice. Small and distant, weak, thin like the sound of an icicle dripping water, melting in sunlight. She called out . . . meekly at first: mom-m. Mom-m. Then as time struggled across the night, the hours grew long and frightening; her voice grew stronger in calling out to her mother. *Mom.* MOM. MOM. No answer was returned.

It was simply not possible for her mother to speak. She had died. Mary Margaret knew that now to be a fact. Her mother's voice had come down from the Spirit World. Mary Margaret could hear her mom, but her mother would not be able to hear her voice. Death was strange. It traveled across all borders. It moved across all light and darkness. And Bear had told her that her mother was dying the day before. She knew her mother was near death. And now, now . . . she was dead. Her body cold and dead. Only her Spirit remained, but remained in the Spirit world where she could no longer hear her children, hear Mary Margaret call out in her lonely anguish. The girl covered her face with cold hands and shriveled into a ball, her arms hugging her feet close to her torso.

This is how she spent the remainder of the long, black night.

She occasionally nodded her head in tiredness. She would often doze off. Then a squeak, another, and then a long bang and the main door of the auditorium opened. Light flashed through the doorway. She looked up and was blinded from the brilliance. She could not see the black figure standing in the open threshold with arms raised as if in supplication. The figure appeared to be a crow in flight. She wondered if it was Bear. She hoped fervently it was Bear. Come to take her home. To take her out of the House of the Faithful. This black hole, this great gaping black monstrous abyss. The figure moved down the aisle toward the stage where Mary Margaret uncoiled from the ball in her chair. Now she felt more frightened of the light then she had of the darkness. The figure was neither a crow nor was it a bear. She hid behind her tight hands.

Sister Agnes Marie stood before the child.

The sister held out a blanket.

"I knew you would be chilled. I couldn't come until now, this morning. I wasn't allowed to come during the night."

Mary Margaret opened her eyes. It was the one good nun, the one nun of the "house" who had any compassion, or seemed to be the only nun who had not only compassion but some liking for the Indian children.

"I am truly sorry, sad this confrontation has resulted in this punishment for you. Sometimes I believe we are all too detached to have a proper understanding."

Her attempt at kindness kindled no warmth in the girl.

"And I am very sorry to bring you bad news."

Mary Margaret stood straight like a tall green corn stalk. "I know your news. I know. Bear spoke yesterday. Mom spoke last night."

"We had word this morning, child. They said there was nothing the doctors could do. She had only slight pain, however . . ."

A growl wrenched from Mary Margaret's very essence, her spirit, her heart, her brain. Her scream shrilled through the auditorium, echo after echo filled the hall, reverberating. It drummed through the corridor beyond the opened door. It rattled through to the nun's quarters. It shook the school's walls. The scream echoed through the child's mind, and the mind of Sister Agnes Marie.

Mary Margaret vowed to get out of there, the "house," very, very soon.

卍

Some say the screams are still heard in the corridors of the "house" and they echo over and again in the auditorium.

Mary Margaret still hears those screams in Montana, her home, as she continues to speak to Bear.

卐

# Bacon

WE FIRST SAW TRACKS IN THE SOFT EARTH. THEY DIDN'T HAVE TOES. We smelled fat.

We listened to sounds. They sputtered and made odd little cackle-like noises, not very pretty. Not sounds like the evening thrush or even mockingbirds.

We watched the two with short legs move around the area. They bustled about, stopped to sniff a flower or stooped to pick a few of our red berries. The two tall ones didn't seem interested in doing much but sat on their haunches most of the daylight.

Once when the two short ones were walking, tramping the grass, one stopped. Her arm flew up to her mouth: a frightening scream. I could see what the trouble was. A little black shrew out for grain perked its tiny head up in the grasses.

Hiding behind thick witch hobble we were cautious, but intense, watching their every movement. They were not to be trusted. The two shorts were picking our berries and breaking off our flowers to sniff and take to their place.

At night we would steal our way off the knoll and stand in the dark outside the place, and look in through a large opening. The shorts were burning things. Good smells rose up from their fire. The two talls sat around on their haunches. One squatted on a little stone with legs. He held a long stick with color at the end. He'd touch a white wall, small and square, and bright reds and blues and greens would magically appear . . . sky, flowers.

Sometimes in the darkness as we stood watching, one of the short ones would bring music to the air and she would twirl like a dandelion would twirl in the wind, or a firefly in the night sparkling in the black. The other three would put their hands together when the twirling one stopped and stood still, then bent over. She acted crazy . . . as if something bit her. One tall seemed to do nothing. Once we watched him scratching with a short twig. One short was always at the burning, but sometimes she would swirl around and look at the other three . . . her arm would go up just above her eyes and brow and she would sweep the arm across the head, the skin. She sputtered. The other three would put their hands together. And she would blow a chicory on the wind.

We particularly liked the smells that came out from the burnings, the fire on their big rock inside, especially just after the sun would rise there in the east. The smell was usually greasy. We could hear drops of water jumping, and then another smell would come out of the space. Another kind of sputter . . . it is very hard to describe. A greasy smell that wasn't the same as fat, but rather sweet.

Once we knew for sure that they were burning birds. Everyone recognizes the smell of burning birds.

We'd be so hungry when three times a day they would burn.

Once she sneaked real close to the house. One short one had brought a smelly bundle outdoors, put it in a large hole-thing. She went down and brought back the bundle. I was right. They had been burning birds. Bones were in the bundle and bits of green things, and tiny round things, small as the smallest pebble you've ever seen. White and soft. Tasted pretty good, too. Especially those with very large, hard bones. Must have been a huge bird. But the taste was different and they would be bloody. We liked what was in the bundles.

One night as we stood watching through the large opening . . . far enough off so they couldn't smell us or see us without squinting into the dark or coming out onto the dewy grasses, the two tall ones came into the light out of a cave. They had black shiny things across the eyes. They danced sort of. Staggered like they had eaten too many elderberry seeds or pokeweed. At certain times pokeweed berries and elderberries can make you stagger. They taste just fine, but you can get a little dizzy, yet you don't care. Tingling, you cuddle closer to her and nudge her a little with your nose and extend out your arms to her. And she cuddles with you.

These tall ones staggered. Smoke spread from their mouths and noses. They were burning. One tall gave the other a short white stick. He put it into his mouth and blew out a thin line of white smoke. Then he sputtered, made a certain noise like a crow or, magpie and staggered around the space. The two shorts also sputtered and made noises. Crows. They both bent over, stood straight, and bent over again as though they were picking something up off the ground but they didn't have anything in their hands when they straightened.

These are strange creatures with weird ceremonies. They reminded me of those who used to live here many, many years ago and that we don't see very often. Grandfather told stories of them. The ones that had flesh mostly and only wore little pieces of deer or wolf. They had dark flesh. It was very handsome. In the summer it would shine under the sun. In winter they would cover it with wolf . . . the enemy even if he is a brother. The flesh people would dance, twirl, too, and they would put a long stick into their mouths and then allow white smoke to blow gently out. There were many.

They did some miserable things. They would chase us into the woods.

Once in a while a very sharp stick would zip into your leg, or belly or even your head. It hurt. It was painful. You'd be sick for many nights. Sometimes you would not get up off the ground. Eventually there would be a pile of your bones.

But these tall and short ones they didn't twirl the same way. They always had colorful things around their figure. They never wore wolf, or deer. Their smoke sticks were small . . . actually hard to see. They appeared like they were going to stay forever in our land and woods. They never went out to get rabbits or birds with the sharp pointed things, but they always had food.

The two talls continued to stagger and put funny looks on their faces. The two shorts continued to bend and sputter. They weren't watching the burning. Good. Maybe it will get black and they will bring it out in a bundle and we can have it. Their food has good taste.

She pushed me. She grunted then. Growled. I was thinking of food and not watching what they were doing. I was in memory, dreams. Dreams are good to stare at. One of my favorite things to do when I'm not out hunting food, or have my hands in an old beehive sucking honey.

She gave me another hard push. I woke up from my dream, reverie. I couldn't believe my sight. My eyes were playing tricks on me. There were two of us in there. The two talls had gone away. Probably sneaked out the back and out into the woods to wet the bushes. There they were. There were two of us in there. They were smoking those short white sticks. The two shorts with skins around their middles were actually twirling with our people.

She knocked my chest. I was then standing tall and straight. She hit hard against my chest. And then she gave a low growl which was followed by a louder grunt. She showed her signs of anger. She started her own twirling. One foot after the other came down on the earth, pound-pound, pound-pound. Like a drum that the flesh people used to have and pound. Their pounding had good sounds. It made you want to get off your haunches

and twirl. At times it made you want to go to the bushes with her. Once it
was so fierce I became mad, stern, angry and looked for something to beat,
pound, hug, kill.

She hit my chest again and started moving away from the big opening.
Far off in the woods I could hear coyote howls. We don't have wolf any-
more in our area. He's piles of bones and not really even bones anymore.
Dust.

I looked at the two shorts. They were hugging our people. Our people
were hugging the two shorts. One of our people stopped and put his mouth
on one of the shorts. She put her mouth on his.

What was going on.

I was excited. I was curious, I could feel a very special sensation run up
my legs, cross my belly and run into my back up into my shoulder blades.

She was at the entrance. She slammed her hand against it.

There was sudden quiet. Silence. Except for coyote matching up with
his mate off on another hilltop.

A light flashed behind me and I turned to see what it was. It was the
moon. We call her Grandmother Moon. Grandmother because she watches
over us. Fish in the stream, coyote, birds, even us, my people. In the bright
Grandmother-light I watched her slam the door. She heaved against it.
Loud noises sputtered from the figures. The two shorts sputtered pierc-
ingly. It hurt your eardrums. The two who belong to our people just stood
there dumb, dead, useless.

In a moment she had the entrance slammed open. She is very powerful.
She went through the entrance and to the burning. The four figures ran out
a different entrance sputtering loudly, piercing noises. It hurt the ears.

She was eating at the burning. Greasy fat was all over her nose, her
mouth, it dripped down her hairy chest. She turned quickly and growled
at me as if to say . . . chase them. Chase after them. See why our people are
with the two shorts.

I came out of the trance somehow which overtook me as I watched her gobble up greasy things in the burnings.

She was right. I chased around the buildings. I chased off in the moonlight down the road after the four figures. In Grandmother's light I could now see the two shorts running as fast as their short legs would take them toward the light way off. And with them were the two talls. Where were our two people?

Momentarily I discovered the why and wherefore of our two people. Something on the ground tripped me. It was no stone, nor log. It was something soft, furry. No raccoon. After stumbling and recovering my footing, I picked up the heavy furry thing. It had no smell. Wait, it did, but faint, the smell mixed with something, odorous, The fur was certainly familiar. It was one of ours. Not far off was the other huddled in a clump. The strippings of two of ours.

She hadn't followed. She was still inside. I grabbed up both the black furs, and went to the house. She was twirling around the burning place. She had sweet things in her hands, something long and yellow. She had something bright red in her mouth, red with small black seeds and green around the outer edge. She was happy. She was happy until she saw the two bundles of black fur in either of my hands. I hunched down onto the floor, growling. She growled and dropped the sweet from her mouth and threw the yellow thing away.

We were pretty angry, tore up everything within. Broke and smashed and threw and turned over whatever there was to break.

Then we went back to the knoll and farther up the mountain.

卍

We woke early the next morning. Didn't wait for the sun to get up. First light we climbed down the mountain to take a stand on the knoll over the place where the two talls and the two shorts had been. They prowled about. I could hear little cries of the two shorts. The two talls were slamming around like she did last night as Grandmother Moon rose. The talls sputtered. I could feel anger in the air.

We'd seen enough of them. We turned and went back up mountain. As we turned our backs I could hear the talls sputtering. I didn't know for sure if I can repeat exactly what they said and how. I'll try:

"Those fucking bears."

# Ohkwa:Ri

## I.

PATRICK FATHERWELL HAD WORKED TWENTY YEARS FOR THE RAILROAD, fifteen of those years he had been an engineer. Most of the time he hauled ore from Henson Mines, or lumber from the Ruppert Pond Forest Area. He had never engineered passenger trains. Only once did he haul corn. That came down through Montreal from western Canada. He thought it curious the States would be bringing summer corn from Manitoba when there was more corn grown in the mid-western states than the food and grain people could even begin to handle. It wasn't his job to question, and so he didn't. He, Patrick, and his fireman simply did their work and never questioned the proceedings. He was paid to engineer the train carrying its cargo in the flats and boxes and nothing else.

Fatherwell's father had worked for the railroad back in the days when things were rushed, prosperous, and it was the best job a young man without an education could ever hope to get. His father was long retired. Now, this year, his son, Morgan, had applied to the railroad and was given a position as brakeman. There were times they actually worked together. And Patrick always took this occasion in pride and would loudly proclaim to all others how the Fatherwells were really the railroad: grandpa, son, and grandson, and they would go on into the next generation and on to the seventh.

Not a particularly big man, Patrick was actually rather slight. Dark hair curled above a very handsome face which had a strong brow, black sparkling eyes, a strong nose, a good mouth with perfect white teeth, and a chin handsomely carved by nature into a shape that a movie star would have envied. This noble head rose on a thin neck over broad shoulders and a powerful chest, over a thin waist. At first look, he might have been considered wiry, but a further look would more than likely suggest the athletic body. And he was, or had been, an athlete, though he never won medals, trophies, or college scholarships. He'd skied, skated hockey, played some football, but really had excelled in lacrosse. With his young son, he hiked and accomplished many mountain climbs—so one could expect all this healthy exercise would keep his body slender and in top shape, with good tone. And it did.

Patrick was most proud of his athletic prowess and success. He was also very proud, in a boastful way, of his blood: French and Indian. Both his parents originally came from Canada to New York State, and both had French and Indian blood; but what their tribal affiliations were neither knew nor seemed to care. When Ross Fatherwell and his bride, Mary, were young, it was shameful to be French with Indian blood. It meant being forced into residential school and being eventually jobless and mired in poverty. Their parents hid from their tribal affiliations, and consequently when Patrick came into the world and was old enough to start learning exactly who he was, his parents could not tell him what his Indian blood was. They just didn't know. They could trace their French lines—not back to Samuel de Champlain, probably, nor the Jesuits, nor even General Montcalm—who eventually lost French Canada to the British. They were more than likely of yeoman stock, good farmers who bred stout offspring with straight spines and heads not totally empty. Patrick had no problem with his French blood, but he did manage to highlight his Indian blood, whatever the quantity.

"Hey look at my cheeks. Look at these good bones. High bones. Right under these almond-shaped black eyes." He was fairly pale, but certain friends agreed he was probably Indian because he was hairless on the chest and the hair of his arms and legs was sparse, as was his light beard.

Folks were always asking him what his Indian name was. He didn't have one, but jokingly answered: "Man of Big Balls."

He had a comic sense as well as a tremendous pride in his obvious maleness. He didn't drink booze often, but when he did, no man could drink him under the table. He carried it well; it only made him more salty with humorous jokes.

"You can't be Indian, Patrick," a railroad buddy said once when they were out drinking in Syracuse, after a twelve hour run.

"Why the hell not? Look at these bones."

"You hold your bourbon too well."

"What the hell does that mean?"

Apart from being a proficient athlete, he won his greatest applause in the woods and at the rivers. His bag was never empty of game. The only animal he refused to kill was bear, even though Colette, his wife, had long dreamed of tossing a bear rug down before their fireplace.

"No, I don't go bear hunting. You want to go into Canada for moose, I'll be the first in the woods. But not bear."

"Why not?"

"I don't know. I just don't know, but a voice keeps saying, 'You don't kill bear.'"

Many and many a night Colette had the pleasure of cooking rabbit, venison, quail, wild turkey, pheasant, or frying bass, trout, or pike. She was a good wife and mother and took very special pleasure in serving at her table the game her loving husband brought home from the woods.

The family rarely ate beef or pork, and almost never hot dogs, except at a picnic.

"Well, Big Balls or not, you don't look too Indian to me."

"Yeah! You wanna see?"

"No thanks, I believe you. You know, matter of fact, I don't think you're even French. Where the hell did you ever get a name like Fatherwell? That's about as French as my Irish prick."

"Intermarriage, over-marriage, hell, I don't know. Drink up, buddy."

And so Patrick often found himself defending both bloods. Patrick's maleness, manhood, masculinity was never doubted and rarely tested by any other male who had a knowledge of his character or muscle power. He never had to prove he was "Man of Big Balls."

As the bear was at home on the mountain and in the woods Patrick was at home within and without of himself. His body, his mind and his spirit were housed in the self. He was satisfied.

## II.

WHEN HE WAS IN HIGH SCHOOL ONE SUMMER PATRICK TOOK A JOB ON A dairy farm. He rose at five to milk 35 head, and twelve hours later he returned to the cowbarn to milk again. He cleaned the gutters of manure, forked hay down from the mows, curried the draft horses, watered them as well, fed the pigs and was often chased from the pen by the boar—huge as a granite boulder, and fast as a bee in flight. When his barn chores were finished he went into the fields: first to cut, then later to rake, and finally to fork the hay onto the wagon and eventually into the mow. Supper was after the five o'clock milking, and after supper his young limbs were so exhausted that sleep overpowered his body before the dark of night could touch his shoulders.

Patrick bunked in a cabin with another hired hand whose name was Joe St. Clair, or Indian Joe, a Cree. Joe was ten or fifteen years older than Patrick and he stood his ground with the adolescent while arm-wrestling, body wrestling, and even forking hay into the high mow, which was dusty and fluttering with frightened barn swallows squeaking their wings.

They became good friends. Joe was generous with his knowledge and expertise, which basically dealt with life and death in the woods and at the river. He was a crack shot, never missed a mallard in flight; he never went home from the river without at least a dozen fish on his string. He taught the youth how to make snowshoes, how to whistle and sing like a thrush and loon. He taught the youth how to cook a fish, a potato, an ear of corn, in the open fire without a skillet. He taught him how to respect the wildlife around him, to respect the earth and the people, too, which inhabited it. He spoke of the spirit world above and the Creator, Grandmother Moon and Brother Sun. He showed him how to tan hide and sew moccasins— "even if it was woman's work." He taught him the leaves and roots which could make good teas, which he could survive on, should he ever get lost in deep woods.

Indian Joe was a college in himself. Even though he had had only two years of schooling. And Indian Joe was Indian, as full-blooded as an Indian came. Joe took him onto the reserve where the youth saw how many men had long hair. Some men braided their hair, Patrick began to let his hair grow—not too long, but the curls did dangle about his ears. Later, once he met and married Colette, he trained his dark hair to hang straight down his back. When it touched his waist he had his wife do his hair up into two braids, which he hid under his engineer's cap at work.

He stayed friends with Joe until the autumn his friend was killed— walking in the woods—by a hunter who'd left his glasses at home on his bedroom dresser by mistake.

That night the moon was high. Patrick went to the woods, found a place on a felled log, and cried.

Joe had not been much of a talker. He expressed his emotions and ideas through action or by setting an example. He taught Patrick how to carve wood figures by carving a wolf or a bear. The only employment Joe ever enjoyed was farm work. Over the years he traveled from one farm to the next, restless.

Patrick never forgot the teachings, and in turn taught his own boy, Morgan.

## III.

THE NIGHT THE TRAIN HAULED THE CORN OUT OF MONTREAL WAS A raw night. High winds whipped the St. Lawrence River. Blizzard snows met the train when it approached the foothills of the mountains. Visibility was so poor that the tamaracks and hemlocks at the sides of the rails could barely be distinguished in the whiteness of the storm. Winter had arrived early and made life and work difficult. Patrick didn't swear much but that night he "bitched this" and "bitched that," throwing in an occasional "bastard" when he saw that "bitching" wasn't getting anywhere. His freight train was late. It simply could not travel very fast, let alone keep up its usual speed. Most of the rail bed was a straight run, but here and there a bend had been laid because of chaparral. Patrick was well aware of these bends, and especially the big bend at the climb at Algonquin Springs. That bend was a horseshoe and on a fairly steep incline. He dreaded the approach. Even in good, clear weather it could be tough to cross with an overload. He hoped the idiots who prepared the cars and boxes had laid things in even so that nothing listed too far to the left.

They passed Maple Bend without problems. The train approached Miners Bend and Timber Bend with ease and again with no problems. One more bend on the road, Sulphur, and then came the last and the worst, Algonquin. Sulphur passed easily. Two miles to go to Algonquin. The train huffed and puffed, and leaning out the window, snow falling on his head and eyelids, Patrick turned back inside and called out to his fireman:

"Here she comes. Hang on."

No sooner had this warning left his lips than he felt a jerk, heard a banshee-like screaming screech and was tossed from one side of the engine room to the other. They had derailed by leaning, listing too far to the left. The cars sprawled in a wide gulch two feet deep in snow.

No life had been lost. But much of the cargo had opened and spilled out on the ground: boxes, barrels, various machines, some timber, mail bags, and two car loads of corn from Manitoba, Canada.

There was an inquiry. Patrick received, as engineer, no rebuff nor suspension. It obviously wasn't his fault. In the gulch was a deep creek which had swollen. It had risen up over the tracks and in the cold of the storm, frozen in humps, causing the derailment.

Later most of the cargo was salvaged and of course the engine and freight cars up-righted. The only cargo left behind was the corn, ruined by the blizzard.

## IV.

SEASONS CAME AND WENT — WINTER TO SPRING TO SUMMER. MANY TIMES Patrick made the run from Montreal to Syracuse. Always the dumped corn was there in the gulch, clear as a sandy beach, too deep for anything to grow up through the mounds. Around late July he was making a run over the gulch at Algonquin Bend and he observed a half dozen bear eating the corn. Well that was a good thing, he thought. No harm to that, the bears needed fat, and corn would give them a good line of fat for winter hibernation. Early August he had another run over Algonquin Bend. The mounds of corn, though lower, were still there in the gulch. Something was amiss. On the mounds he thought he could see huge humps of rotting flesh. He slowed the train for a better look.

"What's the matter, Patrick? Why'd we slow?" His fireman asked.

"Look down there. Hurry up."

The train crawled like a turtle.

"What's that on the corn?"

"Wow! Looks like skinned corpses."

"I'm gonna stop the train."

When Patrick, his fireman, and the two brakemen climbed down the engine and stood knee deep in the corn mounds, the stench of rotting flesh curled their stomachs, and millions of swarming flies dashed at their eyes and mouths.

"It's bear, Patrick. Not human. Look at the paws and feet. Come on. Let's get out of here."

Patrick was incensed at the horror, the cruelty, the wasted lives of these special animals. His anger spoke on the throttle. When they had passed around Algonquin Bend he let the engine out and sped down the rails. That weekend he was free, off the books, and with his son he drove to the small hamlet of Midas where Algonquin cut through the thick forest— and where the bears had been shot and stripped of their black fur coats. A dirt road curved in the woods, following the creek running through the gulch. He braked the Cherokee wagon on approaching the edge, where he spotted an old Ford parked.

He and the boy got out of the car with rifles readied in hand. They gingerly moved closer to the edge, close enough to see a bear on the corn mound, down on all fours, it's muzzle deep in corn, it's mouth and teeth working at eating.

"It's still alive," he thought. He raised his rifle and took aim.

"Don't shoot," cried the man standing behind a large white pine. "Don't shoot." He dropped his own gun, and at the sound of his voice and his gun hitting against the tree, the bear lifted his head, sniffed and scurried off into the brush on the other side of the gulch.

Fatherwell did not lower his gun, nor change his site.

"Come out from behind that tree, you son of a bitch. Put your rifle on the ground."

Most carefully, a leg came out from behind the white pine, then an arm, a second foot, another arm and a head with a face stood before Fatherwell and his son. He bent and slowly lowered his rifle to the ground and raised up again, his arms in the air, his flushed face frozen in terror.

"I oughta shoot you, you son-of-a-bitch, then skin you and mount your head as a trophy."

The boy walked over to the tree and took the rifle.

"You killed those bears and skinned 'em. They wasn't doing any harm to you, to no one."

As the Fatherwells were about to ask the intruder's name, suddenly the man bolted, raced through the thickets and disappeared into the woods. He left his gun behind to the laughter of Patrick and his son.

"He won't be back, and we've got a new gun."

"No. He will be back. He will. Don't trust greed and hate, boy."

## V.

As OFTEN AS TIME AND HIS WORK ALLOWED, PATRICK MAKE PERIODIC trips to the "corn dump" as he soon came to refer to the gulch. No poachers were seen again, no skinned bear carcass was found again. But each trip he made he would discover these black beauties at the corn mounds. He would stand there for hours, his gun racked in his truck, sipping water from a glass bottle, or chewing a cud of leaf tobacco, watching the bears frolic in the high mound of corn. Some trips there would be only one female with a maturing cub, other times he would find several bears bent over eating corn. One whiff of his human smell and they would quickly raise their heads and prance off into the brush, clattering through low brambles which crackled and broke and left a trail.

"You're safe for a while."

Late summer, mid-August, Patrick had a free day. He asked Colette if she'd like to take a drive into the mountains. His wife was overjoyed at the prospect. It had been years since they just drove through the country on a joy ride, or, as Patrick would say, "rubber necking the scenes." As teenagers dating, he would always insist upon taking trips to the beach on Lake Ontario at Henderson Harbor; to Cooperstown to the Baseball Hall of Fame; to Saturday night drive-ins, of course, to neck more than to see movies, and once they took an overnight trip to the John Brown Farm in Lake Placid. After they married, after Morgan's birth, Patrick would assemble the family and they would take excursions mainly to entertain the young boy: Frontier Town, the North Pole, Great Escape, and whatever town had a zoo, especially where there might be cages holding bears.

Fatherwell would stand solemnly before the bears, his hands twisting as to unlock the cage doors. He never said a word. Never lectured the boy about zoos and cages which were, in his thought, jails. But Morgan sensed his father's mind. Patrick would stand there before the bars by the hour. Morgan would run off to see the other creatures, or go for hot dogs with his mother. Upon their return they would find Patrick still standing, legs apart, hands twisting, kneading, before the cage door. Zoos were not the natural homes of bears.

On the morning of their trip to the mountains, Colette packed a light lunch of cold roast chicken sandwiches, dill pickles, her own homemade molasses cookies, and a huge thermos of iced tea for the hot afternoon she knew would be awaiting them in the meadows, even though they would picnic in the cool shadow of a huge elm tree or beech. That morning she chose carefully what she would wear. After all it was a "date" with her man. She didn't often get to date anymore other than to sit before Monday Night Football on the television. She felt young and girlish, almost giddy.

She picked out a pair of apple-pink shorts, a white silk blouse with apple blossoms embroidered on the collar and a sky-blue scarf. Being a tiny woman, even at forty, she appeared at a distance to be a high schooler. Never beautiful in any glamorous, model sense, she was thought by friends and family to be "cute." Colette reveled in this. She was careful with her weight, careful with her grooming, smiled and laughed freely, and maintained a jaunty step. Consequently, she did continue to appeal to her husband. She especially knew his eye would travel. Once an acquaintance whispered that Patrick had been observed pinching the butt of a waitress in the town diner. She knew it was imperative for her to keep up appearances. Besides, she loved the guy.

Patrick packed only a hunk of suet he purchased from the town butcher and his rifle. Unlike Colette, he did not fancy himself up in any particular dress. Jeans and a sweatshirt would do, though his sweatshirt was lettered with "SAVE THE WHALES OF THE OCEANS." A small figure of a whale swam below waves and above sea grass wafting in the liquid flow.

Once in the truck, Patrick headed for the mountains and Algonquin Bend. The drive was pleasant under sunny skies and temperate breezes. His gas tank full, paper cups of coffee in their hands, there was no need to make pit stops. They rolled the highways with ease, Colette making talk, chatter and Patrick not listening but concentrating on the road's summer traffic which was fairly heavy that Saturday morning. Colette pressed up against him still playing the game of the teenager. Once in a while he'd drop his right arm about her shoulder and give a squeeze. She was thrilled and reached up and gave him a quick kiss on the cheek.

With ease they passed out of Watertown to Lake Bonaparte where Colette expressed the idea that Bonaparte would make a great place to picnic. Patrick ignored her suggestion. They flew through Star Lake on into Cranberry Lake where he slowed and made a left turn onto a dirt road just beyond the village limits. He drove maybe five miles down this road and at last came to a stop at a clearing, a meadow formed years before by clear-cutting the forest for lumber.

"What a lovely field," Colette observed, opening the passenger door of the truck, and stepping out. "Paddy, my goodness. Look at the blackberry brambles over there—thick as bees in a hive. Did we bring a bucket?" She carefully, afraid of possible snakes or mice, wandered to the brambles and picked some sweet fruit and popped the berries in her mouth.

Patrick quietly shut his door, stepped quickly up the dirt road, keeping an eye on the ruts he discovered in the soil. There were old tracks of coyotes and scat; he found a glob of rabbit fur attached to a scrawny sapling. He heard wind rustling through the trees, and the caw of a crow high on a white pine. But he did not take his eyesight from the dirt road. A white butterfly flew past, wheeled and lighted on his shoulder blade. He halted in his step, thinking he heard the whistle of a railroad engine rounding the bend at Algonquin. Probably his imagination, but he knew that the rail bed was near by, so close it was only a hop and a skip from the road where he stood. He strained to hear the whistle—ghostly in the woods. Turning about he watched for a moment Colette picking the blackberries. Suddenly she stood straight. Her hand flew to her breast. She turned and raced to Patrick's side.

"There's something in the bush. I heard someone breaking the bushes."

He only smiled.

"What is it?"

"Don't know. Maybe a fox. Maybe a bear . . ."

"A bear?"

". . . maybe a man, or a kid out squirrel hunting."

"Did you see a bear?"

He smiled down gently at her. "Maybe. I don't know."

"Let's not picnic here."

As she made this suggestion he continued his walk a pace or two, stopped, retraced his steps and returned to the truck. His wife, fearful of animals, followed and observed him take down his rifle from the rack. This certainly reassured her that her protector was there and would see no harm came to her. She clung to his left arm, but he shook off her grasp and moved down the dirt road. He had discovered a fresh track, the rut of a Ford—he recognized the tire insignia. Slow but determined, he continued. Colette gathered her fears and strode slowly five paces behind. He was heading towards the area where the dirt road entered the low brush before the old woods actually began.

"Stay here," he commanded.

Before she heard the guns, she listened intently to the caws of two crows flying overhead.

A red fox crossed their path on the road. Its tail close to the ground. Its ears pointed up.

Another shot. They were at the brush. Another shot and Colette and Patrick walked within the shadows of the woods. Another shot was heard and they stopped, finding themselves standing before the gulch and the mounds of corn.

There were huge black humps scattered on the ground in puddles of blood. Colette counted one, two, three dead bears. Horrified, frightened at the sight and smell of death, she threw her arms around Patrick's waist. He untied her arms and pushed her off. As he did another shot, from close range, rang out, echoed in the woods. She watched Patrick grab at his gut, and she watched blood slowly spread across the sweatshirt which covered his torso now crouching over.

"They was all drunk, drunk on the liquor the corn made."

A voice came through the trees:

"Drunk. An' I shot 'em up! They ain't no damn good any way."

Patrick straightened up, the blood still seeping from his wound.

"Don't come any closer or you're as dead as those goddamn bears."

Patrick Fatherwell continued his march towards the gulch, placing one heavy foot after the other, dust rising, blood dripping slowly from his abdomen onto the road.

"I'm warning you not to come any closer. Shit man, I'll kill you."

Now he could see the man. Long greasy hair trailed down his back, dressed in a dirty T-shirt. Coffee and beer stains spotted his chest. He wore filthy Levis, near threadbare, his feet in worn brogans. Under the T-shirt stood out a hump of a belly raising the shirt up from under his belt. Little black hairs covered the man's navel.

"Get back. I know who you are. You're the same bastard who chased me off here once before. Get back."

Colette screamed. She pulled on Patrick's arm almost dislodging his rifle.

"Go back to the truck," he commanded her as he raised the rifle.

From his left eye he noticed one wounded bear rise up from the corn mound and struggle off pulling his left hind leg.

"Go back."

She stood deathly still, took her hand off his arm and began to cry.

"You can't chase me out of here. This is state land. My land. I'm a taxpayer. MY land." The strange man lifted his gun to his shoulder. As he did a shot seared the air, smoke puffing around Patrick. The bullet so fiercely struck into the mush and bone of the head, so swiftly, at such close range, that as the victim was struck and commenced to fall, a spatter of blood hit in his open eyes, and Patrick batted his lids and fired again. There was no need. The man crumbled on the ground. Blood and brains covering the pine needles and the fresh tracks of the once living bears.

She screamed, screamed, and watched Patrick turn and slowly stagger down the dirt road towards his truck, blood dripping from the hole in his stomach.

Colette watched him move through the brush out into the clearing where the stand of blackberry brambles had attracted her attention.

Patrick slumped over on the ground, his rifle still clutched in his right hand.

A crow flew overhead, cawed loudly, and quickly disappeared into the vast sky.

回

# Tortured Skins

"I HATE THE SONS-OF-BITCHES!"

Rudy's anger flared.

"Slaughter 'em, I say."

His bitterness, the cruelty of his words, leaped into the air the same as the tongues of flame from the pit fire leaped into the falling darkness in the sky.

"You're mad as hell," Marvin Heist proffered.

Three hunters squatted before the fire which blazed and spit, sputtered and fumed. Behind them in the lowering light, the peaks of the Adirondacks could be seen withering into the dark. A string, a last ray of sunset painted the slopes pink-orange.

"If there was only one bear left in the whole world . . . I'd kill it. An' hang 'im by his left testicle."

Rudy's two companions laughed as the fire shot shadows across their faces. A blackened coffeepot bubbled a pungent brew.

"What the fuck a bear ever do to you?" asked the third hunter, Charm Beggins, Rudy's cousin.

"Nothin'. I just hate 'em, that's all. The goddamn bear and the wolf both."

"You're a mean man, Rudy Perigrin. A mean and hateful man. And I'd suppose a vengeful man, too. I mean, don't get me wrong . . . I love you, you bum. I like to hunt as much as you or any man. And I particularly like to hunt big game, bear for example . . ."

"Marvin, I . . ."

"Let me finish, Rudy."

"Yeah. Sure."

"Well, Rudy, Charm, too, I ain't got the heart, no idea of, cleaning off the mountains of the teddies."

Marvin sucked on a toothpick and sucked air through an opening between his lower front teeth.

"I couldn't rightly do that."

Rudy refused him a reply.

Marvin Heist had been an excellent shot all his life. A fine hunter since adolescence. He took only the legal limit of whatever game . . . mallard, buck, or bear, when he was fortunate to bag game. Thus far he'd had the luck to kill only one black bear. And he was immensely proud. Its fur lay on the floor before his home fireplace, and its head was mounted on the dining room wall. The rug was immortalized in a photograph of it and his first son, odd, playing with his penis, naked on the glossy black fur.

"You had your way, Rudy, there'd be no bear left for anybody to pop off," Charm injected. "You're a might too harsh there, Perigrin. A might."

"He's got a terrible grudge against the world."

Rudy frowned, proving his age when suddenly wrinkles corroded his forehead.

"Only bear."

The men were all somewhere in their late forties, seasoned hunters, veterans of Vietnam, husbands and fathers, heavy Friday night beer hounds, though none drank when on hunting trips . . . unsafe, dangerous. Charm worked as brick layer, a mason; Marvin as an auto mechanic; Rudy butchered meat in a supermarket. Close to the same age they were also near the same weight and height: five feet ten, a hundred and eighty pounds in stocking feet. Their friendship had formed years before in high school. Marvin was married to Rudy's sister; Charm had married Rudy's wife's sister. Their relationship was tight. They even drove the same kind of truck, a Ford. What differed was their outlooks, philosophies, ideas, on what, where, when, and how much. Plus Rudy was a quarter blood Abnakie on his grandmother's side.

"No, I don't want to slaughter the whole fuckin' world. Just bear. All the fuckin' bear."

"He's a symbol of the wilderness," Marvin stated.

"Fuck the symbol; fuck the wilderness."

"Without it we wouldn't be here tonight . . . in the wilderness hunting your hated bear, or any other game any other time, as far as that goes," Charm injected.

As though the creatures of the wilderness agreed with Charm, a shrill whistle was heard followed by an owl's hoot.

"See. Hear. Even the ol' horned owl agrees."

A bat swooped down from the night, circled the blazing fire and pecked off bugs which had been attracted there. As quickly as the bat arrived, even quicker it swooped away.

The coffee brewed, Marvin reached out with a holder for the pot and poured the steaming liquid into three cups.

"Where's the milk?" asked Charm.

"The Cremora's in the food trunk."

Rudy pulled out the Cremora and a package of shortbread cookies his wife had baked only the day before, intending it would go on the hunting trip. These hard cookies kept well on such excursions. Rudy chomped down on the bread. It cracked apart within his jaws. He chewed as though he gnawed a bear's cooked muscle of leg bone. He cleared his mouth, his tongue whipped out and licked at the crumbs nestling in the corners of his lips.

"There's more than four thousand bears in this mountain country. I aim to shoot every one of 'em."

Charm stirred his coffee that now had Cremora floating on the surface. He pushed back his cap, sniffed the air, balmy for October, scented with the autumn and the earth covered in dying leaves, and leaned over and leered an odd smile at Rudy.

"Perigrin, you have been bear hunting nineteen years now. You have trekked the woods every season for nineteen years, and you ain't shot a single bear, not the first one."

Rudy scowled and broke off more shortbread with his teeth.

"Yeah," squeaked Marvin. "You ain't, come to think of it."

Marvin and Charm giggled simultaneously . . . schoolboys caught dunking flies in an old-fashioned ink well, or hiding a baby garter snake under the seat of a pig-tailed girl in the classroom.

"I've only bagged one, and Charm, here, has gotten two bear over the years. But you haven't shot your gun off, let alone killed a bear. Your story is it's always in flight, or behind a huge granite boulder, or turned out to be a shadow or something. I don't understand."

"Really. A man who's got a hate like yours, and a good eye and, I might add, a terrific aim. Well. Seems to me you should have slaughtered your quota a long time ago. Rudy, you are a strange bag of wind. A big fart from too many beans."

Perigrin did not respond to this belittling accusation. He eyed the men, especially Marvin, and chomped into another shortbread.

Cold silence, touched with bitterness, fell between the three friends. Perhaps Charm and Marvin had gone too far.

The fire, though lowering, continued to flare and lap at the darkness. Again the hoot of an owl, and a breeze rushed through the conifers and the underbrush. A strange, wild smell penetrated the night air. Rudy lifted his head and sniffed the air. His nose seemed to twitch like an animal, a raccoon. Shadows crept across his face.

The men sipped coffee and chewed their shortbreads silently. The cup's rim burned Marvin's lips. He blew air on the steaming liquid and the hot metal.

"What's the clock," Rudy broke the silence.

"'Bout ten, I guess," Charm offered. "Time to turn in."

"Think I'll sit up a little," Rudy declared. "Never know what might be lurkin' around."

His companions nodded in agreement.

"Think a bear might show?" Charm asked quite innocently.

Rudy glanced toward the hump of sleeping bags and their guns, to the left of the fire.

"You never know." He responded innocuously.

Marvin yawned, shot a look toward the sleeping bags.

"You know, I was talking to a ranger at the park last week. He said all last summer, just about every night, the campers were frightened by one bear or two prowling around, looking for goodies, garbage to eat." Marvin curled into a ball of laughter. "You know what they were hunting for?" No one answered. "They weren't looking for the usual bacon that time, nor the watermelon rinds, not even the Cheese-Whiz." Again he rolled into a burst of laughter. "They were draggin' diapers out of the garbage containers. Baby diapers. Imagine that. Baby diapers."

An incredulous grin appeared on Charm's mouth. "Unbelievable. Baby diapers. What the hell were they lookin' for them for?" he guffawed.

Rudy made no offer of a remark.

"Didn't much matter. Just wanted used diapers."

"Why?" Charm pondered at last aloud straight into Rudy's eyes. "They were eating the shit in them."

"Don't jerk me off, Marvin," Rudy stated.

"I'm only telling you what the ranger said. They were eating the baby shit in the diapers. Said they chased two yearlings one night deep into the woods, deep. The moon was high and pretty full and they had brought flashlights. The area was lit up. The forest floor was covered with baby diapers. A truckload littered the ground. Imagine that. Baby diapers. Whatever happened to good ol' greasy, unhealthy bacon. Or watermelon."

The two men, Marvin and Charm, both had other bear stories to tell concerning campers, tourists driving up to the mountain garbage dumps to witness the bears paw through garbage for half-eaten hot dogs, stale bread or hamburger rolls, broken pickle jars, or whatever discarded foods they could ransack out of the dumps.

Rudy remained silent, uninterested. He added no story to his companions' tall tales, absurd stories. He drank his cooling coffee, chewed his cookies, and occasionally scratched his head or his rump. He was utterly unimpressed, uninterested, lost in some other reverie from some other time in some other place.

Marvin's echoing laughter ceased. He yawned, stretched, and rose from his squat by the fire. He picked up his sleeping bag. Charm also rose from his position by the flames, dumped the remaining coffee onto the fire, which hissed, and he went off for his bag. It was now growing late.

"Light's comin' early. I wanna be up at the first crack," Charm spoke to the night.

"Let's go Perigrin. Just stack more wood on the fire." Marvin picked up some twigs which had fallen during last winter's blows and tossed them on the fire. The flames speared high into the night. Sparks quickly blew about the campsite. The moon had begun to rise. The shine caught his cheek.

At last Rudy spoke: "No. Think I'll just sit here awhile and watch the moon rise . . ." which was in view to his right.

"'Night," the men called. "Don't let the bedbugs bite."

"Jerks," thought Rudy.

Shortly the two men rolled in their bags gave off annoying snores.

Rudy remained by the fire. Its glow was waning and the licking flames commenced to sputter. The hard muscle of the campfire was losing strength. It grew weaker as the moon ascended. Rudy rose from the earth, awkwardly. Walked to his own sleeping bag, but did not take it up. He stooped, ruffled around the guns stacked beside his bag and picked up one bear rifle. His rifle. The barrel shone by the moon. It sparkled. He hefted it to his shoulder and eyed through the sight, aiming at the fire. A black rock was his game. It resembled a bear in fetal position, a small ball of black fur. He eyed the trigger of the unloaded gun, pleased, feeling the strength in his shoulder and arm, feeling strength in his spirit, his guts, and his mind. "Fuck bears. Fuck you guys, too." He spoke aloud in a low, non-passionate voice. He slipped back in his seat by the fire, rifle still in his hands. Gently as though it was a small child, a babe who would waken and cry out, he placed the gun beside his thigh. "I'm ready. I know you'll come tonight. I know it. I smell you, you bastard. I smell your stinking ass."

Marvin rolled about in his bag and issued a great grunt. Charm continued to snore, his snores growing louder as time passed. Rudy wiped a yawn from his mouth and refused to admit sleep was slowly overpowering him. "I'll get you, you sonna-bitch. You're there. I hear you pokin' in the brush. I smell your ass. Your breath stinks like dead fish. And I smell it. I smell your fuckin' hide. You ain't comin' for no baby diaper tonight . . . You're comin' for a fuckin' bullet in your fuckin' gut."

Ever since he graduated from high school, Rudy Peligrin had hunted. First with his brothers, Dan and John, for woodchucks, then his dad for deer, and now his buddies for bear. And it was true, much to his chagrin, his embarrassment, he failed every year to drag from the woods the dead carcass of a bear. Not one. Not one single black hair. All the way through junior high he thought of nothing else but killing bears. Woodchucks and squirrels were okay for kids, practice. Later, deer was the aim, and now he thought of the bull's eye. Tonight was the night. A bear was here, nearby. He'd bag his bear tonight.

Something startled him. He stood stiffened, felt for the gun by his thigh. No, he didn't hear footsteps or growls. He heard Linda, his wife, screaming as he slammed the kitchen door that morning going out to the garage for the Ford. "Don't bring no bloody mess home either. You clean the thing out there. You hear?"

A nurse, Linda saw all the blood she wanted to see at the hospital emergency room where she worked the evening shift. She had no desire to see blood on her own kitchen table. Rudy himself saw blood every day at the local Grand Union . . . he being the head butcher. Every morning it was his duty to cut beef, make hamburger, slice out tough cuts for stew, etc. He did not hate blood nor was he squeamish. Actually he liked the feel of it cold or hot moving through his fingers and down his arm. He liked blood, and would thrill with the blood of a bear soaking into the rough skin of his hands, his fingers, his wrists. He had lived for that very experience. He would repeat over in his mind as he sawed through bones or hacked beef muscle. Once he admitted this daydream, this fervent desire to Linda.

"That's sick. What's wrong with you? You, a dear and darling husband. A good father. A caring worker. You don't even miss Sunday mass. You pay taxes. You even give once in a while to charity. So why are you so sick about this stuff, this killing, this killing a bear? Pretending, pretending at work you're hacking up a body, a bear. It's gonna get you into trouble. You'll go nuts with this obsession, Rudy. Nuts. Do you hear me? Nuts."

He would allow her to rave on. It was good for her vocal chords, he'd reason. But he would continue relishing blood on his hands. He never wore gloves like other butchers.

He paid no attention to Linda. She might be right. But who gave a damn. He'd worry about those things when the time came. If they wanted to haul his ass off to the booby hatch, well, go for it. But not before he killed his bear.

Linda would put her arms around his neck, give him a kiss and a hug. "Rudy, I love you. The kids love you. Your mother loves you. The whole world loves you. You love yourself . . . don't you? Oh God, why do you have these horrible ideas?"

It was true, his family did love him; his girls, Cherry and Apple, both adored their father. The townsmen liked him, his boss greatly respected him. The whole world liked and respected Rudy Perigrin, even the garbage collector. In her own fashion Linda adored him. They shared a happy life, good sex, pleasure with their girls whom they childishly named after fruits because they believed their girls were as sweet as cherries and as tart as Macintosh apples. But this one festering pustule Rudy had had for all these years nagged at their lives and relationship. Linda greatly feared it would erupt and destroy their marriage and the family.

Rudy could not hear Charm's snores or Marvin scratching his skin where poison ivy was spreading blisters on his rump from having taken a crap earlier in the day. He could not hear the owl or the breeze. He did not stare at the moon, nor did he watch the coals glow in the dying firepit.

What he now heard was Miss Allen's voice. She was begging and insisting, and at last commanding him to put on the suit, the costume.

"No." He would not give in to his kindergarten teacher's demands. "It itches."

"Rudy, for the last time . . . put it on. The show is going to start any minute. Henry is in his bunny suit and Mary in her lamb costume. Now put it on. Immediately."

Rudy and his teacher were in the boys' room. He stood clad only in his under shorts. The furry suit in his hands, his feet reluctant to step into the imitation fur.

"It won't kill you, Rudolph. It isn't going to kill you."

He broke into tears, sobbed and remained adamant. He would not put on the suit.

At last Miss Allen grabbed him about the naked shoulders and shook him. He bit her hand. She slapped him hard across the cheek.

"Put that bear suit on this moment. No more of this idiocy. I'm telling your mother what you have done." She sucked at the wrist where he had bitten. It was red and swollen with small teeth marks deep into the skin. He did draw a speck of blood. She shook him once more. He complied. He placed first his right foot into the feet of the costume, then the left, drew it up his naked legs and thighs, then his torso up to the neck. Miss Allen helped pull the hood over Rudy's head, lining up the eye sockets with the boy's eyes. She zipped up the zipper, not acknowledging that she nearly caught his skin in the teeth. Rudy immediately commenced to itch and scratch.

Still sucking her bitten hand she called, "What kind of little bear Indian are you?"

"I ain't no Indian. And I ain't no bear." He said in a muffled voice.

He would always remember Thanksgiving and the play of the Pilgrims' first. He would hate the holiday forever. And he would hate teachers, but he would particularly hate bears.

Miss Allen had two small boys carry a cream-colored window curtain out on the stage. She instructed they raise it high to allow the audience of parents to recognize the play had begun. The little Indians came out first. Little boys and girls dressed in brown cloth sacks to resemble hide outfits and with chicken feathers in their hair. They carried a basket of corn and one of squash, and one boy carried a papier-mâché turkey on a platter. The pilgrims arrived in black and white and pretended they had just debarked the Mayflower. With the pilgrims safely on land and about to accept the Indians' gifts, Miss Allen directed the animals to come on stage: the rabbits, deer, a chicken, skunk, and Rudy the bear. He was itching and scratching. Twisting and sobbing in torment. When fully on stage, the boy unzipped the suit and scratched before the audience. First his tummy and then his shoulder blades. This was not meant as a part of the performance. Miss Allen stood horrified in the wings. She whispered instructions to him to pull up his suit. He failed to hear. The audience began to giggle and titter. Rudy's mother sat in the front and sensed something was wrong. And when the suit slipped down to the floor, she screamed, "Stop that. Now."

Miss Allen dragged the child off the stage. She slapped him hard across the face. The heavy slap left a red swatch. When he arrived home with his mother, she too slapped him hard and sent him to his room where he was to wait his father's homecoming from his job at the foundry. His father would take care of Rudy's insolence. When his father arrived home, he climbed the stairs, unbuckled his belt and lashed the boy. His father whipped his buttocks until they ran red in blood.

卍

The camp was quiet, still as a midnight church. Charm had ceased snoring. Marvin had stopped rolling in his sleeping bag. Rudy lay stretched before the flickering glows of the fire. His gun near his prone figure.

There was movement in the brush . . . thick stands of witch hobble and very young sapling fir. A swish, another swish and another swish in the brush. Boughs, limbs parted. A dark figure stood framed by a pine. It edged out of the brush and approached the firepit. It sniffed, loudly. Could smell nothing much more than the boiled coffee and the scent of shortbreads. It noticed the sleeping hunters but made no noise to disturb them. It ambled toward Rudy, and stared down at the sleeping figure. It bent and scooped Rudy into its arms awakening him. Rudy reached down for his gun but it was far from his reach. He kicked and thrashed but made no vocal sound. He was being carried away from the fire, from his buddies who did not stir.

He gasped for breath. He could not suck air into his lungs. He felt his chest cave, it was heavy. He felt his stomach cave. He itched and wanted to scratch the skin where it was exposed. He clawed to breathe. Nothing, no air entered his mouth or lungs.

The night was totally still. No noise of any kind, no sound of any animal or leaves rustling. The moon had dipped and the sky was pitch black. He fell asleep in the arms of the creature who had walked into camp from the deep woods. Silence.

卍

When the light was up in the morning and both Marvin and Charm, having overslept, awoke, they did not see Rudy by the fire in his sleeping bag. The hunters called out, thinking he had gone to the stream for water to make coffee or to brush his teeth or just simply to pee. They called several times but got no response. They took loaded guns and left camp to tramp through the woods to search their friend. They found tracks and followed. No more than twenty yards away from the firepit they discovered Rudy. He leaned against a beech tree, his head slumped, his arms to his side.

Marvin stopped.

Charm asked, "Is he alive?"

Marvin bent over the slumped figure, could not answer immediately.

"I don't know" was all that he could say.

He held up Rudy's head. His left cheek had been bitten. A great hole gaped out at him.

"I think he is dead."

॥

# One More

*Hunters took 827 black bears during New York's 1992 big game season. The total calculated Adirondack bear take of 611 is also above the previous 10-year average of 572. Recent increased harvests come from better utilization of the annual surplus of black bears rather than from a population increase. This harvest will contribute to the maintenance of an Adirondack black bear population which is compatible with natural food production and human land uses.*

—Adirondack Daily Enterprise, 1993

## I.

HE COULD HEAR A DRUM AND A RATTLE. THE DRUMBEAT CAME A LONG way through the birch woods. Beat, beat, beat, beat or rather pound, pound, pound, pound. Soft heads drumming down on the tendered hide of the water drum. And rattle: its shake-shake resembling the sound of rain hitting a tin roof, or sand tossed through a screen.

The pounding of the drum and the shake of the rattle made his old heart feel good.

He sat on a moss-covered log and listened, his back slightly bent, his hands folded in solitude before him, his feet planted on the ground but placed carefully so he would not hurt, damage the spring violet blooming a few inches from the sole of his right boot.

Again the pounding of drum and the steady shake of the rattle. He smiled and whispered a prayer that only the violet could hear. He straightened his back as pride surged through his chest. Out loud he said to the woods and the creatures scattered through the brush and granite stones, the birds on the tree limbs on to the air over head:

"Boy, wish I had a good smoke. It would be a perfect day."

Only a few months earlier he made a solemn promise to Marion he would quit smoking. She'd convinced him it was bad for his health even though he had smoked for 55 of his cumulated 73 years. He managed to cheat, but cheated only himself, not Marion. His grandson smoked, and she never lectured him, but he knew well that elders must never lecture the young. Marion was 71 so she was definitely not his elder, and could nag on him as much as she considered necessary. But not the grandson, even though she did not approve of his cigarettes either.

"What's a man need woman for anyways?" he nearly shouted. "Only fussin' all the time."

He cheated by hanging out near Troy. He'd encourage him to light up, and asked him to blow the exhaled smoke toward him and in turn he'd breathe it into his own lungs. That was bad, and Marion had caught him doing that from time to time. She'd scold and reprimand while smiling at Troy.

Retracting his statement about man needing woman, he smiled in a fey sort of a way, licked his lips and laughed.

"Guess woman is needed by man, many ways. But shouldn't admit it to her."

The drum beat a path again through the thick woods. An ancient rhythm. Again he listened to the shake of the rattle. The Bear Dance, a dance older than any of these great conifers or birch or beech of this forest. Nearly as old as these huge granite boulders surging up through the earth, granite boulders tossed into the air by some tremendous volcanic eruption even before his people came to home these mountains and the river lands below. Rhythms certainly older than him, he nearly giggled thinking the ancient rhythms made him realize he was even less than a mere child cribbed on the cradle board strapped to his mother's stout back, in comparison.

"Guess I'm not so old after all," he decided. "73 ain't old."

He glanced to the end of the log where he sat and found a young chipmunk staring at him while sitting up, holding its paws as though waiting for a gift of a nut.

"Yes siree, little chip. I ain't so old." He reached into his jacket pocket and brought out a peanut for his furry friend. From the left pocket he withdrew an apple, very green, very tart.

"Not the same as a good smoke, but good, and good for me. It'll take the need away."

Again he relaxed and listened to the two ancient instruments. It was Troy and his friend Tommy. Troy was readying for the ceremony in the Longhouse shortly. This made him feel real good that his grandson was a traditionalist, believed in the old ways, the old stories and prayers, not like so many of the young lads and girls. Troy somehow had eluded the booze and drugs. Even graduated from high school. Had sense. Found a good woman to spoon around with and one day would marry and be a good husband and father. Yes indeed, he was very proud of his grandson and his mother, his youngest daughter, who had raised Troy well. Troy—named Troy because he was born in Troy, New York while his father worked iron there; well, Troy had a pretty good job. He worked construction for some white guy over there in Saranac Lake, twenty miles up in the "High Peaks" area. Well, actually, he started to remember, Troy helped to build summer cabins on the various lakeshores for the folks from New Jersey to buy. He had always believed tourists contaminated the land, woods, water—wherever they might hail from. Could not do without fast foods and TVs in the mountains. City stuff and nonsense, he considered. Oh, he thought, it takes all kinds. Must be Troy eats all that fast junk food. Nothing like a solid piece of venison, or a fresh trout from the stream—after blessing and thanking the life taken. No hamburgers or pizza for him. Marion wouldn't cook it anyway. Corn mush with a little syrup was just fine. And corn soup—best food ever invented by the women folk. Marion sure made a terrific pot every moon or so.

"Yeah," he decided, "Venison was good enough for the old folks and it was good enough for him—with a little plate of red spaghetti. Those Italians weren't so bad. Had a good invention there."

His little friend, the chipmunk, continued listening to the old man in the hope, expectation of receiving at least one more peanut.

Henry stared at the furry creature and noticed his left cheek was blown out larger than the right. He had stored the nut away.

"Okay, buddy, one more." He extracted one more peanut and tossed it to the rodent. He then held up the green apple and opened his mouth as if to bite into the shiny flesh, but remembered his false teeth. His hand slipped into his trouser pocket and pulled out a penknife and began to cut off slices of the fruit as if slicing a hunk from a chew of compressed tobacco.

The rhythm of both the drum and rattle ceased. The woods were quiet as though a northern wind had swept through and brushed away all sound: the buzz of mosquitoes, the chatter of chipmunks, the beautiful songs of the birds, even the growls of bobcat and bear. Only the flow of the stream nearby rippled and jumped pushing the rocks of the bed.

"Well, got chores. Best be gettin' back. Now you be careful there, little furry creature, who you take nuts from. Not everybody's honest in this ol' world." The animal scampered off beyond the log.

From behind a dead birch, he fetched up a greasy paper bag—no plastic for Henry. Dust to dust, he thought as he folded the paper bag and slipped it into his back pocket where hung a green handkerchief which he pulled out and made a long hard blow into the cloth and replaced it into the pocket where it trailed behind him as a light on his caboose as he trudged home through his woods.

## II.

"How long's Grandpa been feeding bears, grandma?" Troy asked.

"Since the sun rose. I mean the first sunrise, so long he don't remember."

"But, grandma, can't they feed themselves? Isn't there enough natural food out there in the woods—"

"Well, he obviously don't think so."

They heard the screen door open and shut with a bang and Henry strolled into the kitchen where Marion and their grandson sat at the table drinking cups of sweet coffee and nibbling at cuts of chocolate cake. Rich chocolate layer cake was just about Henry's favorite food. He once said the way a smoker would walk a mile for a Camel, he would hike sixteen miles for a slice of chocolate cake. He had the knack of sniffing a baking cake in a neighbor's oven and had always the time to wait the cooling. Even if he knew, especially, that a family member in town was baking he'd drive to town for a slice. And he disliked town. The village had a population of 5,000 souls, but Henry thought of it as being a huge metropolis, a major city like Glens Falls 200 miles south. He rarely went to town except for food for his forest animals.

"Hey there, don't eat all that there cake. Save some for the old folks."

Troy laughed in great guffaws.

"But Grandad, you always said elders can't tell the young people what to do."

"Yes, sir, you are very correct, but that is in a traditional way. And for your information chocolate fudge cake is not traditional Mohawk. So there, young fellow! I can tell you to save some for the old folks."

He had the boy. Troy knew it. He began to gather up the dirty dishes he had used as Marion sliced a huge portion of cake for Henry.

"Get your bears fed."

"Yes, sir, I did, sir," he responded to Troy's question.

"Who'd you feed today?"

"Well, sir, I left plenty of suet for them all, but only old OCHGUARI showed up to be hand fed. Her cub wasn't with her this P.M. She was fidgety, flighty. Bad tempered. She swatted the suet right out of my hand. Those claws of hers almost got me."

"What was wrong?"

"Well, sir, her cub might be having trouble. Might be sick, or wounded, might have wandered off with another mama bear. Might even of gone off to eat those fresh red cones of the tamarack. They like them, you know. Some say they taste and look like raspberries on the tree."

Outside they could hear a line of tourist cars roar up the road.

Henry stood up and shouted:

"Hey there, you white guys! Slow down! Don't you see those signs I put up: SLOW DOWN/ANIMALS CROSSING."

"Sit down. They can't hear you," Marion proclaimed. "Even if they could hear they wouldn't slow for an animal."

"Probably not even a human, a little kid," Troy interjected as he placed his dirty dishes in the sink.

"Well, sir, I'm much worried about her. She might be sick, herself, too, you know. Didn't stay with me long enough for me to get a good sight on her. Maybe she was in a fight—"

"And got the worst for it," Marion worried.

"Maybe. Who knows. I kept hearing her growl long ways off. But then you boys took out the drum and rattle. She stopped growling then."

"We weren't drumming."

"No?"

"No, we were chopping wood for grandma's woodstove. She's 'bout out of wood."

"I heard drumming and the rattle. The Bear Dance."

"Not from us. What you heard was the ax striking logs."

"Well, that's a drum—of a kind."

"Anyway, Grandpa, are you sure it was her?" Troy asked.

"Naturally. Of course. She had her star. Her blue star was right there on her chest where it's 'spose to be."

Troy laughed at his grandfather.

"Okay, Grandma, Grandpa, we're going to town."

Henry listened for the screen door to slam—which it did. He glanced over to his wife shuffling various objects around the table: sugar bowl, salt and pepper shakers, a small ceramic snapping turtle which once was used as a cigarette ashtray, and a short glass vase holding one white lily of the valley, an early summer flower.

"Good boy. Good boy," Henry exclaimed to no one but himself.

He allowed his thinking to wander back to the woods, the drums and rattle, and his bears. At least once a week he would walk the path into the woods lugging pails and bags of food to feed his animals. He was cognizant of the fact that early spring offered little food to his four legged and winged friends. Grasses weren't tall, no berries or nuts, or even much root to supply their needs. Henry canvassed the stores and various restaurants in the out-lying towns and begged for scraps such as beef bones, tallow, spoiled vegetables, moldy bread—whatever would be tossed out by the proprietors and not composted. He was always fortunate and carried home a goodly load of food. He spent much time picking up Coke and beer cans along the highways and sold the cans for change he'd use to buy grains for the birds. His favorite was the red-tail hawk, but in distributing the grains he showed no partiality. The red cardinal, the blue jay, even the city pigeon who had no business in his woods was cut in for a share. The pigeon had migrated north from the cement buildings of Albany and New York City and they too must eat. Hadn't the Iroquois themselves migrated east from the northern climes of the Midwest? His people, in a sense, were once the pigeons and were starved for food after the long, harsh trek into lands occupied by people ready and willing to kill invaders of their hunting grounds.

When he ventured out to feed the animals and birds, he constantly kept an eye on the forest floor for the sick and wounded. Chicken wire cages behind his small barn almost always held some creature or other in great need of healing. And heal them he would do with food, medicine and prayer. Many a hawk had had a broken wing mended; a baby porcupine or opossum was aided into maturity by a baby's milk bottle and then released back to it's natural home in the forest.

Henry had always wished he had studied to be a veterinarian. But college was too costly. The next best was that his son, David, would become a vet, but Dave chose to be an art major and now taught drawing in the central school. Henry was wise enough, had the need, skill and intelligence to read and study on his own, and he had no fear of calling the local vet for free information on how to care for a fox with a broken leg or a bear holding a bullet in its rear. He learned fast and well and in a matter of a few years he was really as adroit in healing as a college-graduated vet.

That particular morning of the drumming heard in the woods, and the growling of his starred bear—actually the star was really more like a round splash of blue-white fur—turned out to be a good morning. No rescues from possible death by starvation or wounds. His creatures all seemed safe and healthy, even though the word was out that some raccoons in the area were rabid. Not a single crow or squirrel needed attention. That certainly perked up his spirits, and he was able to feed the animals and eat his own apple in good spirits.

Near at hand on the kitchen table rested several books. One was an identification book of wild flowers—Henry never called anything, not even a weed, the dandelion or the purple burdock or chicory. Beneath it rested a volume by Arthur Parker on Iroquois uses of maize and other food plants;

beneath that was a skinny little paperback newly shined, the journal of a very youthful Dutch man of the year 1634–35 titled *A Journey into Mohawk and Oneida Country*. Henry excelled in many intellectual and creative pursuits. He wasn't only a self-taught veterinarian, a horticulturist, and a simple cabinetmaker, but also an astute historian of Iroquois history and culture. A book was never far from his hand. Neither were tools to create a fence, or to carve a log of wood into a face or animal. He had mastered many arts, especially the art of storytelling. He could, and often did, tell stories by night, and mainly to young children.

Most of his life he had held the position of custodian at the central school. He came to love the young children, showing no favoritism to the Indian children over the white. He found himself one day telling a story to a little girl who was suffering a ferocious toothache. The word spread among the kids that Mr. Henry, as they referred to him, was a marvelous storyteller. Shortly his art was in great demand. Schools and art centers, even the college, hired him to tell the magical stories he knew so well. Now in retirement those honorariums came in handy to buy food and supplies for his animals and birds.

He'd made a good solid study of Indian and particularly of Iroquois Mohawk culture and he became widely respected and was consulted by various, considered experts. He was knowledgeable and accurate when citing facts.

He shoved away the Parker book and the wild flower guide and picked up in his knobby fingers the journal of the young Herman Van Der Bogaert for a morning read. He was sure this journal would show some insights into the village and Longhouse lives of his people in the 17th century, when the various Europeans crowded like hungry panthers around those old villages. He had not turned too many pages, the sunlight falling through the window on his face, when his wife came back to the table.

"Just saw your pet out there tramping my day lilies."

"Who?"

"That pet bear of yours."

"White Star."

"That's the one. Better get her out of my flowerbed or you'll be eating her for Sunday supper."

Henry took off his glasses and laid them gently on the table. They were precious to him. He looked up into his wife's eyes and smiled.

"Meat! Meat on this table? I guess not," he joked.

His guns were always ready but had not been shot for many years.

"Well, better do something 'bout her. I don't want her knocking the door down again looking for you, or that cub of hers wandering off."

He cleared his throat and stamped his left foot to the floor.

"I'll go get her."

"Shoo her away from the house. But don't get too close—" she worried, then added an afterthought, "Take a head of lettuce out of the refrigerator to tease her off with, here, I'll get it."

The aging man lumbered up from his chair at the table and accepted the lettuce from his wife's hand as she turned away from the refrigerator.

In no time he was outside. Henry went around the side of the house where the day lilies bloomed. No bear. He went to the barn. No bear. The garage. No bear. By the garage was a healthy blue spruce. It had been clawed and showed signs in the bark of deep bites, tooth marks. Just slightly beyond the garage and the barn, the thick woods commenced. Prints were on the soft grass leading into the woods. He listened for a moment and heard a low moan and then a whine. She was back in the woods. He returned to the kitchen with the cool head of lettuce.

"She's gone. Not too much damage to your flowers."

"You gotta stop feedin' her at the back door."

He laughed showing missing teeth in his upper plate. "You'd rather have her crash the door in?"

"No. I'd rather she stay in her own house—the woods."

He chortled and picked up his glasses to read, satisfied all was right again in his domain.

Suddenly from nowhere, Henry heard the sounds of a human cry followed by a loud grunt and then a dog-like woof.

He was up from his chair as if lightning had struck and out the door. There she was in the middle of the road below the front porch. He stood frozen as he watched the truck brake but still careen into the black lump of bear down on all fours. The squealing tires made a tremendous scream and the thump where metal hit flesh was crunching. Henry felt as though the heavy rubber tires had smashed into his own chest.

The driver of the truck was out of the cab immediately, instantly standing open-legged before the fallen animal and he stared into its glassy eyes.

Henry couldn't move. His legs would not walk on command. His eyes followed the truck driver back into the cab where he took a rifle from the rack. Quickly the gun was cocked and Henry—over the cries of the bear, heard the cracking of the shot. He couldn't believe what his eyes witnessed. The driver returned to the cab, climbed in, started the motor and drove off swerving around the animal. He gunned the motor and sped heedlessly down the Macadam Road.

Henry came to his senses. He raced onto the pavement. Blood was seeping from the bear, its right side, its mouth and from a hind leg. She was still breathing.

He called out, yelled out to his wife who was standing on the porch watching the death of the bear.

"Come down here. Go down to the road and stop traffic." He left the road and disappeared around the house. On his return in minutes he carried his gun. Shaking he approached the animal whose soft cries of immense pain filled the air now fetid from the hot blood rivering the dark pavement.

He approached the animal. Their eyes met. He placed the muzzle of the gun against the bear's head. Shut his eyes and pulled the trigger. The blast was muted but blood and brains smashed against his face, the continuance of fear and horror.

From the corner of his eye he could see his wife start to come towards him.

"No. Stay back. Stay away."

She stopped.

For half an hour Henry stood above the dead animal. A tear welled out of his left eye and as it flowed down the cheek it mingled with and became discolored by the blood still wet on his cheek.

Slowly he put the rifle down on the pavement. Slower yet he bent his torso and knees. He reached out his shaking hands to the bear and lifted the lifeless head up. He was quite sure what he would find.

On matted, bloody fur he saw the white star, the round circle of white fur.

Off to the side of the road stood a young but stout maple. Henry motioned to his wife, and together they pulled and tugged the heavy carcass to the tree and leaned the bloodied creature against the trunk under the fresh green leaves, well within the cool shadows.

## III.

THAT NIGHT MARION SLEPT IN THE BED ALONE. SHE KEPT A LIGHT ON IN the kitchen, a pot of coffee warmed on the stove along with a small pan of corn soup should he decide to come in from the woods. She knew that he would not.

The spring night was fairly warm for the low hills of the mountains. Still, breathless air thick with the scent of pine, rich and bracing. She had climbed in between the sheets and thin blanket with the windows open.

First she heard howling. Then a scream which pierced not only the night and the woods, but her own heart. Then the drum—first soft and almost wooly-like, then as the beat grew louder it seemed as if something was beating, flailing a quiet pool of stilled water. The rhythm could be heard for five or six minutes. Then silences. Beat again and then silence. All night the drum beat was in her ears.

She knew it was the Bear Dance—ancient rhythms.

When daylight passed across her face, she woke and was not surprised to find Henry standing at the foot of their bed.

Her eyes fluttered, and she raised up. Henry stood with shoulders stooped, bent, arms to his side, his gray hair messed as if he'd walked in a blizzard.

She said nothing. It wasn't the time.

Henry shifted his weight from his left to his right foot, and his hands shot out to the bedpost to steady his listing stance.

She left the bed and stumbled to Henry. As she placed a hand on his shoulder and the other at the elbow of his right arm she could not help but notice a broken leaf in his tangled hair. Urging her body close to Henry, she detected a tiny spot of blood at the corner of his mouth and observed tooth marks on his lower lip. Shocked, but not surprised, she helped navigate Henry to the bedside.

"Sleep," was all she said.

"Yes," he whispered, "sleep."

Once she had the old man under the covers, she ambled to the window and pulled down the shade and then left the room.

Henry lay in the bed shivering.

"Yes, sleep."

His old lids closed.

"I'LL BE ALL RIGHT. I'll be all right tomorrow. Just stay here and rest up."

From outside he could hear a loon cry as it flew over the house.
He had made his peace. His spirit was then at rest. His prayers all said.
"Thank you, Great Spirit, for the new day. I'll look at it tomorrow."

# Salmon

WHAT A GORGEOUS APRIL MORNING, ALL THE EARLY FISHERMEN AGREED. Tramping from the shack to shore, the more inquisitive spotted spring's violets in the wooded upland above the river, and a precocious wild iris with opening petals. Several birds sang and a few flies had commenced buzzing in the lemon light now bathing the waters and the sky above the river. Mid-April and the air was fresh but warm. The dews were not too thick on the weeds, but some snake-spit clung to the stalks of the last season's wild wheat and rusted plantain.

As the morning grew and widened, more men tripped downhill to the shore. Some toted bags of beer, six-packs, others containers of steaming coffee, along with all the fishing gear they needed for this sport. Much of the sport was in guzzling beer, drinking, and telling the usual fish lies.

"Last summer I caught a lake bass, the size you wouldn't believe. You know how long my . . ."

Great peals of laughter, and one voice finished the sentence: "Prick is? Well, that was a mighty small bass."

More laughter, which shushed the original narrator.

"Hey, Mike, what about the lake bass? Just about how big was it?"

And bursts of laughter echoed up and down the river channel.

By nine o'clock, thirty men stood on the left bank, sipping beer or coffee, and on the right bank stood another 28 men, the 29th was behind a low pine taking a leak.

"Got your hook on your rod, Pete?" one voice called out to the man beyond the pine. "Won't catch no salmon in the brush without a hook on your rod."

Laughter again charged the channel.

Up river was an old iron bridge over Sandy Creek, just outside the hamlet of Woodville. The bridge must have been 300 yards upstream. Concentrating on the beer and fishing, no man happened to notice the dark figure standing quietly on the bridge staring downstream at the riotous fishermen.

"You guys ain't gonna catch nothing if you keep up this noise," one irate man said as he cast his line into the flow of water. He had neither a beer can, nor soda, nor coffee in his hand, only a pole with its reel and line. The noise had greatly distracted him from fishing. He was most perturbed, with an edge of anger in his words.

"You come here to fish or to party?"

"Oh Joe, shut the hell up," a companion spoke who stood at the shore nearby. "Swore I'd never go fishin' with you 'gin." He took a deep swallow of beer from his can.

Joe looked up to defend his fishing morality, and as he did his glance moved upstream to the bridge. He spotted the dark figure. Joe waved to the figure as if he knew exactly who it was leaning against the iron rail. The figure did not respond with a wave, and Joe turned his gaze back to the river slowly meandering downstream where it would empty into the lake just beyond Ellisbury. Joe, concentrating on the salmon, remembered seeing a dark figure standing off in the thick brush that morning as he trekked down the wide path to the shore. He waved then too, thinking it was a fisherman taking a leak. The figure did not wave back.

"This was old Oneida lands," a man offered.

"Oneida what?" someone called out without too much interest.

"Indians."

The group sang out.

"Indians. There's Indians here?" the disbeliever asked, showing a trace of ancient fear.

"Not an Indian for miles," Pete said.

"Thank God."

"No, man. We got rid of 'em hundreds of years ago."

"Thank God," Pete proffered.

"Sure left us a great river," one voice in the group proclaimed. "And some great salmon."

"Sure did," the group agreed.

"Nope, not a single Indian here. Not one Oneida."

Some of the men applauded at this revelation.

"Used to be. Thousands of blood hungry savages roamed these river shores. Why my grandpa used to tell tales you wouldn't believe . . ."

"Same as the size of your lake bass, Mike?"

"Shut the fuck up, you ignorant bastard."

And the crowd on the right shore roared.

Joe looked back up to the bridge. The dark figure had disappeared, moved on. He thought little of it and was far more concerned with the fact that no man on the river was getting any bites, let alone any salmon.

"I got some Indian blood," one man named Grover exclaimed proudly, lifting his pole high, the line shimmering in the light like little diamond beads as it sliced the air and then cut through the water.

"You got shit, Grover. Shut up and fish."

"I do got blood, dammit."

"Yeah, right! We all got blood."

"I mean Indian blood."

"He was born in India-na," Pete guffawed.

"What the fuck you know?"

"Just fish. Stuff your mouth with that beer."

Noon was fast approaching. No single fisherman on either shore had yet landed a fish, not even a sucker, though several had had strong bites and Pete had come close to netting a salmon, but before his net could get under the fish's belly it managed to wiggle off the hook which was not in the mouth but had caught into the right gill.

"Shit! Shit! Shit again. I lost the bastard."

From time to time the farmer who owned the land in which the river flowed through would make a periodic trek down the hill from his office and check on the quantity of fish caught and bagged.

"Nobody's caught nothing. Good day, too. Rained last night a little. Should be lots of bites, and hundreds in the catch."

"Yeah, an I paid you 15 fucking dollars for this day. Didn't you guarantee a catch of at least ten?"

The farmer was a big man, a huge figure. Not young, not old. Probably about 40 to 45 years. His shoulders were wide, but his arms were fairly short compared to the long legs that lifted the bulky torso and his head high above the ground. He wore a Levi jacket over coveralls, and a red kerchief was tied around his neck to stop whatever flow of sweat his large body might produce. Though his name was Jones, the fishermen suspected it was an alias. He was swarthy like an Italian, a Sicilian. Big black eyes set in deep sockets in his face. A mushy looking mouth protruded over a weak chin. If the fishermen thought that men were handsome like young women were gorgeous, they would undoubtedly consider Jones ugly, especially his mouth which showed large grinders when he laughed.

"Well, boys, I wish ya lots a luck." And he strolled back up the incline to his office. The men shouted obscenities at his wake.

"Fuck you, Jones."

"I want my pissin' money back if I don't get no fish."

"Oh hold on, men," Mike said. "The day is still young."

"Yeah, but you ain't, and that $15 ticket woulda bought a whole lot of beer and fish at the Grand Union."

Jones' figure disappeared as Joe continued every once in a while to glance up at the bridge and search the railing for the figure who stood so long before. "Must be a game warden," he thought. "But we're legal."

Noon came and went. The men grew hungry. Some had had the presence of mind to have their women or wives pack a lunch. Mike pulled a brown paper bag from his tote and opened up a white bread sandwich.

"Ruth make you another cold potato sandwich, Mike?" Pete asked humorously.

"Sure did," Grover responded for Mike. "She put pickle relish on it?"

They roared once more at poor Mike's expense. He was growing very tired of this buffoonery and ridicule.

"Can't waste" is all Mike said.

Two o'clock. The sun stood high and red in the southern sky. Not a single man had yet caught a fish. They were, indeed, disgruntled.

"Your goddamn Indian river is spooked," one man shouted. "Spooked the goddamn salmon. I'm going home." He began to gather his gear, as did several other men on both shores of the river.

Though Joe's day was no different from any of the other men, he had caught nothing, he was not quite so ready to pack up and leave Sandy Creek. To hell with the Indians and their spooking. To hell with Jones and to hell with all these bums getting ready to leave, he thought.

"Let's go," one man called out. Others were by then sitting on the ground drinking beer and still chewing lunches, about a half dozen were standing in various bushes pissing out the beer they had drunk. "It's two o'clock. Let's get the fuck outta here."

"Yeah, an' get our fifteen bucks back from ol' Jonesy."

What's wrong with all of these guys, Joe asked himself. So we didn't get any fish. But holy shit, we've had a great day on the river.

"You retards," Joe called to the fishermen. "Retards. Enjoy the fuckin' sun and the fresh air."

"Piss off," someone shouted.

"I'm gonna try Black River next Saturday."

"An' it's free."

"Yeah, free, but you can't eat the shit that comes out of it."

"Who cares. I don't want to eat the fucking fish. I just want to catch a dozen or two," Pete said.

Several men had their gear in order. They hung around rapping nonsense to the men not yet willing to pull stakes and move on home. Just then Joe spotted the dark figure on the bridge and as he did Mike spotted another dark figure on the shore opposite Joe who moved down the path through the brush. It wasn't too long before Mike realized who the figure was. And in only moments, Joe watched it move down from the bridge and trek the right shore. That figure was trotting fast. Neither walked straight.

"Holy shit," screamed Pete. "We got guests."

All the men shot glances in the area Pete pointed to.

"I'll be a fucked pig," a man standing next to Joe called out. As he watched with Joe a huge burly figure move toward the shoreline.

In no time the men scattered uphill. Many of them left their gear behind. Only a handful had time to pull their lines and race off at a fast clip uphill.

Instantly, the left and right shores were vacated. Not a solitary fisherman stood there still angling for salmon.

On either side of the river a black bear commenced wading into the waters. One bear dipped its paws down deep into the flow and its paws came up with a salmon. The second black bear did the same and it, too pulled a large fat salmon from the shallows.

The fishermen climbed the hill, rumbling noisily through the incline brush. Some still shouted obscenities.

"Holy shit, there's another one," they heard Pete call out. And down to the shore waddled another black bear with a red kerchief tied around its neck. At the same moment Grover appeared on the opposite shore. He was clad only in a red breechcloth, his naked chest covered in sweat but shining from the reflection of the sunlight. His hat was gone and long blue-black hair streamed down his back.

"Who said there wasn't any Indians anymore?"

He sat cross-legged on the earth and watched the bears fish.

On the bridge stood a man alone. He howled a yowl into Grover's ears, who looked up towards the bridge. There stood Joe in a red breechcloth. He pounded his chest.

"Who said there wasn't any Indians here?"

Grover stood up, made a sign to Joe, and waved him down to the shore.

The bears were happily gorging on salmon. The afternoon light began to fall as the spring sun moved west.

# What Did You Say?

*A Conversation*

## CHARACTERS

Rex . . . First Voice

Rey . . . Second Voice

Two young men

## SCENE

A dark stage. A round table center with two telephones resting on it within a bright floodlight. A young man enters, picks up the receiver of one phone, dials. Ring, ring, ring, ring. He places the receiver down and exits. Another young man enters and picks up the second receiver, places it beside the first receiver. Ring, ring, ring, ring. He exits.

## VOICES ON THE PHONES

Rex: Hello. (silence) Hello. (pause) Who is this? (silence) It's your dime, chief.

Rey: Don't call me chief, and don't hang up.

Rex: Who is this?

Rey: Who do you think it is?

Rex: If I knew I wouldn't need to ask.

Rey: Who do you think it is?

Rex: Oh! It is you.

Rey: Right.

Rex: Hey! Where are you?

Rey: Where do you think I am?

Rex: How would I know? Your phoning me, aren't you?

Rey: No way. You dialed me.

Rex: Where are you?

Rey: Where would you suppose I'd be?

Rex: I don't know. Haven't the foggiest idea. In New York? Georgia? Timbuktu? How would I know?

Rey: Would you believe home on the Rez?

Rex: Great. Games again, huh. I'd believe anything.

Rey: If that's what you want, I can play games for you, with you, and on you. Now, then, and tomorrow.

Rex: Besides playing a game on me . . . today, what are you doing?

Rey: I'm mixing a drink.

Rex: What are you doing?

Rey: Mixing a drink, I said. Can't you hear me? Are you deaf? Yes. I remember now. You are slightly . . .

Rex: I can't hear you when you're rattling those ice cubes so loudly in my ear, idiot.

Rey: I'm no idiot. So listen.

Rex: To the ice cubes?

Rey: To what I say.

Rex: But what . . .

Rey: I said I'm mixing a drink.

Rex: I know that. You said that.

Rey: The mouse is nibbling the moon. Spain is cheese.

Rex: We have a very bad connection. What's the weather like there?

Rey: The moon? Or Spain?

Rex: No. Where you are.

Rey: Can't you tell . . . the air conditioner is on!

Rex: Then it's hot there.

Rey: Can't tell with the machine running so cold.

Rex: Huh! There's mold on the latrine?

Rey: There's mold on the latrine?

Rex: What were you doing in the latrine?

Rey: Looking for you.

Rex: Looking for who?

Rey: For who.

Rex: For you.

Rey: You?

Rex: You?

Rey: No, me. I was looking for me.

Rex: Yes, go take a pee.

Rey: No, me.

Rex: Of course you had to pee . . . with all that drink mixing. That's what normal people go to the latrine for.

Rey: Are you suggesting I'm not normal?

Rex: Have you finished with this tomfoolery?

Rey: Are you out of the latrine?

Rex: I have not been in the latrine. You can be a pain.

Rey: On the moon or in Spain?

Rex: I just got back.

Rey: With Jack? Jack who?

Rex: Yes, just called, friend, to say I love you.

Rey: Who?

Rex: You.

Rey: You.

Rex: No, not you . . . me

Rey: You need to pee . . . again?

Rex: Me. Me. Me. ME.

Rey: You don't need to shout and let the whole world know you have to pee.

Rex: Oh! Me.

Rey: No, me.

Rex: You?

Rey: Not you, me.

Rex: Yes, you. This is a boring conversation.

Rey: I'm not snoring.

Rex: I said boring.

Rey: Yes, it is boring.

Rex: Who did you say you loved?

Rey: So you did hear me. Not me, you.

Rex: What did you say? Would you kindly repeat that? We have a bad connection.

Rey: I'm mixing a drink.

Rex: Another drink? You just fixed one. You're really into booze these days.

Rey: Not another. The same one.

Rex: You are either very drunk, or you've dialed the wrong number.

Rey: I picked a number out of the Yellow Pages.

Rex: I'm not listed in the Yellow Pages.

Rey: When? No, no. I haven't seen one in ages.

Rex: No.

Rey: Yes.

Rex: You're drunk.

Rey: I'm now mixing that first drink. You aren't listening.

Rex: What?

Rey: I said . . . I'm mixing a drink.

Rex: Another one?

Rey: No, dammit, no. The same one.

Rex: You sound like my wife.

Rey: That's the most sensible thing you have said this entire conversation.

Rex: I can't understand you. Stop rattling those ice cubes so close to the receiver.

Rey: I've obviously caught a wrong number.

Rex: You've got the right number . . . 555–2222.

Rey: That's exactly what I dialed. And I got you.

Rex: Well, that's the right number. And it is me.

Rey: Then I must have the wrong person. Is this you?

Rex: Yes, it is me. Who did you want to speak to?

Rey: With you.

Rex: With me?

Rey: Yes, you. Are you there? Are you listening?

Rex: Of course, I'm here. Of course, I'm listening. I'm talking with you, aren't I?

Rey: But are you listening?

Rex: Of course I'm listening, when your rattling ice cubes allow me to hear.

Rey: Are you listening intently, intensely?

Rex: Yes, very intently, intensely.

Rey: Well, go to the window.

Rex: Yes.

Rey: Lift up the sill.

Rex: Yes.

Rey: Jump.

Rex: Are you threatening me? I'll call the police. This call can be traced.

Rey: I only called to say hello.

Rex: You sound like a nut. A heavy breather. Are you a heavy breather?

Your wife isn't here. So why bug me unless you are a heavy breather? A deep throat. Sick!

Rey: I'm calling long distance. I'm calling you. And you know I'm calling long distance. AT&T.

Rex: Calling who?

Rey: Who? Who?

Rex: Yes.

Rey: Do you know who you are speaking to.

Rex: Yes. You.

Rey: I know you are speaking to me. But do you know who?

Rex: Who?

Rey: Maria Montez.

Rex: Don't get funny.

Rey: Emiliano Zapata. Richard Nixon. General . . .

Rex: You are not funny. Strange maybe, but not funny.

Rey: George . . . George Washington.

Rex: Very funny.

Rey: James Dean. Rin Tin Tin. Geronimo. Hitler. Oh no, St. Francis.

Rex: You're getting funnier.

Rey: Pope . . .

Rex: Sometimes I wonder why they ever invented the telephone. For nuts like you to hassle busy people like myself.

Rey: . . . John. Right. Just so I could phone you and bother you. That's all I have to do in my daily life.

Rex: But you do not know who I am. You got my number out of the yellow pages while mixing a drink.

Rey: And I'm a heavy breather checking if my wife is in your apartment, or if you are talking with the president.

Rex: Well, I'm not your wife, not your president.

Rey: Nor my husband.

Rex: Then why are you calling me in the middle of the night?

Rey: Is it that late? Is it that late? Am I late?

Rex: Why?

Rey: To tell you I'm mixing a drink.

Rex: Another. You're drunk now.

Rey: I can't hear you. We have a very bad connection.

Rex: Of course you can't with those ice cubes clanking.

Rey: What?

Rex: Because the ice cubes are rattling.

Rey: Are you mixing a drink?

Rex: No, I'm talking to you.

Rey: Who?

Rex: You.

Rey: To you?

Rex: We have a bad connection.

Rey: I don't have a connection.

Rex: You must have a connection. You're talking with me.

Rey: Who?

Rex: Me.

Rey: To me?

Rex: No, to you.

Rey: No, I'm talking to you. You're talking to me.

Rex: No, I'm talking to you.

Rey: You. Me. Me. You.

Rex: Did I tell you I love you?

Rey: Love me?

Rex: Yes, you.

Rey: Are you some kind of faggot? You're the heavy breather.

Rex: No, I'm Delta Airlines. Ready when you are.

Rey: Delta who?

Rex: Air.

Rey: Of course I have hair.

Rex: Air! (Shouts.) Air. Airlines. Delta Airlines.

Rey: That's how I got your number. From the yellow pages.

Rex: You've had enough. You're flying. You've got a connection. Flyin'.

Rey: Where?

Rex: The Moon. Spain. Space.

Rey: Your place.

Rex: But you don't have any hair. Are you bald?

Rey: Yes, I'm glad I called. Give you another call sometime.

Rex: Yes. Nice talking with you even though we did have a bad connection.

Rey: What?

Rex: I need a drink.

Rey: So do I.

Rex: Yes. Bye.

Rey: Catch you later. Bye-bye.


(Silence. Two old men come from left and right stage, pick up the receivers and place them down in their proper cradles. Exit off stage in a slow shuffle. Curtain.)

# Hammer

## I.

MARCUS ASHBY-DREY ARRIVED EARLY IN JULY . . . CARRYING NOTHING but a small black tote bag on his right shoulder.

In the days that followed, I was to learn the tote contained, among other things I was not privileged to know, one pair of white bikini briefs, one nylon red tank shirt, a pair of plum-colored walking shorts, and two pairs of white jock socks. Plus a few books, a notebook, and some ballpoints.

Marcus left the house towards the end of August . . . carrying with him a small black tote bag on his right shoulder. It contained many pieces of clothing, a notebook, ballpoint pens, and other articles or vials I was not privy to see.

I met his bus. It was a scorching day. Humid. An odd day for the mountains which are usually warm, but cooled by a decent breeze, rarely hot and almost never muggy. Actually, I met his bus Tuesday of the first week. He wasn't aboard. When I arrived back home at the house on the hill overlooking the village, the phone rang. He missed the bus. Would definitely be on it the next morning. He was coming from Montreal. Biting my lip I replied that I would be standing on the sidewalk as the bus growled into port. It suddenly occurred to me that I didn't know what he looked like. In the summers lots of young lads and girls come into town for mountain climbing, jobs at resorts, whatever. "Wait. Don't hang up. I should know what you look like."

He responded, "Oh! Well. I'm not too tall, but not too short. I'm heavy, not fat. I'm blonde, sort of curly, and, well, actually, they say I'm not bad looking."

A jock. My first thought, first image that crossed my mind. Just my luck. A jock. A tough kid to spend the summer in my house, and my classroom. Over the years of teaching at the college, I had rented a room to male students. Only once did I have a jock, a hockey player . . . who wasn't bad. Bought his own groceries, made his own bed, cleaned his room . . . sometimes even cooked his own food. A strict physical workoutist, he was usually in bed by ten, up by seven and either at school or on the ice most of the day. I rarely got to see him. He was handsome with a sturdy build. Once he left the bathroom shower dripping wet and wandered across the kitchen to his own room naked. I caught only the skinny round of his butt; he whizzed through fast. Sean was a good kid. Clean, neat, rent always on time, offered me rides . . . as I don't drive . . . to wherever I needed to go, and had a real sweet girlfriend who was always bringing us blueberry-topped cheesecakes. She even washed the dishes when she came to supper with Sean. Nice boy. We've remained friends even though he has long since graduated and entered the world as an adult member of society. I still receive Father's Day cards. No, he didn't marry the girlfriend.

Some of the jock students could be real hell raisers. They drank heavily, screwed anything that wasn't nailed down . . . in your house . . . and collected five-pound Kool-Aid cans they never took out of their rooms from September 5th to commencement. Their rooms smelled of sweaty jocks, sweaty sneaks, and old dried chicken wings. First year away from mom. No training. I guess she expected the college to diaper him, bathe his butt, teach him how to use a fork, and speak words with more than four letters. Let alone attend his games, buy his jerseys, and warm the milk before bed. Not in a teacher's contract. Occasionally a lad would register that you didn't mind warming the milk before going to bed. Occasionally, a really nice kid would come through. Such as Sean.

Marcus . . . he immediately asked me to call him Marc spelled with a "c" rather than "k" and asked if I should introduce him to please just say, this is Ashby-Drey. He was the southern gentleman, accent of peaches and all. He arrived finally on the Wednesday of the first week of July. I looked at all the not too tall, not too stout young blonde men who deboarded the bus. There were several. All in shorts, some in tie-dyes, many with pony-tails. I saw no one step off who was actually not too bad looking. Scanning the bus windows to see if I could spot him, I did notice a blonde head leaning against a tinted pane. The driver was walking down the aisle. I noticed he touched the head, and it shot up. Grabbed for something over-head and almost immediately stepped out Marcus Ashby-Drey, blinking dreaming eyes on the bottom step of the bus, swinging a black tote in front of him.

It wasn't necessary to approach the lad. He stared directly into my face, not my eyes, stepped down and pranced directly to me.

"Professor? I'm Ashby-Drey. Your student and house guest."

Well, not exactly house guest. He was to pay a kind of rent.

This pale blond young man was not too tall at all. He was rather short. I stand five six and he stood at least an inch, possibly two under me. He was not too stout either, in fact, thin to near scrawny. Weighing about 125 pounds. His arms and face were pale. Summer and not a drop of color, he looked liked someone out of a Truman Capote novel. Small wrists, chewed fingernails, bedroom brown eyes as they say, a slight curl to his hair, which was frizzy. Thin shoulder blades but a small round of a belly behind his red t-shirt. His jeans had a hole in the left knee with strings hanging. Blonde hair crept through the pant hole. He was accurate when he said he was not too bad looking, though there seemed to be a few pockmarks on his cheeks. He sported a glossy sheen as though he'd applied some suntan oil, but no tan. He possessed a good brow, a rather pretty, almost girlish mouth, a strong chin. He was clean-shaven and smelled of violet sachet. In general, his appearance was that of a lost boy, an adolescent not very much at home in the world, frightened looking, a young deer pursued by the inevitable hunter, lost in the big woods of the mountains, yet indifferent to the mundane, a quality of the intellectual, the youth of a Evelyn Waugh novel, at Brideshead.

As he introduced himself he handed over his tote bag as though I were the valet come to greet the master's heir. It flopped at his feet. I did not stoop to pick it up.

"It's terribly warm here. Humid."

He allowed the tote to remain on the sidewalk. We shook hands.

"Marcus, welcome to Turtle Pond. I hope you will enjoy your summer stay here."

"I'm sure I will. Where's your car?"

"I don't have one. I don't drive. The house is only a short walk."

I pointed north to the hill where I lived.

"Up there? That high? Can we call a taxi?"

"Not much of a walk. We have no taxis in this town."

"Oh!" he said with tremendous exhaustion in his voice. "I didn't get a good sleep last night. Slept on the bus."

He continued to wait for me to pick up his tote. Which of course I did not do. Finally realizing I was his teacher and host and not the private valet employed by his father, he lifted the tote to his right shoulder as I turned and commenced the walk down Main Street towards the climb of my hill.

卍

Sometime in April the phone calls started. First a small southern male voice phoned to ask would I be offering any summer courses in Native American studies. I replied pleasantly, yes . . . a course called "Introduction to Native American History and Culture," but he, the peach-voice, could receive all the information from either the Director of Admissions, the Director of Student Services, the Registrar's Office or simply by writing to the college for a summer schedule. Two days later another call. Peaches wanted to know the expenses. I repeated the places of information. The next week, Thursday, I believe, another call. Could I suggest a place to stay, a rooming house, or dorm. The following Monday, the prospective student asked if there was a youth hostel or "peace farm" where he could stay free but earn his keep by mowing lawns, washing dishes, etc. . . . . I didn't know of any in the area, but advised him to speak with the Director of the Wilderness Recreation Program at the college. Tuesday night at home the first midnight call. Sorry to have awakened me but had been trying to reach me all day and it was of the utmost importance. Was there a scholarship he might apply for and for board and room as well. No, emphatically. The next call didn't come until mid-May.

"Professor, I've been reading your fiction. You are a very fine novelist. I'd like to speak to you about a certain element in your novel, *Drums,* if you don't mind, sir. Just exactly what is the power, the divinity of the sweatlodge? I mean, you write so intimately and sensitively of the actual experience, but you have the tendency to skip over the great power of the sweat."

Ego will get you into trouble every time. I tried to explain as best I could at midnight having been roused from sleep. I did a weak job.

"When I'm there with you I'm in great hopes we can sweat together. Good night, Professor. Oh! By the by, I'm very glad you are Indian."

It didn't take long for me to consider the fact that I might well be in trouble with this southern gentleman who talked with a mouthful of Georgia peaches. Yet, it was fetching, it was flattering, to hear his words, to taste the syllables, to know that there was at least one living young student who could read and enjoy your words, had interest, and had sought out your books . . . most of which were then out of print.

The next call was the very next morning. Hardly out of bed at seven the phone rang. My coffee wasn't yet perked. My cat, Mira, was not yet fed and she was clawing the livingroom bookcase.

"Sir, there have been complications in my coming to Turtle Pond. I certainly can raise the funding for your two classes in Native Studies, the history and the literature class, but sir, there is a problem. I do not have the cash to rent a room or an apartment. The college can't seem to help in any way. Sir, I could mow your lawns; drive your car; I'm an excellent cook . . . the home-cook has taught me quite proficiently. My parents are both attorneys and we must have household laborers under those conditions."

He was beginning to sound less desirable as the moments passed.

"Sir, would it be at all possible for me to stay in your house? I understand you have extra rooms, and that you live alone. Not married. Are you?"

"No, I'm not married. Yes, I have from time to time rented a room to a student. I have extra rooms. Wait . . ."

"I could move in with you and mow your lawns, or cook, or . . . or whatever. I've been reading, sir. I've been reading various articles and interviews with you. Why haven't you ever married, sir?"

In my right mind unfettered by this flattery I would have put the phone down gently. Ego gets us into trouble. I continued listening to him.

"My understanding is that you are not merely a novelist but also an amateur historian."

He referred to a commissioned piece I had written years before on historical Indian deviancy. It had been popular enough to have been reprinted in several anthologies and widely distributed. I knew exactly what he referred to, and I wasn't the least bit daunted by his reference.

"Sir, it is a good piece. How did you research the contemporary? Oh, we can talk about that when I'm at Turtle Pond, sir. What about it? Would it be possible for me to live in your extra room? I'm quiet, bookish, don't eat much . . . and I'll do all the laundry, mine and yours, too, sir, even yes, dirty underwear," he joked. "I don't mind, sir, Professor."

I was utterly stymied. What to say. How to respond to his request. What exactly was he suggesting? I cared not to spend a great deal of puzzling time on this. However, all the poems and stories I had written began crossing my mind like the life of a drowning man. My travels across Indian America . . . from the home rez to the midwest to the southwest to the far west. I suddenly remembered: the Apache, Chuck, and Little Horse, and . . . What the hell was I doing? This kid was getting into my hair.

"NO, no, no. I don't have an empty spare room at this time."

"Sir, excuse me, sir. But you have no one living in your spare room now."

How did he know? How in the holy hell did this little shit know, this pinched nose, pale cheeked white little bastard know so much about me? I was about to drop the phone as if he were a heavy breather, or a bill collector.

"The college receptionist said you'd rent me a room. I could work for you."

This was too much. A small town is a small town, a small college is a small college, but I'll be damned if my private life should be discussed with a potential student without my permission.

"Marcus . . . I'm sorry, but I must hang up now. I'm terribly busy."

"Is someone there with you, sir?"

"Marcus, I must hang up." And I did. But I must admit I considered his proposition later. Also I commenced feeling guilty because I think I said some rather nasty, perhaps inappropriate things to him before hanging up . . . such as, you little shit, you have your nerve to intimate my immorality in thought and deed. Indeed, indeed, I am a celibate, chaste, innocent, reclusive teacher. I do not give a student an A because she has a pretty butt, or he a manly chest. I was, indeed, to say it again, indeed, insulted, irritated, annoyed, and angry with this completely strange unknown student knowing so very much of my private life. Whatever happened to the element of surprise? Well, perhaps surprise was mine to be. A turn-about.

That was Friday morning. I cooled down. Did give the lad the benefit of the doubt. Began feeling slightly sorry for him. He was truly in earnest. He wanted only to study with one of his favorite authors/teachers. Was I not in life to teach the young? Was that not my responsibility, let alone dedication, ambition, perhaps the true completion of one's academic life . . . to teach as well as one was able? And did not a teacher many years before help me . . . financially? I regretted being so rough on the lad. Well, I had scared him away. I could go prepare the coffee and feed Mira.

Saturday evening the phone rang twice. I ignored the first ring. The second I picked up on. It was Ashby-Drey.

"Sir, have you reconsidered, sir? That's, sir, my staying in your spare room and my working for you. Being with you?"

Weakness. Yes, the house would be empty for the entire summer. And, yes, it is always nice to have someone there to talk with and share a meal. Weakness. I had planned this summer to be alone on the hill so I could finish a project, spend time on the rez with my family, at the festival on the rez, read some old classics, canoe, climb a mountain or two, fish a little in the beautiful trout streams almost outside my windows, and prepare slowly and quietly for my fall classes. I was to teach two five-week summer courses starting in early July. The rest of the summer would be mine to fritter away as I chose. Five weeks, three nights, three hours. No preps because I had taught these two courses many times. And then, then all the time would be mine to do as I wished. In the fall I would teach Native American

Women in History and the Arts, and another course, Woodland Indians: a History. Preps were needed. Re-read, syllabus, etc. . . .

But "Peaches's" voice and interest were grabbing me, and twisting my thoughts from cold steel, hard rock to softness, to flower petals, to warm water.

Sunday morning I picked up the phone on the very first ring. It was . . .

"Ashby-Drey, sir. Have you reconsidered? You're busy, of course. Still in classes and trying to work. And I am, can be, annoying. My parents have always said that. I'm determined, sir . . . to work with you. It has been an ambition of mine to live with you, to record your conversations, your very thoughts, if you would allow. After all, you are the greatest living Native American fiction writer after N. Scott Momaday and Leslie Marmon Silko. Aren't you, sir."

He would not allow me a word.

"Sir, you should be recorded."

I believe, in retrospect, I said something about, oh that wasn't necessary, nor did my work equal or match that of Scott and Leslie.

"My living with you, sir, can be most advantageous . . . for both of us. I'm young and strong . . . I can do much for you. I mean, of course, sir, eliminate stupid and ridiculous household chores or problems. You shouldn't need to take out the garbage, sir. Nor make your own bed. That kind of thing, I mean, sir."

After a pause, I nearly shouted out: "Can you type?"

Not an immediate response from Marcus Ashby-Drey.

"Sir?" The question hanging on the southern "saaaahhh." "I can type and shall do so for you, sir," he replied in a most military manner. Had he attended an academy? If his parents were as wealthy as he implied, he surely would have, coming from the American south. Suddenly my brain was besieged with all the massacres of Native Indian people ever perpetrated on the North American continent. The Mayans, the Caribs, Sand

Creek, Wounded Knee, the smallpox in the Iroquois villages. Death of the Shawnee. Trail of Tears.

"Marcus. Were you a military man?"

"Sir. I beg your pardon. I'm only twenty. Not military, sir. Good breeding and parochial training."

"Your voice just now sounded military."

"I assure you, sir, Professor. I'm a gentleman."

We finally agreed that he would take the spare room off the kitchen. I have a small house . . . only two bedrooms . . . but there would be room for him. My study is the sunporch, a safe distance from the spare room off the kitchen. We agreed that he would come for the five-week school session and register as though he were a workstudy for his room. He could also find a job in town . . . which I agreed to help him locate . . . for his own good. It was done. Finished. I . . . could forget it until the first week of July.

## II.

AS THE HOURS AND DAYS PASSED, AS SUMMER WIDENED ITS BREATH, AS new wildflowers came and went on the brink of my hill, as the young raccoons matured and the chipmunks scampered here and there across the road, Marcus Ashby-Drey became part of my household and, yes, part of my life. He was edging his way ever closer. Yes, I must reflect and secretly admit that he said early on in our phone calls . . . "some say I'm not too bad looking." Basically I could care less how good looking he was. His face grew on you. His blonde hair blonded lighter in the day sun. His slightly pocked cheeks somehow became less pocked. His pretty, girlish mouth, more manly. His strong chin less severe. The military manner of speaking softened to almost priest-like incantation; became ministerial. I even grew used to his North Carolina accent. He wasn't from Georgia. And the flavor of his words really was rather smoky and dark. I noted he was from the Tobacco State. And he chewed Copenhagen. Constantly. Spitting into plastic cups which he was inclined to leave in odd places around the house: my desk in the study, for example. The coffee table in the livingroom. The bathroom medicine chest. This was much worse than all the hundreds of Kool-Aid cans left behind at commencement by the other boys. Time disappears in sleep, dreams. It took its usual course and moved ever so slowly being summer, across the early cool mornings, the lazy afternoons on into the balmy evenings and the beautiful moonlit nights. I grew accustomed to his face . . . as they sing in *My Fair Lady*. And should I stop in the daily rounds to ponder Marc, his changing and softening, I would immediately recall his hands. The touch of his hands. The warm dry fingers that became cold and wet upon the handshake, that first greeting, when he stepped out of the bus. Cold. Wet. The touch of a spider-silk web.

The first evening went along fine. I ushered him into his room which had a glorious view of the mountain range valleying the village. I joked that in New York City that view would cost $1,200. He smirked in disbelief. Supper went well with us. I prepared a simple meal of a husky salad . . . lettuce, avocado, tomatoes, the like. And a cold soup. Beef consommé with sour cream. He appeared content with the fare. When I lit up to smoke he brought out his container of Copenhagen saying he didn't believe in smoking and didn't appreciate my smoking in his presence. However, if I were to continue to smoke, then he would chew. And where was a cup . . . for spitting. After all he said, "I should excuse you for smoking. You are an Indian. Tobacco is sacred to your people." Very nice of him, indeed. After his lecture . . . which I paid little attention to, I suggested he attend the concert down the hill in the village bandshell. He might well meet young people of his age. And he should make friends of his own, were he to stay in town. He agreed. And was off. The concert, a blues group, ended at 8:30. By 9:15 he was home. Said he was quite tired and would enjoy going to bed . . . if I didn't mind and didn't have chores for him. He eyed the clean sink free of the dirty supper dishes. Off he went. I stayed up a little longer and watched some silly thing on television with John Wayne shooting Indians in Florida, Indians wearing Lakota headbands, the flowing feather headdresses worn only by the great Lakota chiefs. From his room, as I was turning out the lamps, I heard his snore, soft and deep, and noticed his lamp shining. He was stretched across the bed. His jeans and socks and shirt on the floor covering his sneakers. He lay straight. His legs and thin arms seemed so helpless to defend against whatever element might enter his room . . . the night wind, a robber, whatever. There was a dark hole in the front of his gray briefs. Dark hairs streamed out of the hole as though the legs of a great insect, a spider, and the belly of the spider, round and soft sat against the flesh. Innocent and vulnerable, he could be plundered. I stared only a moment. He murmured something. Words I could not fathom, understand, words as if in a foreign language. Well, English to an Indian is a foreign language. His chest heaved. I noticed the rose nipples. The bones of his ribs against the skin, white and young. He placed his left hand to his groin as though protecting himself and turned over onto his stomach. I left the room immediately. It all took a second.

In the morning he was fresh and bright. I was fatigued, having wrestled with my dreams and thoughts, perhaps nightmares, most of the night. I fed Mira before tending to my coffee. I glanced at the stove. Water was heating. Coffee was already in place in the filter of the glass pot.

"I know you didn't sleep well. So I started your coffee water."

I was somewhat startled.

"You rolled all night in your sheets."

How did he know this?

"I heard you moan and went in to see if you were alright."

"You did what?"

"You seemed quite agitated in your sleep . . . nightmares? . . . and I was worried. I didn't want to wake and possibly frighten you. I did draw the blanket over you, which had been kicked to the floor. So I made your coffee . . . have the water on. By the way, you have an enormous mole on your thigh, don't you?"

The next few nights I did not sleep soundly at all.

As I said before, days passed. Classes started. Marc turned out to be an excellent student, certainly a solid A student. He wrote intelligent essays, turned in good exams, but could not type. The first day in my office I asked him to type out some work. He placed a sheet of paper in the machine. Turned on the power and sat and stared at the paper. He didn't need to confess he could not type. It was that obvious. That night at dinner before the evening class I said:

"Marc, as you can't type . . . for your room and board, you will need to get a job someplace to support yourself. I can't afford you, but I can help you find employment if you need me to."

He stared at me. Anger flushed his cheeks.

"I will."

I had given him a key to the front door. That night I was deep in sleep when he arrived home and he slipped in without my hearing. I can imagine it was rather late.

Well, he didn't find a job and I won't go into the long miserable story of that. The excuses were of the force of Niagara Falls. However, he continued coming home later and later. I became conscious of his pushing and rattling the key in the lock. It awakened me from a thin sleep. Was he drunk? Suddenly he stopped carousing through the night. Came home from class with me. We walked together. He was working on his research paper . . . the role of traditional women in the Iroquois culture. I began sleeping deeper and waking much more rested. He did manage to do the dishes, pick up things about the house, take out the garbage, but never seemed to go to the laundromat. He washed out his underwear and socks and the one jock he owned in the bathroom sink and hung them to dry on the shower rod. He had only two pair of briefs so one constantly dangled from the rod and I needed always to shove it along the rod in order to take my own shower. That bothered me. It was erotic. I felt, in touching his briefs, that I violated his privacy. It felt as though I had committed an immoral act, especially as the impression of his privates stood out in a large hump from the graying cloth. I dared not ask him to hang them someplace in his own room. And on the other hand, I could not bring myself to take them into my own hands and find a more convenient and private place to dry them behind a door. What might he think, did he know I touched his underwear? He would probably suspect I fondled them. Is that why he left them hanging in my view from the shower rod?

I was being ridiculous, foolish, oldmaidish, schoolmarmish. What's the big deal that an older, sensitive male should take into his innocent hands a young lad's briefs or jock and take them into the kid's room where they should be hanging, not openly, for people to see. No big deal.

I did not remove the briefs. Some mornings both pair would hang from the rod. He was sleeping nude. Well, why not. It was summer and hot. He was secure.

One evening Marc said he was bored with television, bored with reading, bored with his term paper, and yes, utterly bored with the few friends he had made at school or in the village. He had hoped Jim Ryan would come by and take him out someplace. But Jim failed him. Jim Ryan was another of my 14 students in the history class that summer. Handsome young man. He had enrolled with his girlfriend. An absolutely gorgeous young woman. They sat at the back of the room . . . usually hip to hip and legs entwined, thighs opened. From the front of the room where I sat it was difficult to concentrate on the subject. Marc sat next to Jim, his chair as close as possible to Jim's. Before class, after class and during break, Marc would rush in-between the two young lovers. At home, Marc was steadily speaking of how handsome Jim was, typically Irish, and why did he want to go with such an ugly woman. Marienette was beautiful. Marc had to be blind. There was one other young student in the class . . . also a good-looking lad, I think of Italian descent.

"How come Guido hangs around you during the break? He's kissing ass."

"I don't think so Marc. He's seeking added information on the course. Besides, he is looking forward to attending a four-year school and wants advice."

"He's kissing ass."

A certain jealousy.

He made some sort of an engagement with Jim that night . . . go for a beer, whatever . . . and without Marienette. Just the guys. Jim no-showed. As the kids say, Jim blew him off. He decided to go to bed around nine. I followed shortly. I was interested in a new collection of short stories recently published by a good friend of mine, a Mohawk writer, but I was tired. Nothing to do with the stories being boring. They weren't. Actually, they were quite exciting and beautifully handled, masterfully. I was just tired. It was a balmy night. I fell asleep with the book in my lap and the light bright over my head.

In the summer I sleep on the sunporch between eight opened windows. The porch had a beautiful view of the mountains and the river below the house. It was a pleasant feeling to go to sleep listening to the song of the river running over the rocks and down a small falls. Coupled with the low murmur of traffic in the village it was a good help to sleep.

This night I bolted awake, upright. Odd. Strange. Something was in the room with me. And it wasn't Mira, my cat. The light was out. The book I'd been reading and had dropped in my lap was not in my lap, but on the nightstand beside me. Before the house in the front yard stood a young elm flowering in many leaves, through these leaves filtered the street light, dull but moonish, offering enough light that if you needed to rise during the night you would not need to turn on the lamp. Besides, one knows one's house, doesn't one. I lay naked on the bed. I went to sleep that way.

That wasn't odd. What was different was that the sheet and single blanket had been carefully folded and placed at the bottom of the bed. I was exposed. Vulnerable. I had gone to bed in a state of purity, innocence. Had I been violated? By whom? The night winds. A ghost. The cat. By whom? Nonsense. As my eyes became accustomed to the pale light and as their gaze searched the room, I spotted the violator. Sitting in a corner diagonally opposite the bed was Marc. He stared at me. He was clad only in his briefs. His hands lay folded in his lap. He sat straight in the wicker chair staring at me.

"What are you doing here?" I pulled the sheet and cover up to my neck. "Get out of here."

He stood without responding to my command and walked towards the bed and my covered body. He stared down and smiled as if he were the cat that stole the cheese or ate the mouse. He marched out.

For several continuing nights I would awake and find him in the same position in the same chair with his hands folded in exactly the same way. Each night I would pull the quilts over me. I had learned to wear pajamas. One night he sat in the chair completely nude . . . his hands to his sides, exposing his flesh. He smiled like every other night, rose from the chair and walked out of the room, the light from the window striking against his small round buttocks.

It was difficult to approach him. What was the problem? Was he a sex fiend? Did he have a father problem? Was he simply enamored, like some schoolboys become, of his teacher? Was he merely lonely and in need of the company of another human being in the darkness of the long night? Was he a killer unable to decide the method of the kill? I discounted everything, every idea that sprang to my mind.

This situation was totally immoral. If he were . . . that way . . . why didn't he simply go to town and find someone in the dark alleys to love, or have sex with; there were lots of tourists in town, surely he could find, if he searched a little, find someone of his own bend of mind. Not me. Not me . . . I screamed. I am his teacher. I am his host. I am not interested in this boy or any boy for that matter. I wanted only to teach and make my living, meager though it might be, write a few words down on paper, enjoy the beauties of living in this paradise, these old and mysterious and tribal mountains. That's all I wanted. Nothing. Do you hear me? Nothing. I want absolutely nothing else. Flesh be damned. Flesh we ate from a boiling pot before these pinched-nose, pink-faced bastards came to our land. Before these sick minds entered our lives and spirits, our very souls with their wickedness. I want nothing. Nothing. No flesh . . . between the teeth or below the belly.

He had made several friends besides Jim in the village. What if he was talking to them about his nightly visits to my room on the sunporch? What if he told them he sits in the corner chair and stares at me? He naked, naked as the heathens of hell, naked as the day he was born and the day he will be dead. Naked as his god. Staring at me. Watching me writhe in my sleep. Oh, God. The first night he visited me I was naked. Buck naked. Naked on the sheets. God only knows what he might have told the village. I'm a teacher. I could get fired if this were told and misconstrued. Oh my God. What can I do? Throw him out!

I lit a cigarette. In putting the package back down on the stand I accidentally knocked something over. It was his cup. The cup in which he spit the Copenhagen juice. Shit. First I was confused. Then wildly angry; fury rose in me like the warriors of old times going into battle against the European invader. Oh for a lance, a bow and arrow, a tomahawk, any weapon to protect myself from this monster that has invaded my very being. The violence in my mind released, the fury subsided. I squashed out the cigarette and fell soundly to sleep. I would talk to Marc in the morning. I would ask him to pack his little black tote and leave, not only my house, but also the college and the village itself.

In the morning Marc was not there. His black bag was in his room. His bed was cleanly made. His few books on the shelf. His clean briefs hanging on the doorknob. His notebook and pens placed neatly on the bed table. His one extra tank shirt hung on a hanger in the closet aside several new summer sport shirts I had given him. His one pair of dungarees also hung there. I didn't think too much about his not being there. He often rose early and went for a hike up a mountain or a stroll around the lake. Perhaps he found a job and had forgotten to mention it the night before, being so vexed at Jim not showing up.

I started to leave the room. My hand was on the doorknob to close it behind me. A knife shot through my back. I was stabbed. Pain screamed through my flesh and bones. The village had been attacked by the British again. The warriors were out hunting, all but me. And I was stabbed. The pain reached into my body and traveled up the nerves to my eyes. For a moment I could not see. I was blinded. And then the light came on. I turned and stared down at the bed. Yes, it was made, army fashion, the quilts tucked in, by the book. The pillow rested at the top of the bed where it was supposed to be. There was an impression imbedded into the white cloth. A few blonde hairs stood out from the impression. My gaze traveled down the length of the blanket. The impression of a body, Marc's body, as though a spirit, a ghost, lay into the blanket itself. Two arms, a torso, a buttock, two legs parted, feet. Where the buttock was impressed between the thighs, and I could just about feel the heat from his flesh, from those thighs, rise from the cloth and bathe my lowering hands, my face where the buttocks were impressed which anatomically, frontally, would have been his groin and privates . . . there, right there was a jockstrap, darkly spotted with moisture of semen and urine. There before me was Marc's soul.

He didn't return that day. He didn't make class that night. He wasn't home in the evening. He had not come before I went to bed early to read further into my friend's book, stories of Cree Windigos, ghost stories. His key wasn't in the lock by the hour when I turned off the light, crushed the last cigarette of the day, shoved the coffee mug further from the edge of the table. As I touched the mug, I remembered the horror of entering his room, the shock and startle, that dreadful moment of truth as they say in fiction lingo, terminology. I went into the kitchen. The coffee was made. It was hot. Marc had made my coffee. He doesn't drink coffee. But he made it for me. It was hot. It was good, very tasty, as well made as I could ever make it. He didn't drink coffee. I had fear then that someone besides Marc had been in my house that night. But . . . no, no. No one.

I shivered, needless to say. Went for a baseball bat I kept in the closet, lay it down beside the bed on the far side. There would not be any sleep that night.

What weirdo had he picked up and now chummed with? Was it his classmate Jim? Don't be ridiculous. Guido? Impossible. He disliked Guido. Who was it? The devil. An evil spirit. God knows we know about evil spirits. We were brought up on spirits, good and bad, lurking in the woods, behind trees, behind great boulders waiting to take a pinch of our skin, a fingernail, a strand of hair to create evil magic with, halt life if necessary. Did Marc bring an evil spirit from hell to sit in my room with him and . . . and make my coffee that morning. Go to sleep. Too much sci-fi. Too many TV mysteries, too many horror shows. He is a young lad without a woman . . . or man, and young lads without a woman . . . or man, masturbate in funny kinds of ways, imagining. To masturbate one needs to imagine richly. It isn't much fun . . . alone. But that's what he did. But what if he masturbated while watching me sleep, and then left his jockstrap on the bed. Did he want me to find it? Know his loneliness, his being alone, his disappointment that Jim had blown him off the night before. Was he giving me a message? Who the hell knew what he was doing, or thinking?

His face came into my vision. The soft pale cheek with the one pockmark. Pockmark. Marc. Mark. Mark of Cain. No, soft cheek with lots of pocks. Closeness had changed, colored, or discolored the reality. He was definitely pockmarked. Not badly though. He was not too bad looking, as he was wont to say.

Thinking of his cheeks, his mouth, the strong chin, the rose nipples, and forgetting the wet jockstrap, his staring at me in the night, I fell asleep. Not for long. I was awakened. Something was on the bed. Not Mira. The street light was out. No moon shining either. Someone was on the bed.

"Marc? Is it you? Go to your room."

"Shuuuuuuuuu."

"Marc, go to your room," I demanded.

His hot, whiney breath fell on my face, it skimmed my right cheek, it touched my mouth and lips, it curled down my throat and wavered over my exposed chest. My pajamas had been unbuttoned and tossed to either side. My pajama bottoms had been untied and my belly was naked. The warm, and somehow unhappy, breath rolled down my chest and lay upon my belly flesh.

"Shuuuuuuuuuu. I just want to sit here and look at you."

"Go to bed. We'll talk about this in the morning."

"May I touch your hair?"

His right hand touched my hair.

"May I touch your cheek?"

His hand rested on my cheek. First one and then the other.

"May I touch your chest and your belly? Just touch. Just touch. Only touch. You're old, but soft. You're older than me but soft. You smell good. May I touch you?"

I had told him to go to bed three times. He wouldn't go. Insisted upon sitting on the edge of my bed and touching me. What was I to do? Scream. Push him off and away. Sock him in the jaw. It was dark. Who knows what weapon he had in his hand or at his feet?

"I'm going to press my mouth on your lips. I'm not going to ask you."

The wine came to my mouth. He pressed his mouth against mine. What the holy shit was happening? This dumb fucking freak was on me. He was kissing me. His tongue reached between my lips and tried to part them. I tried to shove him off. Then he rose straight.

"I wanted to kiss you from the first time I heard your voice on the phone. Last April. Remember? No, I don't love you. You think I love Jim. But I don't love Jim either. I only wanted to touch him, like I touch you. I only wanted to kiss him like I just kissed you. I don't love you. Or Jim. I wanted to touch Jim. So I touched you in the dark. You could be Jim . . . in the dark."

The poor sad child.

I wasn't frightened anymore. I was safe with this young lad sitting on the edge of my bed, touching me, touching my brow, my cheek, my chest, the nipples of my chest, my belly, my . . . And I allowed his hand to travel over my body, slowly with care and sensitivity, not erotically, not sexually. With care, but not with love, only with a sense of mystery, of understanding, as though this was the first body he had ever touched with his hands and his mouth.

I sat up.

"Marc, I think you should go to bed."

"No, not yet. Don't send me to bed yet. Not yet. I want to touch you."

"You have touched me, Marc. You have even kissed me, which I didn't want you to do." I was as gentle as I could be, kind, soft, concerned with simpatico. I wanted him to go not just to his room, but go, go out of here, out of this house, this town, this life, my life. Go. Dammit, go. Now. "Marc, you have touched me. I really think you should go to bed. We can talk in the morning."

"I don't want to talk. You think I love you. You think I'm gay. You think I love Jim too. I don't love you or Jim. I'm not gay. I only wanted to touch you."

As he said this, he gently maneuvered my body to the far side of the bed. I realized his chest was against mine. His thighs against my thighs, his arm around my shoulders. He was hugging me.

I'm a man. An adult. A teacher. A celibate, as I laughingly say to my daring students when they inquire about my sex life. And they do. After all I'm not ancient. Just because I'm a college professor that doesn't make me ancient. Forty-two isn't ancient. Though to a nineteen-year-old it is. I've made a strict rule of not looking at the young women in my class other than to see if they are awake. The slightest side look and this town would raise a red-blooded Indian on the gallows swinging from his left testicle. Or burn him at the stake, stripped and raw of flesh like in the old days when the British and French invaders wanted to teach us a lesson, the lesson being: die and give up the land. Now, here I was in my own bed, my very own bed, and I was giving up my flesh, my manly flesh, my spirit, to this weird sad poor child, this lost unicorn, this unhappy earthling, this strange boy from outer space, this cadet of hell. It simply must be a dream, a nightmare. In my entire life this seething, corroded, mind-boggling, yes, embarrassing, unethical, immoral . . . I couldn't think of sufficient and timely epithets enough to shroud the extremity of this most horrible of experiences. A student sliding into my bed, a male student sliding into my bed and pressing his flesh, his hot wet skin to my body. "Get the fuck off me."

I smelled his mouth, his armpits, his groin. He hadn't washed. The day had been hot, very hot for our mountain August, muggy. He hadn't washed; the acrid smell flooded my nose. I started to gag. As I did he climbed off the bed. He stalked to the corner, sat down in the wicker chair and stared at my confusion, yes, my dread, annoyance.

"Marc, we'll talk about this in the morning."

He strolled nonchalantly out of the room.

Dawn was creeping into the eastern sky.

## III.

I HAD RESOLVED THE SITUATION.

Marcus Ashby-Drey was to pack his little black tote bag and leave in the morning, head out for the hills, or the valley, or the river. I didn't much care which. I would be blunt, blunt as a hard instrument; I'd kill with the first stroke of words. No excuses, Marc. Go. Get the fuck out of here. Now. This minute.

As I said to pack his bag and leave, he rose from the kitchen table, where he'd been eating a banana and Wheaties, and came to me standing in the doorway of the kitchen and living room. I was fully dressed. White shirt, tie, jacket, slacks, loafers. He was in his briefs.

"I thought we had an understanding of last night."

"No," I was adamant with my harsh no. "We did and do not. What kind of understanding do you mean?" I was giving him room. That was wrong.

"I . . ."

"Touched me. Is that the understanding? You kissed me on the mouth. Is that the understanding?"

"But you . . ."

"I was trying to be kind, Marc, as I'm trying to be kind now."

Tears were in his eyes. They didn't fall. He reached out but I stood too far off for his hands to reach my arm.

"Kind. I don't need your kindness. I don't need your body. I don't need your old body. No. Not yet. Not yet. You'll have to wait, wait and wait for me to need your old body."

He exploded but without emotion. The words, as if rehearsed, came with certain modulated passion, but no anger or disappointment, as though he were lecturing a small child, a misbehaving child.

"You of all people should understand what my need is. You are an Indian. I don't need you, you the man in the jacket and tie. I need you the Indian in the breechcloth, or sitting naked in the sweatlodge teaching the power and the divinity of power, teaching the secrets of the universe. You know, and you won't tell me. That's why I came to your room. I thought you might breathe words of great wisdom through your sleep dreams, words you'd denied me here at the table or in the classroom. I want you Indian, red. Jesus Christ I want you red. RED. I want you stripped of all these white man foolish clothes we are all forced to wear. I want you naked, naked so I can see your hairless body, and know the beginnings of life, when the moon was created, and the stars, when the waters rippled out of the mountains, and sun hung brother in the sky, when the earth rolled and thunder thundered and mountains were born. You were to tell me how the earth was born on Turtle's back. You were to reveal the stars and the mysteries of heaven and hell . . ."

"Marc . . ."

"What kind of Indian are you that you would not accept little brother into your arms, your life? I had to coax you, and sometimes lie to you, to gain a room to sleep in. I left semen on my bed in my jockstrap for you to find and try to understand my needs. Sex, hell no, not sex. Not love. Not to be embraced by your arms. Sex, I can get sex anyplace, anytime, anywhere with anyone. I am beautiful. I thought you were beautiful, too. I read your words, all your books, your precious beautiful words. I thought you were a king, a chief, a holy . . ."

"Marc . . . stop it. Stop it right now."

"Let me finish. I entered your life. I tried to enter your spirit. I only entered your body. When I kissed you I knew you would breathe the words, the truth, the reasons, and the mysteries into my mouth. I didn't kiss you. But I did. I did, and that's all that happened. I kissed you. My mouth touched yours. And nothing happened. I didn't feel a thing. Didn't touch a single word that you have locked up inside your Indian self. Your red flesh. One night I sat by you. I held a holy feather in my hand, and I touched you, your groin, your penis, your stomach, your chest, your throat, your mouth, your eyes, your brow where your great brain, your marvelous mind lives. And I prayed. I prayed. Holy Jesus, I prayed that you would relent, open and give me what I needed. The fucking truth."

He was saying it all. There was nothing I could say to this child. This wounded boy. This scared youth. This blind earthling living in the darkness of his visionless life.

"Yes, I will go. This house is empty. You are empty. Life is empty. I must now fill life as I tried to fill this house and to fill myself as I was in turn filled with the great and beautiful power of wisdom. My little black tote bag . . . as you call it . . . it is filled. It is a medicine bundle. You, Indian, insist it's a little black tote bag. Nothing of yours is in it. Nothing. Not the shirts you gave me, nor the books, not even the strands of your hair I have collected, not the nails that you pared from your fingers. Not even the vial of your urine I took one day when you forgot to flush the toilet. Nothing is yours."

"Keep the shirts. You need them. Keep the books. Just . . ."

"Do you have a hammer?"

## IV.

It was only later that I gained an understanding of his need for a hammer.

Marcus Ashby-Drey left the house that afternoon. Well, not exactly. Neighbors said they saw him sleeping on the steps of the fire escape several nights. Actually they reported I had left a bundle of old clothes on the steps . . . and they looked dangerous, might flame, and hence the phone calls.

Eventually in a day or so Marc found a place to stay until the end of his two classes. He literally bumped into a man of the cloth, a certain Reverend of the Unitarians. My student informant claimed that Marc had shed many a tear on this good man's shoulder while ragging on my hospitality.

I had thrown him out of the house. He couldn't understand why. It must have been due to the fact he had so many studies that he needed to stay up late with his books and essays. I also had not fed him even though I would sit down to the table with great bowls of food before me while he was asked to remain in his bedroom hungry. I was indeed selfish and greedy. The rules that I had imposed upon his stay were outrageous, he ragged: in bed before ten . . . and he was 20 years old; one shower every other day . . . as water was low in the reservoir; household tasks galore and beyond just washing up the dishes and carrying out the garbage . . . I had him scrubbing the floor on hands and knees. Well, the truth of that matter is that one night he came home drunk as a skunk, vomited on a brand new light blue rug. I must I admit I pushed his face in it and told him to scrub it clean, until every trace of the red wine had disappeared. Etcetera, etcetera.

The good Samaritan took him in.

For food, Marcus Ashby-Drey went to a Deli near the college; swore he lived in my house and was taking two classes from me at the college. He was given a charge account. The silly owner lost out. He failed to call me for verification.

Finals came. He took them. He passed the courses. He wrote two term papers for me. He held back at the end of the second final, to speak, to say good-bye.

"I just wanted to say . . ." as he attempted to embrace me, "that I, that I, well, I just wanted to say you are a good teacher, a great writer. And, and, that I still love you. I will remember you always."

"Good-bye, Marc" was my response.

With the black tote bag slung over his right shoulder . . . heavier now again with the acquisition of newer articles (who knows what), he slumped out of the classroom. From the window I watched him wind his waxened way down the hill from the campus. He became quickly a red dot. Then a memory.

Some two weeks later I received a letter, or note rather. I trembled on opening it, remembering those horrible, somewhat frightening nights that Marc lived in the house and paid midnight visits to my room standing in his briefs, his touching my flesh, remembering him saying how he touched the various parts of my body with a feather. I opened it slowly . . . down the edge of the envelope. I hesitated before pulling the folded sheet of paper out. I blew into the envelope, nervously dropped the thumb and index finger into the envelope. It smelled of lavender sachet. Unfolding, smoothing out the letter, I took quick notice that in the far-left corner was either a coffee or a Copenhagen stain. On the lower left corner another stain. I wish to think it was not semen.

After much gibberish about what a great writer I was . . . the ego was cold, frozen to this hustle; what a lovely home I had and how fitting it would be for two; what marvelous courses I had offered that summer; if only Guido had not been enrolled, etc. I got to the stone heart of the center. It is that one sentence I shall carry in my mind every night on going to bed and switching off the light:

"I hated you with a passion and wanted to smash your head in with the hammer you handed me."

If I had turned my back. If . . . I had turned.

The "P.S." was even more frightening than the smashing of my head with the hammer:

"P.S. Professor, I will come to visit you again someday. We can still be . . . friends, or . . . well, friends anyway."

I burnt the letter and the envelope. There was no return address.

# Forked Tongues

*For Mary Dickson, who camped a terrorized night in the empty valley of Sand Creek*

CAST

Monahsetah, *Young Indian Woman*

Six Indians, *Males of varying ages*

Six soldiers, *Males of varying ages*

Jack Smith, *Young Half-breed*

Black Kettle, *Chief of all Southern Cheyenne*

Colonel John M. Chivington, *Former Minister and Cavalry Officer*

Man in White, *Moderator*

John Simpson Smith, *Fur Trapper and Scout, Father of Jack, Indian trader*

Off-stage voices

NOTE

Monahsetah, Jack Smith, Lieutenant Cannon, Colonel Chivington, Black Kettle, and John Simpson Smith were historical characters. All others are purely imaginary.

The speech of Black Kettle has been taken from *Indian Oratory*, compiled by W. C. Venderwerth, University of Oklahoma Press, 1971. All other speeches of the characters are imaginative.

TIME

Late 1860s, or any time


PLACE

The Colorado plains


SETTING

A room, not unlike a court, but within the lodge-skins of a large Indian tipi. Center stage is a desk raised high on a dais. Directly below the dais, in a half-circle, are six straight chairs, suggesting the curve of a tipi. Buffalo robes have been tossed within the wide spaces between the chairs. Stage left, at the proscenium, is a very comfortable leather chair with soft, pretty cushions. Stage right, at the proscenium, is another dais, raised slightly, covered with a red blanket.


# SCENE I.

(*Lights are dimmed and faintly blue with a pale red glow. Off-stage a woman calls:* "Pte, Pte, buffalo run." *Crack of thunder is heard in the auditorium, followed by off-stage rifle shots and loud screaming and yelling. Sudden silence. Blue light rises. A young woman,* MONAHSETAH, *crosses from stage left. She is dressed in a deer-skin dress. She wears soft moccasins, a single black feather hangs in her braided hair. She carries, silently, a dead child in her arms. Another rifle shot is heard off stage and the stage darkens. Blue lights are extinguished; only a red glow lights the stage. Frightened, the woman turns about and hurries off stage. Red lights grow fiercer. Slowly a group of six* INDIANS *cross stage from left, wrapped in plum red blankets, each wearing a single feather . . . the ends red as if with blood. They squat on the floor between the wooden chairs. The* INDIANS *are followed by six cavalry* SOLDIERS *who take seats on the chairs. A YOUNG MAN of 21 enters left, and takes a place at the feet of the first* INDIAN *in the half circle. A huge hulk of a man, dressed in the garb of a minister but wearing jangling spurs, enters carrying a Bible in his hand. He takes a seat in the leather chair and pulls a wolfskin robe about his legs.* BLACK KETTLE *enters. He wears only a blanket, no feathers in his braids nor paint on his face like the preceding six* INDIANS. *He sits on the dais covered with the red blanket. Finally an old but spry man, wearing a white suit and with a great white shock of hair enters right stage and sits at the raised desk. Great screaming and yelling is heard off-stage. One more rifle shot and then a great painful wail rises.*)

YOUNG MAN: (*standing, facing the leather chair*) I . . . was . . . (very slowly to a crescendo) . . . murdered!

SOLDIERS: (*together*) You were not. It was an accident. Your own people did it. You should have been. Damned half-breed. Bastard.

YOUNG MAN: I was murdered. Yes. Shot in the back by the henchmen of that man. (*pointing to man in leather chair*) You had me murdered. Shot! And my body dragged around the village.

MAN IN WHITE: Jack, that is not pertinent to this hearing! Sit down!

JACK: (*Takes former place, but glares at* MAN IN WHITE, *then glares at man in leather chair.*)

FIRST SOLDIER: What about my wife, you bastard! You butchered her!

MAN IN WHITE: That is not pertinent either! Shut up!

INDIANS: (*chanting in unison*) Po-no-e-o-he, Po-no-e-o-he, Po-no-e-o-he.

SECOND SOLDIER: (*rising*) You, sir, said you wouldn't let them do that anymore.

MAN IN WHITE: Stop complaining! You're supposed to be a soldier in the U.S. Cavalry. You Indians stop that moaning. Never got you any place before.

JACK: And it won't now, either.

FIRST INDIAN: We were only trying to state the pertinent facts, sir. Ponoeohe, little dried river. Remember Sand Creek?

MAN IN WHITE: I know what's pertinent and what is not. Why can't you all be nice and quiet like Colonel Chivington there, and Chief Black Kettle? They don't say anything.

SECOND INDIAN: Would you listen if Black Kettle did say something?

THIRD INDIAN: He said it long ago, and nobody heard it then. He's still saying it.

FOURTH INDIAN: Ain't nobody listening now, either.

FIFTH INDIAN: If Black Kettle talks, you'll only quiet him like last time . . . "Shut up, savage!"

SIXTH INDIAN: He lets pony chief talk.

MAN IN WHITE: Enough petty wrangling. For your information, if I let Chief Black Kettle speak, the soldiers would call me an Indian-lover. Now,

I ask you, would that be fair? Would that be nice or honest? Colonel Chivington got infuriated with Jack Smith, and the Colonel screamed out.

CHIVINGTON: (*Light grows suddenly very dim, only a faint glow outlines the frozen figures on the stage.* CHIVINGTON *rises slowly as the force of his speech builds.*) The farm held nothing for me. My older brothers would squabble over the land. My father would die and I would be thrown out with nothing. I had no education. I could hardly hold a fork and knife. Then when I was still young, I met God on the road, and he took me by the sleeve. I learned to read and write out my name. I became a minister of the gospel. Sinning was rampant, and the sinner suffered. I was determined to alleviate the agony, that suffering of the sinner. I took a wife. She bore me children. We moved from town to town in the Godly state of Ohio. We moved west. And I found sin every where. And poverty. Glory to God! We were poor. She bore another child, and we crossed the Mississippi. Gold had been discovered in the mountains, and miners were sinners . . . suffering the agony of greed, drunk on rotgut, and full of ridiculous dreams of wealth. With my brood and a mule, I trekked to Colorado where I preached to the heretic souls of the damned, spending God's time at the creek edge with a pan in one hand and a jug in the other, an Indian squaw under the belly. The young town found a place for me (*rising*) and a hall in which to preach. No one would believe the amount of sin in that town of Denver . . . greed, lust, avarice, drunkenness, thieving.

VOICES OFF-STAGE: John! John, remember the Indians?

CHIVINGTON: (*turning as if searching for the* VOICE) Yes! Indians. Yes! Heathens. They were there. Sinning with the white men. She walked into the miners' camps and came out with a bottle in her arm and a baby in her belly. Her drunken buck came back to kill the man who took his squaw there on the hard, cold ground . . . ground soaked with the sweat and stink of sin.

VOICES OFF-STAGE: John, what about the Indians?

CHIVINGTON: Yes, Indians. Savages. Naked. Conical pimples on the ass of the plains. And they needed to be punished for their sins.

VOICE OFF-STAGE: What about Jack Smith, Colonel John?

CHIVINGTON: Oh! He was there. That little bastard was there all right, panning out his daily gold dust at the coattails of his reprobate father. Taking the fold, thumbing his nose, his greed as large as any man's. He staked a claim and panned his dust. Sullen little bastard. Under the treaty, he could have owned the land the town of Denver was raised on. He had enough Indian blood to claim the earth where my church stood, God's church. We fought in the courts for the land we soaked our sweat off to build upon. The Indians charged thievery and warhooped us to pulp. We paid them what they wanted . . . pots, vermilion, sugar, whiskey. They wouldn't have used the gold anyway. And those savages repaid us with depredation after depredation. Killings, scalpings, mutilations . . . our women raped, babies brained in their mother's arms. And so I put off the cloth and took up the sword of the Lord, filed the edge and charged. I marched my troops against those forces of heathen evil.

VOICE OFF-STAGE: Colonel, the troops are ready for inspection.

CHIVINGTON: Like Christ in the temple, I grew a powerful anger, a powerful thirst for savage blood, and slew the Philistines. There would be no peace on the plains until the savage groveled before me . . . until every lodge was burnt, every whore that sold her body to the miners had been flamed in redemption, before every buck of the tribe had been humbled and castrated. I would march and sweep those plains clean of the murderous heathens . . . open the roads to history. (*returning to chair*) And then Black Kettle held up a white flag, and Jack Smith filed a claim to the land. But we rode and fought our way to fields of glory. Denver was proud of her sons. (*He sits. Lights come up. Action resumes as if without pause.*)

MAN IN WHITE: Colonel Chivington is well aware that he's supposed to be just as quiet as Black Kettle. You're right. (*pointing to the* THIRD INDIAN) They both talked long ago. Where did it get them?

FIRST SOLDIER: That's not pertinent, either.

MAN IN WHITE: All right. All right. Let's call roll.

FIRST SOLDIER: (*standing as do the others in their turn*) Private Jones!

FIRST INDIAN: From Rockaway!

FIRST SOLDIER: (*waiting for laughter to stop*) Killed two very brave braves, killed one papoose, and while raping a squaw was shot in the head in the crossfire of Chivington's 100 Days Volunteers. My own company!

MAN IN WHITE: Sit, sit, sit! Next. Let's roll this along.

SECOND SOLDIER: Corporal Smith. I gotta lotta squaws and a couple of old men. I was sick with diarrhea . . . our rations were that bad . . . and as I was squatting in the bushes a goddamed green recruit saw movement and shot the shit out of me. I was killed.

MAN IN WHITE: No graphics. Very well. Next!

THIRD SOLDIER: Sergeant Polinski. I didn't kill anybody. I was busy see-ing that the troops were supplied with ammunition. Some sneakin' savage got me with an arrow.

MAN IN WHITE: Are you sure it was an arrow?

POLISKI: Sure I'm sure. You want to see the hole it left? (*Begins to unbutton blouse.*)

MAN IN WHITE: No, no, no! No nudity, please. Next!

FOURTH SOLDIER: Private Green. I shot and scalped that old man over there. (*pointing to an* INDIAN *across the stage*) He was called Big Man.

MAN IN WHITE: Is this true, Big Man? Is this true? He didn't tell us this in earlier roll calls.

GREEN: I didn't recognize him before.

BIG MAN: He got me. I recognize him. Indians don't squeal like a stuck pig.

MAN IN WHITE: This is highly irregular. We are not supposed to have direct enemies here. I'm not sure whether I should dismiss you, Green, or not. Or you, Big Man. Surely this fraud can't go on.

JACK: I propose, disturbed Sir, that we keep them both. They've both been with us for a month. (*Sits.*)

MAN IN WHITE: I suppose you're right, Jack. Though it's not according to Robert's. Proceed, Private Green. How were you . . . ehhhh . . . exterminated?

GREEN: I killed and scalped Big Man. Then I had enough killing and scalping. I was scared. I was just a kid . . . a green recruit. They shot me for desertion!

ALL: Booooooooooooooooooooooo!

INDIANS: Never saw an Indian desert.

SOLDIERS: Didn't have the sense to.

MAN IN WHITE: O.K. Cut it out. No wrangling, I said before.

GREEN: I wasn't the only one that deserted.

MAN IN WHITE: I'm sure you weren't. And I'm equally sure that Colonel Chivington dealt correctly by the book with you all. Next, please! Time's getting on. I have a dinner engagement. My wife flares when I'm late.

FIFTH SOLDIER: Private Black.

MAN IN WHITE: How is it that you soldiers are all non-coms, and the Indians are practically all chiefs?

FIFTH SOLDIER: Because our officers were hiding. (*pointing to the soldier next to him*) But he's an officer.

MAN IN WHITE: Yeeees! He's an officer! (*a slight sneer in his voice*) Go on, Black.

BLACK: Private Black, sir. I am forty-eight years old, sir. I was tired out from the long march, sir. Tired and sick on the bad food and the freezing temperatures, sir, the weather. I didn't harm a hair, sir. Not a hair. Never lifted a scalp nor a wig, sir. But I died of natural causes on the battlefield, sir.

JACK: (*popping up*) He can't use that word. You said they couldn't use that word. Strike it, or . . . !

MAN IN WHITE: Strike battlefield!

BLACK: I died, sir of natural causes before the bloody massacre.

JONES: It wasn't a bloody massacre!

MAN IN WHITE: Strike bloody. Meaning struck for Indians; color adjective struck for soldiers. It wasn't bloody! What did you die of, Black? What natural cause?

BLACK: I am forty-eight years old . . . I was very tired. I had a . . . a heart attack.

ALL: Ooooooooooooooooooooooooooh!

MAN IN WHITE: Be more specific! Before, during, after the . . . the encounter?

BLACK: Aaaaaaaaah!

MAN IN WHITE: We're waiting.

FIRST INDIAN: Too much time for this coward.

MAN IN WHITE: A natural act of death does not signify or brand a man a coward. When did you die?

BLACK: When the bugle blew to charge. (ALL *laugh.*)

MAN IN WHITE: Sit, down, private.

BLACK: Yes . . . sir.

MAN IN WHITE: I guess you're next, Lieutenant.

LIEUTENANT: Lieutenant James D. Cannon. I was, like Jack Smith there, murdered. Also by Chivington's henchmen after the massacre. I didn't much like killing peaceful Indians. And as I knew too much of the Colonel's vindictive plans, he had me poisoned in a cheap Denver hotel room. They poured whiskey on my clothes and left empty bottles scattered about the room so it would look like I was drunk and careless.

CHIVINGTON: (*Rises to contest the Lieutenant.*)

MAN IN WHITE: Colonel Chivington! Be seated, if you please, sir!

CANNON: I was murdered long after Smith and Silas Soule, who were gunned down in the streets of Denver by Squires . . . the Colonel's henchmen.

MAN IN WHITE: No particulars, Lieutenant. Particulars aren't important here. Lieutenant Cannon, you are decidedly prejudicing the jury.

JONES: There isn't a jury. There isn't even a judge.

FIRST INDIAN: We only have a moderator.

MAN IN WHITE: In a sense there is a jury. (*Points with the flat of his hand to audience. All but* CANNON *and* BLACK KETTLE *rise to look and bow at the audience. Rifle firing is heard off-stage. All sit immediately, simultaneously.*)

SMITH: I didn't know we had a jury.

SECOND INDIAN: I didn't know anybody was listening.

GREEN: I didn't know anyone was there.

THIRD INDIAN: I didn't know anyone cared enough to come here.

MAN IN WHITE: Gentlemen!

BIG MAN: Lieutenant Cannon is all right. He didn't kill any of us.

SECOND INDIAN: So was Captain Soule. He refused to fire on us.

MAN IN WHITE: All right. All right. The cavalry has responded to roll call. Now I think we can proceed to our next step. I do wish, Colonel Chivington, that you would refrain from flailing your Bible . . .

FIRST INDIAN: You didn't give us a chance at roll call. We get a turn, too.

MAN IN WHITE: Well, with you all yelling and whooping like a pack of Sioux . . . strike that . . . we certainly all know that you're here. I didn't think it necessary to hear your accounts again. Most of your testimony is irrelevant and not pertinent. But if you must . . .

JACK: (*Jumps to center stage. Looks sullen. Hands in pockets, hat at a rakish til*t.) Jack Smith. (*shouting*) Jack Smith. Son of Uncle John, trader and friend to Indians. He was an interpreter. Married Na-to-mah, my mother, killed at Sand Creek. I was murdered by Meshane . . . the sick one (*pointing to* CHIVINGTON *who is absorbed in his Bible*) I was murdered. Shot in the back in War Bonnet's lodge . . .

MAN IN WHITE: See what I mean, Jack? You've told us this every half hour for the last . . . can't you give us more pertinent facts?

JACK: (*Lights dim. All freeze in position.*) What do you want? You want me to go sniveling on my hands and knees to that son of a bitch? Beg him? And thank him for murdering my mother, a dirty Indian Squaw? Thank him for butchering our leaders, for burning and sacking the village? You must be sick! And you call yourself my father!

VOICE OFF-STAGE: Jack, for God's sake, shut that talk.

JACK: Charlie Bent's right . . . a whole lotta people are going to feel a nice clean blade rip through their belly . . . I'm going to hold that knife . . . if I live.

VOICE: Oh! God! Jack, what now!

JACK: I said wait. Hold it. (*as if pointing to his father, the* VOICE *off-stage*) You stop your sniveling. You had your chance. Don't give me the pity of your whining now. You and Will Bent could have stopped this killing . . . before it ever got started. You're both as bad as Chivington. (*As before. Lights go up.*)

JONES: He's long-winded. I thought Indians could only say 'ugh.'

MAN IN WHITE: Stop! Enough! I won't let you fellows have roll call. You must be brief! It's costing your government money. And the Department's got to have this report. Besides, the jury is falling asleep. They are spending costly time, you know. Sit down, Jack, and let the First Indian have his say.

FIRST INDIAN: Small Man. Killed and scalped by Private Jones.

SECOND INDIAN: Biggest Man. Killed, scalped and mutilated by Private Jones.

JONES: I didn't kill 'em all. Some of the other guys got some shots in, too.

JACK: Tell them how and where you were mutilated.

MAN IN WHITE: Gore, Jack, isn't necessary. He can speak for himself.

BIGGEST MAN: He cut off my prick and waved it in the air on the end of his bayonet.

JONES: I did that? (*pause*) I did not. Never saw the man . . . the savage . . . before in my life. If I'd cut off his prick, I'd recognize his face.

JACK: And made a tobacco pouch out of his scrotum.

JONES: His what?

JACK: Yeah! Scrotum! That little bag between your legs that holds your . . . a man's legs . . . that holds his testicles.

MAN IN WHITE: Jack, Jack Smith. (*gaveling*) Don't be clinical. No filth, Jack, no graphics. More of this trash and I'll clear the court. Proceed.

THIRD INDIAN: Died from hunger and exposure on the march up-creek from the attacked village. I had been routed from bed in the cold dawn. Slipped naked from the tipi and discovered myself in the line of fire.

GREEN: Naked! Shameful savage!

CANNON: Idiot! He was exposed to zero temperatures and crawled starving towards the Arapaho camp seventy miles off. That isn't weakness, Mr. Green. That's defiance, perhaps dignity . . . the Indian way.

MAN IN WHITE: No histrionics, Lieutenant. Sit down! Littlest Man, how many soldiers did you kill and mutilate?

LITTLEST MAN: None! I had no weapons or ammunition. In the surprise of the attack I had left my weapons in the lodge. Anyway, my work was to get the helpless ones safely out of the line of pony soldiers' fire. There was only a handful of warriors in the village. Our main force was miles away on a hunt. We were starving. The army made us camp by the creek, but refused to give us food. The army sent out men to hunt.

MAN IN WHITE: When you say . . . the helpless ones . . . you, of course, mean . . . women . . . children and the old and feeble?

LITTLEST MAN: Yes.

JACK: (*screaming*) Cowards! You are all cowards! Just who was the cowardly bastard that called the surprise attack on a peaceful village of women and old men while the warriors were sent off to hunt?

MAN IN WHITE: Stop! Soldiers! Indians! Please . . . do not create double lives for yourselves. Don't take yourselves too seriously. And do remember the jury. (*reaching for a glass of water*) Proceed. Next Indian.

FOURTH INDIAN: Big Man. He killed me, Private Green.

MAN IN WHITE: I suppose as you were leading the helpless ones away also. Proceed.

BIG MAN: He killed me . . . Private Green. He said so himself.

MAN IN WHITE: Oh my God! It's like a record.

BIG MAN: I stood like an Indian in the cold waters of Ponoeohe . . . my arms crossed, symbolizing my wish for peace. I was unarmed.

GREEN: Were you a head chief?

BIG MAN: I was an old chief. I loved you whites once.

GREEN: But unarmed . . . there in the water, I mean?

BLACK: Some of you Indians must have shot some of us. There were nine of us found dead and an awful lot wounded.

BIG MAN: We didn't have to kill you . . . you were killing yourselves in the crossfire or by heart attacks, or were shot for desertion.

SOLDIERS: You lie.

MAN IN WHITE: (*As* SOLDIERS *and* INDIANS *rush each other*) I will not have this. I will not warn you men again. If I must . . . you're finished. Now, the fifth Indian must muster to roll call and we'll get on with this fiasco.

FIFTH INDIAN: Bigger Man. I was a great chief once, and went on many war parties against our enemies, the Utes and Pawnees. I went on war parties against the whites when they stole our lands and drove off the buffalo. I was killed by the gun of a white man. After he killed me, he hacked off my fingers for the rings I wore. Black Kettle can testify.

BLACK KETTLE: (*Lights grow dim, characters freeze.* BLACK KETTLE *rises slowly, pulls his robe about, clutching the folds in loose fingers. There is a slight smile on his lips, but weariness in his voice and posture. He speaks with great dignity.*) There is a cold wind in my heart. (*pausing*) My heart is empty except for this bitter wind, as are the lands of my people, the Cheyennes of the south, empty. Their lodges no more stand to greet the Great Spirit with the pearl dawn of morning. Our voices do not rise with the cottonwoods along the banks of Ponoeohoe. The white man has made his many roads through the buffalo grass. The buffalo has trailed back into earth from where he came. There on the plains are only the bones of my people and their cries on the winds. In a vision I saw all the ponies fall, and all the buffalo and the people fall. The water spirits spoke and advised that I should carry peace to the council fire. I washed the war paint from my cheek, and dressed my lance in beaver skins, and had the women of my lodge place it safely away . . . for I would never take it up again. I went to the white man's head chief, and the wolf chief, there, (*pointing to* CHIVINGTON) with his leaves of the Great Spirit. My brother, who has now spoken, and others took the road with me. Meshane would not give me his hand to hold. The head chief would not give me his hand to hold. I returned like night to our village. In the moon of the hard frost, Meshane came and wiped out my people . . . old men, withered like leaves of dying trees, the women, and small ones in their arms. Now only a hungry coyote hunts the ancient lands of my mother, earth. (*Sits.*) The words my brothers make in the air are true. (*Lights up, all as before.*)

SIXTH INDIAN: Smallest Man. I was drowned in a little pool of the creek. The soldiers' ponies knocked me down and trampled me to death in the cold waters. I have no more to say.

JONES: At least he's honest.

MAN IN WHITE: Honesty is not pertinent here!

(*Blackout.*)

## SCENE II.

(*Same as before. Immediately following. Harsh bright lights.* SOLDIERS *and* INDIANS *mix together, laughing and talking.* JACK SMITH *talks with* CHIVINGTON *and* MAN IN WHITE, *center stage. Only* BLACK KETTLE *remains seated, squatting.*)

MAN IN WHITE: (*Harsh light burn out, and soft blue lights rise slowly and meet in the glow of hot red lights.*) Places everybody. Intermission is over. (*going to dais*) You Indians and soldiers separate. We can't have this fraternizing. (*pounding gavel*) Jack Smith! Come away from Colonel Chivington before I have you shot myself. Jack, give the man a little peace. (*All move to former positions.* CHIVINGTON *offers his hand to* JACK, *but* JACK *spits on it. He walks center stage, drops to knees and stares shamefully at* BLACK KETTLE. *He turns sullen at* BLACK KETTLE's *indifference. He raises and stands with his hands pushed into his pants pockets.*) Let's start.

JACK: I was murdered . . .

MAN IN WHITE: Not that . . . we just went through that.

JACK: I thought I deserved a little emphasis.

MAN IN WHITE: Bring on the girls . . .the women, I mean. (SOLDIERS *stare as if about to see a troop of dance hall girls come out.*) Bring in the helpless ones. (INDIANS *grow sad.*) Let them be exhibit A . . . marked and labeled. (*Rifle shot is heard off-stage.*)

INDIAN WOMAN: (*Young girl who began* SCENE 1. *She enters crying, gashing her arms and pulling at her hair. She is dressed in buckskins.*) Oooooo! Oooooooo!

MAN IN WHITE: Stop that, young woman! Stop that instantly. This room will not tolerate this obscene, primitive display of emotionalism. Look how you are agitating our Indians!

INDIANS: Leave her alone. She's our kinsman. Monahsetah. She mourns for us.

MAN IN WHITE: How can she mourn for you? She's dead. The living cannot speak in this room.

LITTLEST MAN: She is my cousin. I know her well. She died after Little Big Horn.

MAN IN WHITE: Not pertinent. She had to die as a direct result of Sand Creek.

LT. CANNON: Chivington's hate, his war, produced more deaths than just those at Ponoeohe.

INDIANS: (*moaning, chanting*) Ponoeohe, Ponoeohe!

MAN IN WHITE: We struck out moaning and groaning an hour ago. (INDIANS *stop immediately, simultaneously*.)

POLINSKI: You said only the dead could talk here . . . you're speaking, you're living!

MAN IN WHITE: That's different. I'm the exception to the rule. I must speak, being an impartial observer. My duty is to locate and find the truth. Pin it down as if it were a butterfly to be waxed. How else could we discern the truth if I were not prodding and plotting its course? That is my function . . . I cannot digress. I would like to get this over. There are some rather important government officials waiting dinner on me. And, too, I always spend an hour with the children before dinner . . . the children's hour. Nonetheless, the dead cannot know the truth as it is . . . nor tell it should they know. Dead men tell no truth.

JACK: Does that mean living men tell no lies?

MAN IN WHITE: Don't try to confuse me, Jack. Don't misconstrue my words. I never said that, exactly that.

JACK: But it was implied.

MAN IN WHITE: There is Colonel Chivington there on the right. It is an established fact that he is living.

SMALL MAN: His kind will always live.

MAN IN WHITE: Irrelevant! (*Clears throat.*) There is Colonel Chivington . . .

CHIVINGTON: (*Lights dim, characters freeze as before.*) I had to be a hero. (*dejected*) A hero to the peoples of Denver, the miners in the gold fields. I was a hero to the wary and the weary emigrants crossing the plains of the west. I was a hero to the trader selling his wares to murderous savages. I was a hero to the harassed cavalry and its valiant officers. I did instigate and accomplish no more or less than any white man under the given circumstances. I fought Indians. (*flailing his Bible in the face of the* INDIANS) I (*jumping up*) killed Indians. Justifiably, proudly. As I slew the other enemies of my country, the Southern Rebels, at La Glorioeta . . . with that turncoat Silas Soule at my side. I shot and scalped and mutilated sinful, savage Indians. I held the word of God as my guidon, and I was protector of innocent men and women and little children. My battle cry rang like a bell across the plains that winter morning . . . "Kill all, little and big. Nits make lice." And so they did and so they would . . . were they still there living on those infested lodgeskins. I was a hero, I say. Didn't you read my report? I killed six hundred flotsam of scum. Read the newspapers. (*dejected*) Then the rats turned on me, and I was hauled off to court. But I fooled them. I was mustered out of the volunteers before they court martialed me. But no one can deny that I was a hero. (*Lights up, all as before.*)

MAN IN WHITE: He may speak, but he must not speak, for he is living.

LT. CANNON: What kind of hogwash is that?

SMALLEST MAN: If he spoke, Chivington, he would not necessarily speak wisely or truthfully.

MAN IN WHITE: Don't be impertinent.

JACK: But that's honest!

MAN IN WHITE: You are dead! You were murdered in War Bonnet's lodge by the henchmen of Chivington, weren't you? (*White light flashes harshly and burns out instantly.*) You've told me that a thousand times. You are dead, dead, DEAD! I'm losing my control, Jack, my temper. Chivington murdered you, as you say.

INDIANS: Amen! First word of truth ever spoken by a paleface.

MAN IN WHITE: (*Caught, embarrassed. To Jack*) You say you were murdered. Your killer has not admitted the crime nor signed a confession.

JACK: He can't! He's living! The living can't speak. You made the rules.

MAN IN WHITE: Because there is nothing for him to say. Oh! Jack! Please, sit down. We're getting nowhere this way with all this wrangling and all these many interruptions. You've hogged the entire show. Go talk with Black Kettle for a while, and let the young Indian maiden have a chance.

JACK: (*sitting*) Bets made, cards called, but you don't show.

MAN IN WHITE: You, Jack were always a difficult boy. Uncle John, your father complained bitterly. Always moaning and groaning around camp in the village. You had every chance in life, more than any other Indian boy did. Your father was a rich trader and gave you everything. But you amounted to not much more than a complaint. And remember, my hot-headed young friend, you helped guide the soldiers to Black Kettle's village, even though it was your own people. That's exactly like putting the gun in their hands and pulling the trigger.

JACK: Lies. LIES! (*running to* CHIVINGTON) This minister of God forced young Bobby Bent; he forced ol' Jim Beckworth. He forced and harangued and threatened until everybody but full-blooded Indians cowered before him on the plains, loaded rifles and armed themselves with his hate . . . pure, unadulterated hate. All of them squirmed to kill. Remember his little slogan: "Kill big and little, nits make lice. NITS make lice." This bad man, (*knocking Bible from* CHIVINGTON's *hand*) this Meshane, this sick one, bribed the United States Cavalry to spill his rotting hate of Indians for him . . . to lie, kill, rape, steal . . . cut off the poor mutilated prick of old Big Man. This insect inflamed his vile henchmen to gouge out the dark privacy of womanhood and had his men stretch it across the pommel of a saddle, laughing, tickled they got one. Holding Big Man's prick high on the point of a saber, they marched into the city of Denver . . . the poor bloody thing a guidon for his troops. He lied and cheated and murdered. That was not war. It was his personal vengeance with a passion. He should be the prisoner at the bar . . . not us . . . six soldiers, six Indians and one half-breed.

MAN IN WHITE: (*gaveling for order*) Jack!

JACK: His hate spewed across the plains that freezing dawn. He not only massacred a peaceful band of Cheyenne camped on Sand Creek that

morning by the order of the cavalry . . . he murdered and scalped and mutilated every white man who died on the plains after the War of 1864.

MAN IN WHITE: (*Gaveling. Everyone but* BLACK KETTLE, *who remains calm
and passive, is in an uproar*.) Jack!

JACK: Who murdered Custer? (*Instant silence.*) Whooooooooo killed Custer?
Colonel John Milton Chivington killed Custer. Man of the cloth, leader of
lambs, he bloodied the field of Little Big Horn with Custer's guts.

MAN IN WHITE: All right, Jack. You've had your say. But strike it. It's
irrelevant. Not pertinent to either this inquiry or the fact. You'll be asking
me to call Custer as witness next. Colonel Chivington and General Custer
never had the good fortune to meet. Consult your history books on that. I
know . . . I've had a little learning, a fair amount of college history. Some-
body take him away. (JACK *sits quietly near* BLACK KETTLE) Now! Any
more such outbursts of emotion and I'll clear the room. The idea, coupling
Chivington with General Custer! Accusing Chivington of the Custer di-
saster, the massacre. Creating a new note to the Custer myth. Everybody
knows Custer dropped his own thumb into his own soup. No! No! It simply won't do. Strike it! Strike it out!

LT. CANNON: Sir, you are out of your head. This is a total farce. How the
hell much, sir, have they paid you?

MAN IN WHITE: Who? Who paid who what? (*rising, very nervous*) I must
plead for a moment. A slight . . . intermission. Nobody leaves his place.
(*going to footlights*) Pay no attention to anything he may say. He's a drunk.
Thank you. (*returning to dais*) Once more we will attempt to proceed. Calmly,
coolly, and, I may add, objectively, with detachment.

LT. CANNON: You, sir, prejudiced the jury.

MAN IN WHITE: (*ignoring* CANNON) Now for the girl. You may step forward . . . not too close. This is merely a credibility test.

INDIAN WOMAN: (*turning to audience*) I am known as Monahsetah. My mother was killed at Sand Creek. My sister was spiked on the point of a saber there. My father was a great chief. He was killed in the massacre on the Washita. After the murdering there on the Washita, I was taken captive. I was sent to Custer's tent, and in the Indian custom married to him. I was his Indian wife, his Cheyenne. I warmed his coffee at dawn, and after the day's long march, I warmed his flesh in the cold night. I betrayed my people. My dead father, Little Rock, and my mother. I led Custer's soldiers to my people's camp. I am guilty.

MAN IN WHITE: What is this about Custer nonsense! Strike all that out! Not pertinent! Stick to the facts, girl.

SOLDIERS: Yeah! Who the hell cares about Custer's cold feet?

BIG MAN: Let the girl speak.

SMITH: But she ain't dead.

INDIANS: She's dead.

GREEN: But she didn't die at Sand Creek.

MAN IN WHITE: Absolutely! I'm not sure she qualifies. But get on, and mind, keep your statements to facts.

MONAHSETAH: To love is difficult. To hate is very easy. My husband took the life of my father. That man (*pointing to* CHIVINGTON) took the life of my mother. I find it easy to hate. I think in the thing they call a heart . . . I think that there was a . . . a little love for the man . . . this, this, Long Hair Custer. My people called him Creeping Panther. My husband, Custer, crept into the Indians' village. He crept within the furs of my robe. Yes, I confess . . . in that heart there was love for that Yellow Hair Custer.

INDIANS: (*saddened*) Ohooooo!

MONAHSETAH: Then his white wife came and he sent me away . . . back to my people. I carried with me presents, and the seeds of his plant. My womb swelled with his lust. Under the moon of falling leaves his son, Yellow Swallow, named for the yellow guidon that fluttered in the breeze like a bird, came to play in the bright light of morning. In pain and in blood the child of the white man, Long Hair Custer, entered the village of my people in disgrace.

MAN IN WHITE: Disgrace! Son of a great and noble general. They should have been proud, joyful.

MONAHSETAH: There were those who conspired to kill my son. He brought evil, bad medicine upon the village. There were those who plotted to kill me . . . for I had brought shame upon the name of Cheyenne. Friends protected me, and so my son and myself were spared death awhile . . .

MAN IN WHITE: Dear girl, this is all very beautiful speech-making, very poetic, very . . . tragic, but . . .

BIG MAN: Let the girl speak.

MONAHSETAH: Many sleeps and many winters we trailed the plains with one band or another; many summers we journeyed along the rivers. During the moon of rising grass we found ourselves camped on Greasy Grass. Or what the white man calls the Little Big Horn. There I cried. Not for my son. Nor for myself. Nor for the father of Yellow Swallow. But I cried.

MAN IN WHITE: Get on with it, woman. Get on with your story. It's not relevant, but . . .

BIGGEST MAN: Then stop interrupting her.

GREEN: It's not . . . pertinent.

POLINSKI: It's got nothing to do with Sand Creek . . .

SMITH: . . . and Indian depredations.

MAN IN WHITE: You're right. That is correct. It has nothing to do with Indian atrocities, or Chivington's raid. But it is American History, boy, American History. I could suggest we salute our flag at this point. The girl is telling tragic American history . . . poor, poor Custer's rub out.

(INDIANS *and* SOLDIERS *quarrel with each other.*)

MAN IN WHITE: (*striking gavel*) Stop! Stop! STOP! Or I'll commit a massacre here myself. We are way off the trail to Sand Creek. I'm simply being indulgent and giving this girl the opportunity of righting her wrongs. A gift of a moment or two will do no harm. Generosity is the true spirit of man.

BIG MAN: Her wrongs? She was the victim.

MAN IN WHITE: Shall we finish, or not? Proceed.

MONAHSETAH: With my adopted mother, Mawissa, old Black Kettle's sister, we found him dead. There was a dark wound in his breast. There was a black wound in his head. Black and full of blood. I cried, and turned to the old woman with me and said; "I do not love this man anymore. He has harmed the people again. But he is our kinsman. Let his flesh be, let his hair hang, let his heart dry and wither . . . for in his death he will now listen. In his darkness he will now hear."

BIG MAN: And what will he hear, Monahsetah?

MONAHSETAH: When we spoke with him, long before in Indian Territory, on the banks of the Sweetwater River, he promised never again to aim his guns against the Cheyennes. Now in his darkness he will hear and he will answer. He will not break that promise again. I left him there on the hillside. I left him there for his people and his white wife. We washed his body clean of mud, washed his hair of blood, and closed his eyes.

POLINSKI: The story of a jealous woman.

LT. CANNON: The story of a wronged woman.

MAN IN WHITE: American History or not, this testimony is not pertinent. For all intents and purposes this is not the Little Big Horn. This is the Sand Creek Massacre.

MONAHSETAH: May I continue, sir? Out of my sorrow sprang Crazy Horse; out of my disgrace came Two Moons and Dull Knife; out of my hurt came the hurt of Sitting Bull and Lame White Man, and Big Foot; out of lies rose Chief Joseph and Geronimo. And from it all stepped nations of drunk-ards, wards of the state, men without strong hearts. From my sorrow came my son, Yellow Swallow, who fluttered like his father's guidon an hour and died. Who died like buffalo, the earth, the heavens. All is dead . . . (*weeping*) that is all . . . that is all.

LT. CANNON: You must be tired, Monahsetah. Rest now.

MAN IN WHITE: Yes, do, good girl. Go out side and rest, if you like. (MONAHSETAH *walks to* BLACK KETTLE *and drops a hand upon his impassive shoulder. He ignores her. She exits.*) The rest of you might as well go. I don't see how we can continue now. This session's finished. (SOLDIERS *exit.*) Colonel Chivington! I'd like a word with you, please. It's about Jack Smith. Col . . .

JACK: (*Lights dim low. Characters remaining on stage fade into background.* JACK *returns to the stage.*) I'm sick, I tell you!

JOHN SMITH: (*One of the* SOLDIERS *impersonates* JOHN SMITH.) Jack I . . .

JACK: If those sons-a-bitches don't shoot me, I'm likely to shoot myself.

JOHN SMITH: Foolish boy . . .

JACK: I'm sick I tell you. Sickness stinks in my heart. Let them kill me. Let Chivington kill me. He'll kill us all because the bastards in Washington put guns in his hands, and hate in his blood. So that you, my father . . . a sniveling fool who stuck your nose up an Indian's skirt . . . can get rich and richer, and sodbusters and cattlemen can steal land from under the buffalo's feet.

JOHN SMITH: Jack I . . .

JACK: Jack, Jack! Is that all the hell you can say?

JOHN SMITH: You're accusin' me . . .

CHIVINGTON: Uncle John. Ho! Uncle John Smith. You in there? The boys said you wanted to see me.

JOHN SMITH: It's Chivington, Chivington's here. He won't let anything happen.

CHIVINGTON: Uncle John, I came to see you.

JOHN SMITH: (*Goes to* CHIVINGTON.) Colonel? Is that you, Colonel Chivington? It's Jack! Some of your boys got a little hot in the head. They been hollerin' how his mother's a Cheyenne, an Indian and all, and that he ought to .   Colonel, now I know you are a generous, fair man, an' can call your dogs, your men, I mean, off my boy.

CHIVINGTON: I told my men to take no prisoners, Uncle John.

JOHN SMITH: But Jack . . .

CHIVINGTON: I told them to take no prisoners. I guess they are going to shoot your Jack. Your son and Charlie Bent were part of those savages. Their depredations have been vindicated here at Sand Creek. (JACK *has been squatting, but now stands.* SOLDIERS *sent by* CHIVINGTON, *surround the tipi and raise rifles. At a blast,* JACK *crumples. He is dead instantly.*) And justice will . . .

JOHN SMITH: Oh! My God! Jack! (*Lights come up.*)

MAN IN WHITE: It's about Jack Smith, Colonel. Personally, I think he's a show-off and probably just hamming it up . . . but for all good purposes, I think you had better write him out of the script. Can't we leave him a smudged footnote to history by not having him murdered? We'd get rid of him better that way. He's very difficult to handle. (MAN IN WHITE *and* CHIVINGTON *exit arm in arm.*)

BLACK KETTLE: (*Stands. Stares proudly about him as if looking across the plains to the mountains.*) Your soldiers, I don't think they listen to you. You bring presents, and when I come to get them, I am afraid they will strike me before I get away. When I come in to receive presents, I take them up crying. Although wrongs have been done to me, I live in hopes. I have not got two hearts. The young men [Cheyenne] when I call them into the lodge and talk with them, they listen to me and mind what I say. Now we are again together to make peace. My shame [mortification] is as big as the earth, although I will go as my friends advise me to do. I once thought that I was the only man that persevered to be friends of the white man, but since they have come and cleaned out our lodges, horses, and everything else, it is hard for me to believe white men any more. (*pausing*) Nothing . . . lives long, but the earth and the mountains. This is all by Black Kettle. (*He crosses to center stage. His blanket slips. Stage flashes with bright lights . . . red, white and blue. He stands center, his blanket has slowly dropped off his shoulders. He is naked.*) Nothing lasts long. (*Gun shot.*)